Men of Whiskey Row Series

NO GREATER *Love*

D.A. YOUNG

No Greater Love

ISBN-13: 978-1727779189
ISBN-10: 1727779185

Cover Design & Interior Formatting—T. E. Black Designs; www.teblackdesigns.com

Editing—Little Pear Editing Services/ latrisa@idea-lity.com
Copyright © March 2016

Proofing—Ideality-Consulting / latrisa@ideality-lity.com/
Copyright © April 2018

Proofing—Sean Leck

PLAYLIST

Say You Say Me – Lionel Richie

Strip Me – Natasha Bedingfield

Maps – Maroon 5

One More Try – George Michael

Million Reasons – Lady GaGa

Brand New Day – Sting

Little Lies – Fleetwood Mac

Devil Inside - Inxs

Wild World – Maxi Priest

Body & Soul – Anita Baker

Listen to the playlist on Spotify!

AUTHOR'S NOTE

I can't believe we're here! Book *five* in the Men of Whiskey Row Series! Mind blown, seriously! Thank you all for enjoying and loving this series as much as I enjoy writing and sharing it with you. Alexei & Vivienne Romankov. I *love* this couple's strength, determination, and loyalty! I hope you will enjoy their journey as they fight for their much deserved happily-ever-after.

Special thanks to Little Pear Editing and T. E. Black Designs for being so amazing and easy to work with. Sean Leck, you're a lifesaver and I appreciate your dedication and hard work.

SINCERELY,
D. A. Young

"For the strength of the pack is
the wolf…and the strength of
the wolf is the pack."

-Rudyard Kipling

PROLOGUE

Late '80s

San Francisco, California

"WHY ARE WE STILL HERE? Have we nothing better to do than babysit this group of tired old bitches while they bake?! There is not even a tempting one among them that I could wet my cock in."

Alexei Romankov heard the contemptuous talk that came from behind him, as did the "tired old bitches" who stopped making pastries long enough to shoot the culprit looks of pure disgust, which he was oblivious to. Alexei gave them all a reassuring look, and they nodded respectfully to him and continued to work. Not bothering to turn around and address his foolish companion face to face, he softly uttered his warning.

"Shut. Up."

"Why must I, Wolf? You know as I do, that what I speak is the truth!" Taras Boykov sneered. "All day long, we stay in this shop and eat ponchikis, sharlotka, tea cakes, and Napoleon pastries while waiting like fucking lapdogs to be recognized by Vanya. We wait for a

woman. Bah! I have had enough! Tonight, I will be fucking. Whether the bitch is willing or not!"

He laughed lecherously, and to Alexei, the sound was the equivalent of nails screeching down a chalkboard.

Drawing a measured breath, he studied his large hands, willing himself not to form them into weapons as fury coursed through his powerful body. If that happened, then Alexei could not be held entirely responsible for what happened next. These fists were the main reason he was here in this sleepy Russian neighborhood. Two months ago, Alexei had lost his temper one too many times and impulsively killed a man for refusing to give up information Alexei had requested. Thus, his father had sent him here to be council for his ailing childhood friend Vanya Izmirsky.

"ALWAYS SO TEMPERAMENTAL, ALEXEI! DO not worry. I have a way to assist you with that! You are to go to your Tsyo Vanya's for a month and listen to the problems that plague her people. Lately, the neighborhood has been experiencing a streak of violence by an up and coming Irish gang," Boris explained disdainfully. "You must go and resolve all their worries without resorting to fists with these animals. A dose of diplomacy will do you some good. You will live up to your name and learn restraint at the same time. "Alexei the Defender". It has a nice ring to it, da?"

NO, IT DID NOT HAVE A fucking nice ring to it, but one didn't dare to question Boris Romankov without having a contingency plan, such as perhaps, killing yourself before he got to you. Hah! And his papa had the nerve to criticize his actions, Alexei mused with a scowl.

Subsequently, he came west, and his 'thoughtful' father sent Taras Boykov, one of his more brutish enforcers to accompany his son, knowing how much Alexei could not stand the arrogant hothead with a barely contained sadistic streak. There was no love lost between the two men, and Alexei knew this was another of his father's tests regarding his patience — to keep Boykov in check without losing his temper.

There was no question in Alexei's mind that Taras lived up to the meaning of his name as a mutineer, rebel, and transgressor. Yet Boris did not see it that way, especially when Taras eagerly put in the time punishing those who tested the Romankov family. He also relished in the blood that was spilled— the gorier the better. It was the reason he'd risen swiftly through the family's ranks. In Alexei's opinion, Taras could not be trusted and would fuck a snake to have Boris's ear, which wasn't going to happen on his son's watch.

"You will stay put, Taras," he ordered coolly. "It would seem that you are suffering from a memory lapse on this fine morning. This is MY operation, and no one else's. You will not make any moves without my approval first."

Alexei could feel the malevolent waves coming off the other man and smiled, ardently wishing Taras would give in to his darkest desires. Boris had said nothing about using his fists to defend himself.

"Whatever you say, Wolf," Taras responded with thinly veiled insolence.

Alexei felt a sharp pang of disappointment realizing that the fool would not be outright defying him.

"It is, isn't it? And what I say right now, is that you run along and fix these hardworking women some coffee and a tray of Danish," Alexei commanded with an imperious snap of his fingers.

"W-What? Is this a joke???" Taras spluttered in outrage and the women smiled amongst themselves to see the zhopa resorted to doing what he thought was women's work.

"It is almost time for their break, and I know they would be happy to know you appreciate them by performing this kind gesture. Off you go," Alexei dismissed him, before walking through the swinging doors and into the tea shop and bakery to make sure everything was in place before they opened for the day. He walked the floor and inspected the immaculate tearoom carefully.

It was a beautiful, quaint shop decorated quite opulently in the era of old Russia. The curtains were made from a heavy burnished gold brocade, and the walls were painted an emerald green. The booths were navy blue and the tablecloths were pinstriped emerald green and gold. Delicate blue and gold painted

Lomonosov porcelain tea sets were placed on each table. A mural of all the churches in St. Petersburg, Russia covered the entire ceiling from which gold chandeliers elegantly hung.

Idly, he wondered if she would stop by today. His body throbbed with want at the thought of her. Those large, exquisite eyes and the elegance and grace with which she moved made that delectable body appear as if she were floating. Alexei longed to grip her slightly flared hips and plunge as deep as he could into her while ravaging her pouty lips with his own. Aside from this shitty-ass assignment, that image was all he could think about in the two weeks since he'd first laid eyes on her.

A bright flash of color caught his eye. Alexei's eyes narrowed on the hulking figure standing outside the locked doors. The stranger's fiery orange-red mane was highlighted by the morning sun. Other waiting customers eyed him warily and gave him a wide berth. The man's pale skin was lightly freckled, and he was built solidly, like a tank dressed in a black tracksuit. Alexei recognized him, by the country flag patch on his jacket, as a member of the Mulroney Hill Gang, the largest Irish gang in the Bay area.

Founded by Jamie "The Gent" Mulroney, they'd recently migrated from Ireland and were the ones responsible for the current wave of trouble the neighborhood was experiencing. The shakedowns for protection had started two months ago, and when people refused to cower and pay, their businesses were broken into and ransacked or firebombed with Molotov cocktails.

The elderly were terrorized, and the men jumped and brutally beaten. Some of the ladies had even claimed sexual assault while law enforcement looked the other way, themselves too afraid of the Mulroney Gang's retaliation.

Pussies.

Alexei leisurely strolled over to the gold ornate doors and unlocked them. He held one open and greeted the arrogant govno who smiled cockily at him. His thick Irish brogue was annoyingly cheery to Alexei, and he found it a toss-up on whom he disliked more: this idiot or Taras.

"Who the feck are you?" Irish asked curiously as he looked around the shop. "I thought I'd stop in and pay my respects to old Vanya. She around?"

"She is not."

Alexei did not bother with introducing himself and simply smiled and nodded in greeting as regulars filed in. The bakery side of the shop quickly filled up and soon flowed into the tearoom. An introduction was not necessary. The bastard would find out soon enough who he was.

"Perhaps there is something I may assist you with, Mr...?"

"The name's Danny Flannigan, boyo, and as a matter of fact, yes," the Irishman arrogantly replied with a congenial smile that didn't reach his hard, green eyes. "I'll be needing an answer on when she can start making her payments. The sooner she falls in line, the quicker the other owners will follow. 'Tis for their own good. I'd hate for a cash cow like this to remain

unprotected and something dire happen to it. Do ya ken?"

Alexei heard the underlying threat in the bully's tone and willed himself not to retaliate to it in the Romankov way. The fucking Irish were always so hardheaded and stubborn. He was just about to respond when the door was flung open again, and a regal-looking woman with a willowy build entered the shop. She glanced around superiorly, and her wide sky-blue eyes widened when they settled on Alexei. Immediately, she smiled at him coquettishly and headed toward him.

Her long wheat-blonde hair hung down her back in a single French braid, and her pale, translucent skin was devoid of makeup. Her pink bow-shaped mouth parted, and the bakery was filled with her lilting musical voice, heavily accented with Russian cooed, "There you are, Alexei! I hoped I would see you today! I'm working on a new dance for my solo in the ballet. Please say you'll come by the studio this evening! I would love to show you what I've come up with."

Nadia Stanislav was an unquestionable beauty, no doubt, and as Alexei scoured the shop, he noticed that all the customers appeared enchanted by her, including Danny Flannigan, who was practically drooling as he sized the lithe dancer up. Normally Alexei's type, she should have already been in his bed, and he would have been branding his name all over her pussy, but not anymore. It would seem he had a new type...

Apparently, she'd come alone, which was a huge disappointment to Alexei. He opened his mouth to decline her invitation, but the door was flung open again, and this time, his eyes clashed with a pair of lovely molasses eyes that snapped with ire. They belonged to the honey-skinned beauty Alexei had been obsessing about. Today, she was dressed in a leopard print sheath that molded to her amazing body and a deep merlot-colored wool coat that matched her heels. Her black hair was pulled away from her fine-boned face into a high ponytail. She looked every bit of the successful career woman that his investigative reports said she was.

"Yes, I'll be there," Alexei found himself saying.

VIVIENNE PEMBROOKE WAS IN THE mood to beat somebody's ass as she threw the door open to Imperial Crown Tea Shop. But not just any ass would do. She specifically wanted ballet dancer Nadia Stanislav's bony, snooty one. Her boss, William Gallagher of Gallagher Public Relations had assigned her with the menial task of babysitting his firm's most difficult client. From the instant she'd met the prima donna bitch, there was no love lost between them.

The ballerina needed constant adoration from those around her, and Vivienne refused to cater to her or that supersized ego. She had a job to do here, one that would look amazing on her resume, but Nadia was making it very difficult for her to accomplish it. She was under the impression that Vivienne was there to pander to her every need and called her at all hours of the day with ridiculous requests that included walking her teacup poodle, picking up her laundry, and making daily runs to Imperial Crown for her fix of citrus spiced tea and cinnamon raisin coffee cake.

"You have an assistant, Ms. Stanislov. I suggest you take advantage of their assisting skills," Vivienne sarcastically reminded her daily. "Or perhaps train your dog to fetch. I do neither. My job is to keep you on the straight and narrow while you promote your play for the San Francisco Ballet Company."

Well, today, she'd failed her job because the silly twit had given her personal driver the slip, and she hadn't bothered showing up at the press junket, thus making Vivienne look like an even sillier and incompetent twit. The hysterical driver had called her and wanted to know where he should start looking for her, but Vivienne had, had enough of these antics and knew exactly where to find Nadia.

Vivienne noticed everyone in the shop staring with curiosity at her dramatic entrance, and she struggled to compose herself while looking around for her troublesome ward. Finally, she located her standing in a corner with two men, staring up at the black haired one adoringly. He was the real reason that they had to travel out of their way to this gaudy little hellhole for some pastries and caffeine. He was also the reason Nadia couldn't think straight and all she talked about with her big eyes twinkling as she spouted her 'Wolf this' and 'Wolf' that' bullshit.

His blue eyes met Vivienne's from across the room, and not for the first time, she was struck by how deep a blue they actually were, like liquid indigo, and framed by thick black lashes. His black hair was kept on the longer side and fell around his head in thick waves, and that strong, slightly crooked nose and square jaw only enhanced his good looks. His eyes traveled over her intently, and he quirked those supple lips as if he knew a secret joke at her expense. It caused Vivienne's stomach to plummet and awaken butterflies she didn't even know she had before encountering him, each time he did it. But she'd be damned if she gave him the satisfaction of knowing it. His tall, muscular form was sheathed in a black suit that had to be custom made, judging from the fabric and the way it fit him superbly.

Vivienne rolled her eyes at him. Hard. Just to show him she was immune to his brooding sexiness. Sort of. She approached them, briskly speaking, "Hello Nadia! Fancy seeing you here instead of at your press conference. It's time to go. On the way, you can explain to me why coming to this place was worth jeopardizing your career."

The other man standing with them spoke, and Vivienne found it hard to decipher what he said due to his thick Irish accent.

"What's your hurry, luv?"

His lascivious look made her skin crawl, and before Vivienne could shut him down, he turned to the silent Alexei with a crude laugh.

"Wish I'd known this place was crawling with beauties, I would have made a personal visit a long time ago, eh?"

Alexei's eyes flashed dangerously at him. "Excuse me, Flannigan, while I get them situated. Come with me, ladies."

His frigid tone brooked no room for argument as he turned away, and they followed behind. Apparently, Flannigan was hard of hearing because his hand shot out, and he grabbed Vivienne's arm. She stared at his pale digits curled around her arm and raised frigid eyes to meet his lewd ones.

"Release. Me. Now."

He smiled cruelly and instead, tightened his grip. Flannigan was disappointed that the beauty showed no reaction. Pity, he liked a good tussle with a whore, before taking her.

"Or you'll do what, lass?" he jeered.

Vivienne's other hand slid into her purse, and she swiftly pulled her small black baton out. Flipping it open, she brought it down viciously on his wrist, and he quickly released her with a curse.

Flannigan shook his injured arm while advancing on her with a sneer. "I do like a feisty bitch! I'm going to enjoy the way you fight for your li -"

The swift, sharp jab to his Adam's apple with the end of the baton stunned him, and he clutched his throat and dropped to his knees, grappling for air. Vivienne smiled icily above him, twirling the weapon expertly. She laughed with delight as he glowered up at her.

"Personally, feisty bitches don't do a damn thing for me," she drawled, glossed lips curling in disgust. "They're all talk but crumble like fresh-baked cookies at the first sign of trouble."

Vivienne gasped with surprise as she was yanked against a hard form and her startled eyes rose to meet Alexei's furious ones.

"You have overstayed your visit," he growled menacingly in that deep baritone thickly laced with his Russian accent. "How dare you disrespect my place of business! Go now!"

Alexei tried to ignore how hurt she looked at his harsh words, but he needed to focus. If he didn't, Flannigan was a dead man in front of all of these witnesses for daring to disrespect and touch her. He could feel her soft, pliant curves through their clothing, burning into his side, and up this close and personal, her sumptuous skin was indeed without flaws. Flecks of gold danced in her feline eyes, and Alexei longed to discover if that glossy mouth was as succulently soft as it looked. White hot awareness sizzled between them, and his cock ached, demanding for him to find the release that Alexei now knew only she could give him.

But now was not the time or place for pleasure.

"I don't stay where I'm not wanted," Vivienne whispered, shocked by the warmth of his hand through the layers of clothing. Sex. It was all she could think off as the seductive notes of sandalwood and musk in his cologne surrounded her. Hot, sweaty, nasty, thigh-and-back-aching sex as he fucked her any way he wanted it. It didn't matter what she wanted because Vivienne knew he would make sure she found pleasure in it. And with that thought, she found herself swaying towards him even as she defiantly commanded, "Take your hand off me!"

Alexei's touch felt so right, that Vivienne immediately felt bereft when he reluctantly removed it. His cool breath washed over her face, and she longed to rise on her tiptoes, to mold her mouth to his and see if they fit together as perfectly as she suspected they would. His eyes lowered to her lips, and her breath hitched as he slowly licked his.

The spell was broken by the bane of her existence.

"Let's go, Vivienne," Nadia said sharply and pulled her away from Alexei. "Izvinitye, Wolf. We did not mean to be disrespectful toward the Romankov name."

"Spasibo, Nadia." Alexei nodded regally, his eyes still locked with Vivienne's as she was dragged out of the shop.

"Fookin' black bitch!" Flannigan jeered spitefully, struggling to his feet, his accent more pronounced with his anger. "When I get my hands on 'er, I'm going to teach 'er a lesson she'll never ferget then fook her 'til she's speaking in Gaelic tongues!"

"Please come back at four, Flannigan," Alexei said abruptly. "We can talk about the protection price then. Use the backdoor. Thanks to your gang, the police have been heavily policing the neighborhood. Bring your boss with you."

Alexei waited until he left and then retreated to the kitchen where he found the women hovering together in the corner instead of baking bread. Their expressions varied from disgust to fear. Puzzled by this, Alexei looked around and realized Taras was missing. He glanced back at the ladies in question, and they pointed to the bathroom just as Alexei heard a triumphant groan.

Two minutes later, Magda an older motherly figure stumbled out of the bathroom in a traumatized daze, clutching at her torn blouse. Around her neck were red handprints. Jovial whistling filled the air, and then Taras appeared, wiping his hands on a paper towel.

His eyes met Alexei's, and he smirked arrogantly, secure in the knowledge that he had Boris's support and no harm would come to him.

Neither man said anything for a long moment before Alexei lowered his head in defeat and Taras' chest puffed out like a rooster's. "We must prepare for a meeting with Mulroney this afternoon."

He walked past the shocked women and out of the kitchen without another word.

LATER THAT AFTERNOON, ALEXEI OPENED the back door to an even cockier Danny Flannigan and a smaller older man with thinning brown hair and a receding hairline. The man's features were nondescript, save his pale gray eyes that were glacier cold and menacing as he sized Alexei up while Danny made the introductions.

"Boss, this is Wolf...oy, I dinna catch yer name?" Danny tried to laugh off his mistake, but it fell flat under his boss's steely gaze. "Well, erm, this is my boss, Jamie "The Gent" Mulroney."

"Pardon, my eejit of an employee's introduction, but whom do I have the pleasure of doing business with?"

Although spoken in the most dulcet of tones, it would have frozen the blood of a lesser man. Alexei was no such thing. He gave a welcoming smile and graced them with a respectful nod of his head.

"My name is Alexei Romankov."

He gestured to Tara's standing by the table on which bundles of money were neatly stacked. "This is my father's most loyal and trusted employee, Taras Boykov."

Alexei took note of the way the Romankov name gave the men pause, and they exchanged uneasy glances. Throughout the world, his family name was well- established and known mutually in the underworld and in the business one, as was the Romankov method of approaching both with a quiet but savage ruthlessness. He held the door open wider.

"Please come in. I am ready to deal so that we may leave this godforsaken place and return east. I've spoken with the other owners and tenants and convinced them that you can be trusted."

Warily, they passed him and looked around the large utility kitchen with even more caution. Seeing no one, they relaxed slightly.

Alexei shut the door quietly and pulled out a chair at the table. "Let us sit and break bread while we figure out the details of this deal."

He poured them tea and listened to Mulroney arrogantly speak as a scornful Taras fumed silently and sipped his tea.

Boris would not have made such a bitch move, he thought derisively watching the younger Romankov sit docilely like a lamb and sell his people out. Alexei always tried to do everything by the book and strategized before making moves. Taras didn't believe in hesitating; it's what got men killed. This morning, he'd shown Alexei who was boss and without his father to hide behind, the man had backed down like the coward he was.

As Mulroney paused, a wave of lethargy suddenly hit Taras, and he emitted a garbled moan that startled him as much as his hand that held the small teacup suddenly hitting the table did, causing the expensive porcelain to shatter on the wooden table. Alexei turned to look at him as bits of the broken cup and tea splattered everywhere.

"Are you alright, Taras?" he asked politely.

Taras opened his mouth to respond and realized he couldn't.

A wave of panic crashed over him as he tried to stand, but his limbs were useless. His eyes flew to Mulroney and Flannigan, but they were completely still just like him. Only Alexei was able to function normally as he rose gracefully from his chair and turned both men's chairs to face Taras. He met their gazes and knew the terror he saw there was reflected in his own eyes.

That bastard Romankov had drugged them!

"It is called Sux-something or other - Chloride," Alexei explained to them in a sotto voice. "Bah! I always

forget the name, though never its purpose. It's used to induce muscle relaxation and short-term paralysis. You are left awake and alert for the duration of our time together, just unable to move. Good times, da? Let the games begin!"

Alexei placed a hand on Taras' shoulder and patted him fondly as he addressed the Irishmen. "This man is an excellent soldier in the Romankov family! He goes above and beyond his duties. My father is very pleased with his performance and loyalty. Good men like him are hard to find, eh?"

Drenched in sweat, a panicked Taras could not move as Alexei walked away from him. Suddenly he could hear the roaring, crackling flames as the great oven was opened and knew that he'd gravely underestimated his boss. Panicking, Taras tried again to move, yet no matter how hard he tried, he couldn't.

Alexei came back, donning a pair of rubber gloves and dragged his chair toward the oven. Taras could only stare up at him as Alexei peered down at him, his blue eyes glowing sinisterly as he leaned down further until they were nose to nose. And in his eyes, Tara could see the Devil possessed and knew this was why Romankov was called "The Wolf". Like the predatory animal, Alexei had quietly studied and stalked his prey ruthlessly before going in for the kill. He'd known Taras' arrogance would be his downfall.

"Did you really think you would get away with disrespecting me and my family name, Taras?" Alexei taunted, momentarily leaving him to grab a long sharp cutting knife from the dish rack. "And that it would be

meekly tolerated? You are but a foolish child! Romankovs tolerate no disrespect! Nor do we kowtow to anyone!"

Alexei bent down and met Taras' horror-filled eyes, holding the knife up, the blade gleaming evilly under the kitchen lights. Swiftly he brought the knife down, blade first and stabbed Taras in the genitals and twisted it, causing a large bloodstain to spread across his lap. The excruciating pain flayed every one of Taras' nerves alive as Alexei withdrew the knife and tossed it aside. He hoisted the enforcer up effortlessly and then shoved him head first into hell. Flames licked hotly at Taras' head just as feeling was starting to come back to his body, and his last moments were truly spent in Hades as the blazes overtook him.

Dispassionately, Alexei watched as the fire consumed the bastard. Soon the room was filled with the acrid smell of burning flesh. He pushed more of the disintegrating body into the flames until he was finally able to shut the door completely. Alexei turned back to Mulroney and Flannigan and laughed. The deep, rich sound was so at odds with the sickening smell emanating from the oven, and it chilled both men to their cores.

Alexei noticed that both of the men's crotch areas were now soaked with urine, and he shook his head mournfully as he took the gloves off and washed his hands.

"What a pity. It couldn't have happened to a more deserving fellow."

He returned to them and grabbed a small teacake from the tray of sweets on the table. Taking a bite, he placed a foot on his chair and braced his weight on it. He gestured to Mulroney with the cake as he chewed enthusiastically.

"Except no matter how loyal Taras was, he was disrespectful, just like you, Mulroney. You come to this country and think you can do whatever you want and damn the consequences, right? Surely, you didn't think that it would be so easy to overtake this neighborhood and do whatever you like?"

Alexei finished the teacake and grabbed a cloth napkin. He slowly wiped the sugar from his mouth and hands, walked over to the pantry, and retrieved a small metal case. Whistling Depeche Mode's "People Are People", he opened the case and pulled black-coated gloves out. Alexei slipped them on before turning the case toward the men and revealing the small clear vials with an excited smile.

"In this neighborhood, we are good, honest, and hard working people that refuse to cower to the likes of you," Alexei continued conversationally as he picked up a vial and uncapped it.

White fumes rose from the top.

"So no, we will not be paying protection money to you or anyone else, Mulroney. Before tomorrow night, I predict that your gang will have found a more desirable spot to set up shop. Far, far away from here if they are smart."

Alexei approached him and gave a careless shrug, his eyes glowing diabolically. "But I know you Irish are a stubborn, pigheaded bunch and don't always learn the lesson the first time."

He tapped the middle of Mulroney's forehead with the bottom of the vial. "That is okay with me because I'm a patient man with plenty of time. But you, Mulroney? Not so much. Your time has run out."

Jamie "The Gent" Mulroney could only watch with helpless dread as Alexei pried his mouth open and poured the contents of the vial down his throat. Although he knew it was pointless, Jamie tried to scream, but couldn't while his body was engulfed in an agonizing blaze of pain as the corrosive nitric acid expeditiously demolished his organs. It was brutally barbaric, but if the Irishmen had bothered to do their homework, they would have known that it was nothing less than expected from Alexei "The Wolf" Romankov.

Danny Flannigan shit his pants when Alexei turned his chair around, pulled his gun out of a concealed holster, and faced him. He gave a maddening grin as he crossed his arms across the back and placed his chin on them.

"And then there was one," Alexei remarked softly, enjoying the way Danny tried to avoid his lethal stare. "How would you like to go, Flannigan? By fire, bullets, or acid? Maybe a little of each?"

It didn't matter where Danny's gaze landed, death was everywhere. His eyes were beseeching as they bounced back to the commie bastard whose own stare never wavered. They stayed locked on him until finally, Danny had feeling in his fingers, then his hands, and finally, his body.

He tested his mouth and a mangled sound came out before he threw up all over the kitchen floor. "P-P-Please dinna kill me! I beg of ye', Romankov!!! Ye'll get no more trouble from us! Consider us gone!!"

Flannigan blubbered and pleaded for his life to unnerving silence. Nerves shot to hell from wondering what his fate would be, he tried goading and insulting Alexei but only received silence.

Only when he hung his head down in defeat did Alexei speak.

"Today is your lucky day, Danny Boy. I will spare your life because you've shown me what a good messenger you can be. You will tell the tale of what happened here and inform your people that if they want a fight with the Romankovs, they will get WAR. It is my specialty and I never lose. Get up."

Eagerly, Danny struggled to obey the order, but the sudden rush of feeling through his limbs caused him to collapse in his own waste. Grimacing, he tried again, and this time, he was successful.

"I promise we'll leave tonight! I'm the second-in-command, and they'll not question me. It'll be like we were never here!"

He stumbled toward the door, eager to smell his freedom and celebrate his reprieve from death, but it was short-lived as Alexei spun him around. Danny's eyes bugged out of his head at the sight of the large meat cleaver in his raised hand. The sharp blade glinted in the light.

"We have one more thing to clear up, Flannigan."

"What might that be, sir?" Danny asked fearfully as he inched toward the door.

"The woman that you disrespected so blatantly this morning? She belongs to me. Any disrespect toward her is a personal insult to me. And as you now know, such an offense will not be tolerated."

He grabbed Danny's hand, and despite the big man's struggling, Alexei easily dragged him back to the table. He set the hand that had grabbed Vivienne on the table and quickly brought the cleaver down.

Thwack!

The Irishman's ungodly scream filled the shop. He fell to the floor, writhing around and clutching at where his hand had once been. Blood fountained out while Alexei stood over him with a twisted smile.

"Now, you may go."

THE SCENE FROM IMPERIAL CROWN Tea Shop was at the forefront of Vivienne's mind as she observed Nadia practicing. Although the hour grew late, not once since picking the ballerina up had the P. R. agent left her side. They had a meeting tomorrow with William and the ballet company. Heads were sure to roll, but Vivienne was damned if hers would be one of them, which was why lately, she'd been considering branching out on her own. The thought of being her own boss appealed to her greatly, especially when William spoke to her in that condescending 'assholian' way of his.

Her tension headache increased, and she scowled, pulling the hair clip from her hair, allowing the ebony waves to tumble around her shoulders. Vivienne sighed with relief as some of the pressure receded from her temple.

"Why are you still here?" Nadia sulked, twirling past her gracefully. "Have you nothing better to do than gawk at me??? Is it not enough that you embarrassed me today with your high-handed American ways?!"

Do NOT lose it on this Barbie doll, Vivienne pleaded with herself, feeling her body temperature soaring at a level to rival the sun's. Think of your job, girl! Besides, you don't even have bail money because you're wearing it on your feet!

Vivienne glanced down at her Michael Kors shoes and smiled with contentment. They were a splurge she'd indulged in when she'd received a bonus two weeks ago prior to her life being shot to hell. Technically it wasn't like she was destitute or even needed to work. Vivienne Pembrooke came from money. The only problem was that it was illegally gained, and she'd sworn not to rely on it as she made a career and reputation for herself.

"Actually, I do have better things to do than babysit your spoiled ass, Nadia," she bit out. "The sooner you stop prancing around, the sooner we can talk, and I'll finally be able to leave."

Nadia abruptly stopped and wiped the perspiration from her outraged face.

"PRANCING?!" she screeched. "You think that all I do is prance about? How dare you mock the dance of

life! You sit there with your face fixed as if eating lemons and dare to stare down your nose at me?!"

She drew herself up proudly and passionately declared, "There is no joy or love in your soul! You are only interested in getting to the top, by any means necessary!" Nadia eyes raked over her scathingly and she spat, "Your aura is as black as your heart. It is I, that cannot believe I am stuck with you!"

"Hold that thought." Vivienne calmly rose and took her Carolina Herrera coat off, laying it carefully on the chair. Who did this prima donna bitch think she was talking to? Ol' girl was surely gonna die tonight.

Vivienne jumped in Nadia's face and damn near took her eye out, shoving a manicured finger into it.

"Fuck you and the carriage you rode in on, honey! You must be out of your goddamn mind to talk to me like that after all I have done for you! You are so focused on YOU that you have no idea what a nightmare you are to deal with! Your shitty attitude has driven every assistant and P.R. rep assigned to you away! Hell, I'm on my way to being an alcoholic because I need several drinks after our touch bases. I am the ONLY one who has stuck by you, Nadia, and if you don't get your act together, I will put my foot so far up your ass -"

She stopped when she saw the glisten of tears in Nadia's eyes before she turned away defiantly. "Then go, Vivienne! Go and be just like everyone else in your American rat race."

Nadia was lonely but too proud to admit it, Vivienne belatedly realized. For the first time, she considered what it must have been like for the ballerina to come to the United States alone. It was probably the reason Nadia took the trip across the city to be with familiar sights, smells, and sounds at the tea shop. A twinge of guilt pricked Vivienne's conscience. If she hadn't been so obsessed with making sure her ducks were in a row, then she would have picked up on it. Instead, she'd skimmed Nadia's dossier and focused only on the complaints, basically writing her off. The twinge of guilt expanded into full-blown indignity.

"I'm not going anywhere," Vivienne said with finality, and Nadia turned back to her, light blue eyes glimmering of hope. "You and I are going to work this shit out. Yeah, I'm sure we'll butt heads from time to time, but I'm no quitter, Nadia Stanislav, and neither are you. So, go dance your heart out, and I'll watch instead of work. I promise."

Nadia clapped her hands with delight before throwing her arms around a startled Vivienne and hopping up and down.

Unsure of what to do, Vivienne stiffly patted her back and tried to ease herself out the exuberant embrace.

"There, there..."

"Thank you so much, Vivienne! I promise you will not regret it!"

Gone was the reserve from her face as she spun away in a graceful pirouette. "I shall play something American just for you!"

Vivienne silently exhale of relief as she sat down again. That could have gone so differently. She should have paid closer attention to her client. After all, that was her business, wasn't it? Vivienne had grown lax, daydreaming about an insanely sexy Russian whose eyes promised her hedonistic pleasure that she was absolutely certain wouldn't be legal in any country.

She snorted delicately, imagining him, so strong and virile in the shop's opulent surroundings. Tea shop owner her ass. The man radiated vibes that screamed: "Fuck with me at your own peril". Vivienne had been around enough men of that caliber to know what it looked, smelled, and felt like. The Russian was the real deal.

"He likes you a lot, you know."

She looked up in surprise, but Nadia was too busy flipping through her record collection to notice.

"I beg your pardon?"

"Wolf likes you," Nadia explained patiently as she finally selected a record and pulled it out of its sleeve. "In Russia, women watch him, and he is oblivious. Here in America, he watches you, who appear to be the obtuse one. Many women want him," she gave a self-deprecating smile, "myself included, until today when I saw where his attention has been focused."

Nadia threw Vivienne a censorious look and chided her, "You should be honored by the attention."

"Hardly," Vivienne replied sarcastically even as her mouth went dry at the possibility of capturing Alexei's attention. Her damned heart longed for affection so badly that it would embrace any seductive lie if she foolishly allowed it. "Cool your tits, girly. You speak of him as if he walks on water. He's just a man, darling. Nothing more, nothing less."

"For a smart woman, you are willing to play the fool and believe that, eh Vivienne? "The Wolf" isn't and could never be an ordinary man," Nadia said cryptically as the strains of Lionel Richie's "Say You Say Me" filled the room.

Vivienne rolled her eyes at the song, and Nadia laughed at her disgruntled expression.

"I believe this song to be a fitting tribute to you and I, Vivienne. Come dance with me! I will show you some simple moves."

Say you, say me say it for always
That's the way it should be
Say you, say me say it together
Naturally

And that was how Alexei found them.

He stood outside the studio's glass doors in the foggy San Francisco night. For once, Vivienne's exquisite face was freed from the rigid and uptight mask she always had in place. Instead, laugh lines creased the corners of her eyes, and she glowed with pleasure as she moved with effortless grace and followed Nadia's lead. Never had Alexei seen a more exquisite sight. It soothed his savage beast like nothing else could as the words to the song resonated within him.

In his line of work, Alexei lived in darkness, had accepted it as his penance for what he did. He knew that eventually, he would take a wife, approved by Boris of course, whose graceful and calm demeanor would be the soothing balance to counter his underworld turbulence. Together, they would eventually breed to keep the Romankov bloodline alive. It was expected, and by now, Alexei should have acknowledged it, but he didn't want that. He wanted fire and passion blended in with that calm and grace.

He wanted Vivienne.

I had a dream; I had an awesome dream
People in the park, playing games in the dark
And what they played was a masquerade
And from behind of walls of doubt, a voice was crying out...

VIVIENNE CALLED HER GOODBYES TO Nadia as she exited the studio. She stopped short at the sight that greeted her. Alexei was leaning against a burgundy Mercedes convertible, and his shuttered gaze was intently focused on her. He looked like a dashing international spy with the charcoal trench coat over his dark suit and his midnight hair blowing rakishly with the light wind. Her body hummed with pleasure at the sight of him.

"You move like an angel."

His deep baritone was made even more appealing by the thick Russian accent that he spoke with. The sound of it made her knees weak with longing.

"What are you doing here?"

Vivienne winced, not recognizing the foreign high, wispy sounds that escaped her throat. Oh, God; he'd turned her into one of those women. What would she do next? Twirl her hair and simper like a silly, vapid airhead?

This. Was. So. Not. Her.

Alexei contemplated her words carefully while trying to stop the lust from slamming through his body like a freight train. Yes, he wanted to fuck her like crazy until his hunger was slaked, but he needed so much more than that from Vivienne. He needed the solace that only she could provide after he returned from an assignment. Her gorgeous smile to soften and smooth his jagged edges. In the end, Alexei decided to keep it as simple as it was complicated because he knew that she was worth it.

"I am here because I want you," he replied in his brutally honest way. "I have great responsibilities, and there is not enough time in a day to handle them all, but for YOU, I will find, and make the time. You have my word, which I do not give lightly if ever at all, Vivienne. You will not regret taking a chance on me. This is my promise to you for always."

Clear as day, Vivienne recognized his yearning for her raging unguarded in his eyes; it matched her own. Even though the words were music to her ears, she remained in place like a cautious animal sensing a nearby predator ready to pounce. Words were just words until you turned them into actions, which developed into patterns. That was what Vivienne looked for in a man. She'd been more than hurt in the past by a man who'd shown her that repeatedly until she'd finally accepted that painful lesson.

Breath suspended, Alexei watched uncertainty take up residency on Vivienne's face, her teeth worrying her bottom lip. The regretful twist of her head sent her black hair flying back and forth around her face, and her words were an unchecked blow to Alexei's gut and ego.

"I'm sorry. You just aren't my type."

"And what type is that?" Alexei challenged as fury coursed through his veins. He straightened from his casual stance on his Mercedes, primed to do battle and wear her down. "Because I'm not black?"

Taken aback by the abrupt change in his demeanor, Vivienne warily replied, "No you're not. I've never dated outside of my race, but that's not what I was referring to."

She looked him up and down with regret, still unable to believe what she was about to do.

"I don't date gangsters. Ever. You're wasting both of our time if that's what you are, and I don't believe in my time being wasted, Mr. Romankov."

Alexei bit back a grin. So much fire in her! He could not wait to make her his in every sense of the word.

"I do not know what you've heard about me to give you such an impression, but I can assure you that I am not a gangster. I am a businessman, complete with a degree."

He wondered if she would be able to make the distinction in their words. Technically, he wasn't a gangster. The correct term for his profession in his circles was assassin, but at least he hadn't lied about having a degree. He just didn't use it that much. Except for her, Alexei would make the necessary adjustments to his lifestyle and destroy anyone who got in their way or between them.

"What's it going to be, Vivienne Pembrooke?"

Her instincts were screaming run.

Do not skip, or power walk away from this man! Take your high heels off and shatter Florence Griffith-Joyner's track records! Why are you still standing here, bitch?! It's really not that hard to do. Just put one foot in front of the other and repeat the process!

And Vivienne did, until they put her right in front of the tall, dangerous Russian because her greedy, eager heart was another matter altogether. She couldn't lie to herself and say she didn't want him. Alexei's eyes gleamed with triumph as she warned him, "Don't lie to me, disrespect me, or take me for dumb pussy! I am my own person and in this until I decide I don't want to be. Do you understand that, Romankov?"

Solemnly Alexei nodded his head. "May I kiss you now?"

"Yes-mmmph!" Vivienne sighed as his warm firm lips claimed hers ravenously. His tongue glided between hers to sensuously sweep her mouth. She softly cried out in wonder as he bit her lips, soothing away the sting with the velvet touch of his tongue. Sooo damn good. Powerlessly, Vivienne clung to him as her tongue did some exploring of its own and curled around his.

Alexei yanked her by her hips into him as he dominated her soft mouth. He couldn't get enough of her sweet-spicy taste, and his hands slid up into her hair to yank her head back as the kiss raged out of control. Still, it was not enough for him. He pushed Vivienne back against the Mercedes and dropped his hands down to her ass, growling into her mouth as he cupped the perfect globes and squeezed them firmly before slapping a cheek sharply.

Her sharp cry of surprised pleasure brought Alexei back to reality and their location as people gave them disapproving frowns. Over Vivienne's shoulder, he met their stares. His lethal one dared them to protest, and they hurriedly averted their eyes and scurried away. Alexei dropped his forehead to her shoulder, desperately trying to find some semblance of control as he rubbed her hips and ass possessively. Drawing in a shuddering breath, he pulled back to stare into her drowsy, desire-filled eyes then her pink swollen lips.

In the cool night air, underneath the scent of her Chanel perfume, Alexei could detect the decadent fragrance of her arousal, and his mouth watered voraciously for a taste.

"You are wet for me?"

Wordlessly, Vivienne nodded, and he traced his finger from her forehead to her high cheekbone down to her parted lips and she sucked it into her mouth teasingly, loving the way his eyes darkened to a shade of blue-black as her tongue wrapped around the digit and she bit down.

Alexei's body clenched uncontrollably, demanding he stake his claim tonight. He could no longer ignore it. Gripping her elbow, he escorted her to the passenger side of his car and held it open for her.

"Then we must do something about that. Get in the car, Vivienne."

She jerked free of him with a defiant glower as she walked past him and got into his car.

"As long as you understand that it's because I. Want. To. Not because you think you can order me around! I am my own person, and if you don't understand that now, Romankov, trust and believe it's gonna be a problem for you later."

Alexei squatted down until they were eye-level. "And as long as you understand that you are MY woman now, Vivienne, and there is nothing I won't do to protect you, even from yourself, we won't have a problem, da?"

His lips claimed hers ruthlessly, and Vivienne clung to him ardently and gave as good as she got.

Truer words had never been spoken by either of them as they would come to discover in the years that followed.

CHAPTER *One*

Washington D.C.

THE INTERCOM BUZZED ON VIVIENNE Romankov's desk. Tersely she answered it with, "Raeann, I specifically told you that I wasn't to be interrupted and to hold all my calls. Thank you so very much for not adhering to my directives, even though that's what I pay you for."

Silence met her reprimand, and she sighed impatiently.

"Raeann? I can hear you breathing, so I know you're not dead, honey. What is it that you wanted?"

Her new receptionist emitted a high-pitched strangled sound before speaking in her thin, reedy voice. "I do apologize for bothering you, Vivienne, but Dr. Klaus is here. She's insisting that I inform you that she is not taking 'no' for an answer today. She also said to tell you that if you refuse, she will break her client/patient confidentiality agreement-"

Vivienne disconnected the call, rose from her chair, and swiftly exited her office. She stormed down the long corridor of R.R. & S. Relations to the front desk as the smooth baritone of Nat King Cole crooned the "Christmas Song" from hidden, overhead speakers. Vivienne didn't even linger to admire the newly hanging gold and silver deco mesh wreaths with the silver reindeer ornaments positioned on each office door. Normally, those, along with the fresh white poinsettias in burnished gold urns at both ends of the hallway, would put her in a festive mood, but not at this very moment. Not Vivienne had a nosy, interfering shrink to kill. Not even the sight of the ten-foot-tall flocked Fraser fir, gorgeously decorated in white, silver, and gold ornaments and bows, brought a smile to her face as caterers hustled and bustled around preparing for tonight's office Christmas Party.

Her laser-like focus was solely on the woman clad in a pair of dark jeans, tucked into black boots, and a white button-down dress shirt covered by her long, black overcoat. Atop her head sat a knitted black beanie with a fur pompom. She was a natural beauty, who never wore a stitch of makeup. Of Japanese descent, her facial features were delicate and serene, making her seemingly approachable to her patients. Currently, she was gaily singing along with the rest of the staff, who quickly scattered when they saw Vivienne's thunderous expression.

Laura Klaus finally noticed her dear friend glaring at her and remained totally unfazed as she glanced around the now empty area, save Raeann, who was doing her best to blend into the reception desk. Laura smiled merrily, and Vivienne knew her eyes were alive with humor behind her tinted reading glasses.

"You sure know how to clear a room, sweetie! It's good to see you!"

Vivienne tried to hold onto her stern expression, but it was hard to do with Laura's infectious personality. She came forward with her arms outstretched and hugged one of her closest confidantes tightly.

"You're such a huge pain in my ass, Laura! What the hell are you doing here? I thought you'd be on the plane with your family by now to Japan."

"Well, I would be if someone wasn't avoiding me like the plague," Laura returned eloquently as she side-eyed Vivienne, who avoided her gaze as they walked down the hallway to her office.

Carefully she scrutinized Vivienne's appearance. There were no outward signs of distress, but when it came to her willful sister-friend, the signs were rarely obvious. As usual, Vivienne was impeccably dressed in a fitted, knee-length black turtleneck dress with a black, red, and white abstract-printed boyfriend blazer. Her black hair was perfectly curled and pushed away from her face with a thin black headband.

"Per usual, you're runway ready. I love those knee-high boots, but I'd break my freaking neck in them! I don't know how you do it, Viv."

"Yes, you do," Vivienne returned lightly. "No one knows better than you how important appearances are to me."

"What's your saying? Never let them see you crack? Which completely contradicts that other statement of yours that you're fond of saying when I compliment you. How does it go?"

"Are you referring to "Black don't crack"?"

"That's the one!"

They shared a laugh as they entered Vivienne's office and she shut the door.

Laura settled onto the pink sofa and patted the spot next to her. "Please have a seat and tell me why you're avoiding me."

Vivienne remained standing as she vehemently protested, "I'm not avoiding you! I just have heaps to do before Christmas. The office party is in two hours. I have tons of shopping to do and two client meetings before leaving for Whiskey Row on Monday, and—"

"And this is the time of the year that your best friend was murdered," Laura reminded her gently, causing Vivienne to fall silent. "The time that Moira was murdered and your marriage fell apart."

"Alexei and I have reconciled and are doing fine," Vivienne stubbornly refuted. "Everyone is doing well, so please do me this one favor and drop it, Laura."

"Just because people are well doesn't mean that they can't still be works in progress. Are you really going to tell me that you and Alexei have addressed all of your issues?" Laura challenged her with knowing eyes.

"The boys make the time to talk, especially Casey, but you've been M.I.A. for a couple of months. If you tell me that you have no doubts or fears about your relationship, then I'll stop prying. Nevertheless, please remember that I'm not just your therapist; I'm your friend as well, one that cares deeply about you."

Laura watched as Vivienne stalked to her desk and picked up her meditation balls, rolling them with a thoughtful expression. She allowed her words to sink in and waited in silence. Her heart went out to her dear friend who hadn't exactly started out that way. There were moments in the beginning of their relationship where Laura feared the other woman would stab her and smile and laugh while doing it.

She could still vividly recall the day a much younger Vivienne banged on her office door before throwing it open and stepping in, holding a crying baby in her arms.

EYES SHINING BRIGHTLY WITH UNSHED tears, Vivienne boldly announced, "I heard you're the best this town has to offer, Doc, and that's what I need. I refuse to settle for anything less."

Laura studied the stunning but defiant woman who seemed as though she were trying her damnedest to keep it together and warily replied, "I don't know about that, but I'll certainly do my best, Miss. How can I help you?"

The woman sniffled and almost collapsed with relief at her answer, finally allowing her tears to fall. She wiped them from her eyes, and Laura's concern grew as she noted that those lovely eyes were the windows for the bottomless pain the stranger carried.

"That's good." She cleared her throat and this time her answer was almost childlike as she whispered, "Because I need you to fix me, please."

Although Vivienne said she wanted help and showed up to their weekly meetings promptly, it would be another month before Laura actually broke through her impenetrable shell.

"I'm afraid I can no longer see you, Vivienne," she announced, watching the restless woman go through her usual silent routine of pacing the room back and forth for the hour while she clutched at the pendant dangling from her neck. "While I do appreciate the money that I get just to watch you perfect your catwalk, I feel that neither one of us is spending our time productively."

The look Vivienne gave her should have scorched her to a charcoal briquette. "Is that what you think of me, lady? Are my looks all you see?! You're supposed to be helping me! Just know that while you are silently judging me, I'm silently judging your "Little House On The Prairie" hairstyle and outfits!"

"I happen to like my clothes, Vivienne," Laura managed to speak calmly even as she fought the urge to get up and go change her clothes.

"But this isn't about me; it's about you, and the problems you won't address! You have a child, and I'm

concerned for both of your well-beings with all of this tension in your house."

"What do you want me to say?!" Vivienne shouted as she began to cry in earnest. "Do you want me to tell you how my best friend was murdered by her husband and that I blamed my husband?! Or how I can never go back to him, no matter how much I want to?! How about the fact that my friend left behind three wonderful boys that, my husband, our friend Ian, and I are now responsible for, and that they'll also need your help too? I'm trying to stand on my own two feet and get my public relations firm running, and my daughter has developed colic! I'm devastated, heartbroken, sleep-deprived, tired, and scared! I feel like I can't do anything right, and it's killing me!"

Laura was speechless. On the outside, this woman appeared as if she didn't have a care in the world and that men should be tripping over themselves to get to her, but on the inside, she was the equivalent of the Chernobyl Disaster. She rose and grabbed a box of Kleenex, passing them to Vivienne and leading her to the chaise. Exhausted, Vivienne fell on to it.

"This is good, Vivienne. I know you're overwhelmed, but we made progress today. We will get through this together. I promise you, brighter days will come."

"MY HUSBAND AND I KNOW what we have together. We're committed to making us work," Vivienne finally said. "We love each other, and I could never see myself with anyone else. *There is no other man for me.*"

"And does he feel the same way?" Laura asked.

She'd encountered Vivienne's husband on numerous occasions throughout the years when he brought the boys to therapy and had always been intrigued by Alexei Romankov. He was a devilishly handsome man and always charming to her, nonetheless Laura could sense there was so much more to him. She could read the questions regarding Vivienne swirling in his eyes, but not once had he ever vocalized them. His pain was virtually tangible, and he wore it like a heavy cloak.

It was wrong of her, Laura knew, but once, she'd left out a magazine, opened to an article featuring Vivian and her friend and business partner Ian Rusnik when she knew Darby was coming to visit and left the room when they arrived. Upon her return, he and the magazine were gone. When Alexei came back to pick Darby up, he'd stared at her for a long moment and then inclined his head in silent gratitude before soundlessly disappearing out the door.

"That there is no other man for me? As a matter of fact, it was he who informed me," Vivienne joked, but Laura did not smile.

Her friend rolled her eyes. "Yes, he does feel the same, Laura. I trust him implicitly. I'm sorry that I haven't been by, and you're right; I'm nowhere near done, but our being back together has made me open to whatever the future brings because I know we'll be together! The family is continually expanding, and for the first time in a very long time, I don't feel so...*bereft* during this time of the year. The boys talk about Moira more, and it doesn't hurt them like it used to."

"That doesn't change what occurred, Vivienne, and you know it." Laura stood up and gave her friend another hug. "I've got to get going, but I'm glad we talked. I just want to leave you with one more thing, okay?"

"Lay it on me!" Vivienne urged with relief, now that she didn't have to think about all the things that were still unsaid and simmering on the back burner between her and Lex.

"You weren't the only one who was hurt, Vivi. Alexei may adore, and love you beyond reason, but he was hurt by your breakup as well. A word of caution: His pain *will* manifest itself, and when it happens, it will not be pretty, my friend."

Laura kissed her cheek. "Merry Christmas."

"Merry Christmas," Vivienne returned automatically and walked her out. They chatted about the Sullivan brothers' Take A Stand foundation and their families, ending the conversation with another hug as they parted ways.

Vivienne's walk back to her office was a preoccupied one as Laura's words echoed in her head.

"His pain will manifest itself. When it happens, it will not be pretty, my friend."

THE HOLIDAY OFFICE PARTY WAS in full swing, and everyone from the D.C. office was having a festive time as the deejay spun Christmas music mixed with top forty hits. Employees noshed on fried green BLT sliders, buttermilk fried chicken tenders drizzled in hot honey, sweet potato crispers, truffled deviled eggs topped with smoked prosciutto and gorgonzola, lobster and avocado crostinis, and beet and orange frisee salad with cranberry vinaigrette. Servers passed around signature holiday cocktails-Christmas Sangria, Plum & Thyme Prosecco Smash, and Rudolph's Tipsy Spritzer. Per the firm's mandatory clause, employees could only indulge if they drank responsibly or accepted a ride from the car service Vivienne hired.

They took pictures with the well-built, good-looking Santa Claus' and indulged in the assorted cookie and hot chocolate bar while getting facials, pedicures, and manicures by the spa service Vivienne hired for the event.

She enjoyed listening to her employees' chatter as she worked the room. When they were on the clock, Vivienne was tough and uncompromising. If she was working, their asses had better be working, no excuses. She'd grinded and paid her dues and expected them to do the same. No one had handed her anything in her career, and Vivienne was proud of all that she'd worked for. Yes, she'd had a trust fund from her father that she received when she graduated from college. But she'd never touched it until she decided to go into business for herself.

There was also the money Alexei had deposited into her account every month after she left him. While together, he'd insisted on paying for everything, and the thought of her paying for anything caused terrible rows between them. Once, during their separation, she'd tried to move the money from her account into trust funds set up for the boys, but by the next day, the sum was back in her account. Vivienne didn't even want to know how he discovered something like that, but she hadn't attempted it again. She'd never touched it and only used her salary to support herself. Alexei was very adamant that *he* paid for everything concerning his children, whether it was at his house or hers.

It was fun to listen to the conversations also as she moved through the crowd. It gave Vivienne an inside peek into her employees' personal lives, letting her know how they were doing outside of the office without her having to get all up in their business.

"I don't know if Mike and I are going to last! I feel like he's only using me as a bed warmer!" Jalissa from accounting complained to Sonya and Andrea from marketing. "I mean, the sex is amazing, but...how foul is that, right?"

Vivienne rolled her eyes as Sonya and Andrea made appropriately sympathetic noises.

Seriously? You're complaining about getting some?! Jesus, complain if he attempts to use you as a bulletproof vest instead of for sex. Damn girl; don't complain about getting quality dick! That shit is harder to acquire than a female president in the White House!

There was an awkward silence, and she realized that the women were staring at her with shocked expressions. It was only then that Vivienne realized she'd actually said the words aloud.

"Sorry! I was just walking by, and I happened to hear your conversation," she murmured waving her hand dismissively before walking away. "Carry on!"

Shortly after Vivienne received a call from Terrell Weston regarding his agent and cousin, baseball superstar Vincent Weston, whom R. R. & S. had just taken on as a client. The ruggedly good-looking athlete was a public relations nightmare that no one was willing to touch. Somehow Vivienne had convinced Jack and Ian to let her take a shot.

"Two words, Jack: Inez. Gaines. She made all those reality stars look like Mother Freaking Theresa. Just look at her now! She's now branding herself as a lifestyle guru, and people love her! We can get him on track. I KNOW I can do this."

It wasn't that Vincent wasn't a likable guy. He was. In addition to that, he was also charming, extremely talented, a philanthropist, and in love with his wife, who happened to be his high school sweetheart. They had two adorable children, and the media loved them. Life was charmed for the Westons until Puffin Adams, a well-known porn star, came forward and proved that she'd been having a five-year affair with the athlete. Devastated and humiliated, his wife filed for divorce and took the kids. Vincent hadn't been able to function since. His batting average had decreased, and he'd been missing plays in his shortstop position. As a result of the scandal, Vincent had lost several major endorsements because he'd broken their morality clauses.

Vivienne knew what his *real* problem was. He was a ho who liked to do ho-ish things, plain and simple...just not with his wife. Sure, he probably loved her and was a first-class bastard for what he'd done to his family, but that man had no business getting his hot ass married. He knew it and so did the entire world. Now his game was suffering because he was trying to live like a monk and get his family back when all he wanted was pussy galore.

"Hey, Viv. I hate to bother you, but I just wanted to let you know that Vince has been talking out of his ass for the last couple of hours, and I kind of feel like if he doesn't see you, he'll flip out and do something to cause a bigger scandal for himself. Any chance you could meet me at our family restaurant LuLu Belle's? All that hard work you put into him will be for nothing if he spirals out of control, you feel me?"

Shit.

Vivienne was supposed to meet Alexei at home in an hour and a half. They were going to spend the weekend here in town before heading back to Whiskey Row. She really didn't want to prolong their separation any longer than necessary but felt it was best to address Vincent's issues before starting her Christmas vacation. The holidays could be an especially stressful time on those missing their loved ones.

No one knew that better than her.

"I've never been there, but yes, I'll meet you there. Give me an hour to officially close down the office. And Terrell?"

"Yes, ma'am?"

"It's your job to keep him sober. So, if he's been drinking…by the time I get there, he *better* be sober. Are *you* feelin' me?"

Terrell cleared his throat nervously. "I gotchu, Viv."

"Glad we understand each other."

Vivienne disconnected the call and stared at her phone with dread. She hated to make the next call but knew transparency was necessary in keeping the lines of communication open. She scrolled through her contacts and found the one Alexei had input himself. As always, she smiled like a schoolgirl with her first crush when she saw "Love of My Life". Vivienne pressed the call symbol and listened to it ring.

Please don't pick up, she thought but did so half-heartedly. She loved to listen to her husband's rich, cultured voice…except when he was annoying the hell out of her by bossing her around.

"Vivi."

It was only her name, but the way he said it made it sound like it was the password to all of the universe's secrets. Before him, she'd always just been plain old, practical Vivienne, who'd just wanted a normal, safe life. But the moment she'd agreed to be with Alexei and he'd thrust so deeply into her and groaned, *"Vivi, my sweet, Vivi!"* Vivienne had felt *special.* Like being "Vivi" was her super power.

"How are you doing, Mr. Romankov?" she greeted him, touching the quickening pulse at her throat. Just speaking to him caused her body to react uncontrollably. Even after all these years, she was still too sprung on him. "I miss you."

"As I do you." His voice lowered an octave. "I'll show you exactly how much as soon as I see you. Please make sure you're up to it."

'Yes, about that..." she hesitated. "I'm sorry, but something's come up-"

"What's the problem, Vivienne?" The warmth had evaporated from Alexei's tone as he challenged her. "I thought we were in agreement that *nothing* interferes with our time together. When did that change? I do not recall conceding to a revised agreement."

"Nothing has changed, Lex. I just have a client that I need to touch base with," she explained patiently. "It will be quick, I promise. The office party is winding down, and I'll just dash over there before heading to the house. An hour tops." Vivienne raised her gaze toward the ceiling, praying asking for a miracle as she waited for his response.

The silence lengthened before Alexei finally responded. "Have you eaten?"

"I haven't. I was waiting for you to get in," Vivienne answered with relief as she gathered her coat and purse before locking her office. "I wanted to cook for you tonight."

"Don't bother. I'll pick up some food when I get in to save us some time." Alexei responded decisively. "I guarantee that you will enjoy it, and the place isn't that far from the house."

"That sounds like a plan. I'm starving and not just for food," Vivienne teased provocatively.

"Likewise, my dear. I'll make sure to order larger portions so that you'll be well-nourished. You will be needing all of your strength for our time together."

"This time, no biting! If the marks were discreet, where only you and I could see them, then that would be different, but since you don't play fair, NO BITING, Lex. I mean it!" she insisted obstinately.

Alexei's warm laugh came down the line, and the sound sent a flow of desire through Vivienne, causing her to lean against the wall for support. Lawd, she couldn't wait to love up on her man...

"I put them where everyone can see so there is no mistake of how well-loved and cherished you are, Mrs. Romankov."

Just listening to the honesty of his declaration made Vivienne's resolve weaken. "Well, damn, babe, when you put it like that..."

"Oh, I do. Do not keep me waiting longer than necessary, my love," Alexei stated arrogantly before ringing off.

"I can't wait," Vivienne whispered to herself before heading back to the party with a spring in her step. In less than two hours, she would be back where she'd always belonged.

In Alexei's arms.

CHAPTER *Two*

GRADUALLY THE TENSION EBBED FROM Alexei Romankov's body and was replaced by relief when he ended the call. *Vivienne wasn't canceling their plans.* He leaned back in his chair and looked out of the window of his private plane, seeing nothing but darkness. It matched his mood moments ago, and he felt foolish for jumping to conclusions without hearing Vivienne out. *Christ, could anyone really blame him, though?* After years of living apart, false hopes of reconciliation, and her avoidance every chance she could, they were finally back together again and had remained solid for several months.

Running Romankov Industries kept Alexei extremely busy, but nothing came before Vivienne and their family, and he knew it was the same for her. That was why the weekends were sacred to them. They rotated which city they spent them in to accommodate their work schedules and family, and this weekend he was looking forward to taking her out in D.C.

Alexei stared down at his phone's screensaver. It was a candid shot of Vivienne, Ruby, D.J., and baby Jack sleeping in their massive bed, and it brought a smile of contentment and peace to his face. It had been taken Thanksgiving weekend, and they'd pretty much been gift-wrapped from their eager parents when they'd pleaded to come over. Alexei found he could not deny any of them a single thing. Especially little Ms. Ruby Aileen when she held his hand and fluttered her eyelashes at him. His own daughter, Kat, affectionately called her "The Incorrigible Con Artist", but in Alexei's eyes, she could do no wrong.

He was still amazed at all the changes that had happened in such a short amount of time. He now had grandbabies to spoil silly and one more on the way. That weekend had been a particularly wonderful one as they all clamored for attention from him and Vivi. At the end of the night, the trio had fallen asleep between them as he and his wife held hands above their heads and smiled at each other, content with the chaos. It was nice to have the estate filled with their chatter and laughter. Their housekeeper had loved cooking and baking for them and spoiled them silly with treats. Alexei had taken them to the petting zoo he'd reopened when it was just Ruby last Christmas, and he'd shown them his massive dogs that patrolled the estate with the guards. He'd been absolutely adamant that under no circumstances were the children to go near them, and it was the one time he'd refused to give in to Ruby's pleas.

"WELL, WHY DO YOU HAVE the dogs then, Papa?" D.J. asked. As usual, he was brimming with curiosity regarding everything around him. It was not surprising that the massive canines that towered above him and came to Alexei's chest on his six-foot-six-inch frame was at the top of his list of things to know about.

"The Caucasian Ovcharka is a guard dog and is meant to defend, not pet or play fetch with. These, dear boy, are the dogs used in Russia to take down bears and protect your flocks from predators. They will guard you with their lives as long as you are family. But if not, the results are seldom pretty. Can you understand that, young D.J.?"

"Yes, Papa," D.J. replied without taking his eyes from the massive furry creatures. "Have you ever had to use them in that manner?"

"Not I, but my father did all the time," Alexei replied, thinking of Boris's old saying:

"Some people are born with loyalty; others, you have to instill in them through fear."

ALEXEI REMEMBERED THOSE WORDS AS clear as day as he and his father stood and watched the dogs play with their toys.

He was just settling into his town car when his phone signaled an incoming call. Alexei glanced down and grinned when he saw that it was from his daughter-in-law, Noelle. While other parents might have issues with their childrens' spouses, Alexei adored all three of his bonus daughters. Like his wife and daughter, they were successfully smart businesswomen, with kind personalities. Noelle, Sidra, and Avery also loved their significant others fiercely. He truly could not have prayed for better women for his sons.

"Hello, Noelle."

"Hi, Alexei! I hope everything is going well. I know you're on 'couple time' so I'll be quick. I just wanted to make sure that when you and Viv call Ruby later tonight to find out what she wants Santa to bring her, *please* do not agree to anything beforehand." Noelle's voice ended on a desperate note that had Alexei struggling not to laugh.

Clearly, Ruby was asking for more than the sun, stars, and moon combined. It had to be most outrageous if her mother was forewarning him.

"That bad, eh?"

"Please just tell me parenting gets easier," was all she begged of him before hanging up.

Now, she had Alexei curious as he drove through the crowded streets of a merrily illuminated D.C. toward Vivienne's residence. *What could be so terrible that he was being asked not to spoil his darling girl?* He remembered when Casey had begged for a Gila monster, and Darby wanted his lip pierced. Kat had bypassed Vivienne and asked his permission for a new hairstyle. She'd come home with half of her hair shaved off by her best friend Autumn. Jack was the only one who'd never asked or done anything ludicrous.

Alexei pulled into the well-lit, busy parking lot of LuLu Belle's, and his stomach automatically rumbled at the taste of their infamous bacon-wrapped filet with gruyere-cauliflower and potato gratin. The jazz supper club was a place that he'd discovered by accident while waiting for the boys to finish a therapy session. This particular location was new to this area, but since Alexei knew the owner personally and that they were here overseeing the place, he knew the quality of the establishment and the food would be exceptional.

He valeted his car and nodded at the doorman as he entered the low-lit club. The intimate and elegant lounge was filled with well-dressed patrons having a good time as they listened to the smooth R&B the band onstage was playing.

"As I live and breathe, is that Alexei Romankov?"

Somehow, the smoky voice was heard above everyone else and the patrons parted for the owner, LuLu Weston. She was making her way toward him, her ample hips swaying, and her arms held out with a lovely smile of greeting for him.

"Ms. LuLu." Alexei gallantly bowed over her hand and kissed it before giving her a warm hug and kissing her smooth dark cheek.

The platinum blonde, eighty-year-old woman's tawny complexion grew flushed and she laughed bashfully, tickled pink by his charming demeanor, and squeezed him to her. "It's been awhile, baby! How ya been? Ya look real good!"

"Yes, it has. I have been well and you?" Alexei surveyed the club thoroughly before his gaze lowered to hers. "No sign of trouble?"

"I haven't had any trouble since the day you stepped in and helped a damsel in distress out!" she sassed, winking at him.

"That is always good to know. Should that change, you have my number. Please don't hesitate to use it," Alexei urged her warmly.

Their friendship was one that neither had expected more than two decades ago. While waiting for Casey, Alexei was sitting in his car, listening to Fleetwood Mac sing about "Dreams" when he'd spotted two thugs mugging an older woman at knifepoint. Instead of cowering, she'd tried reasoning with them. Enraged by her stalling, one of the men slapped her to the ground. That's when Alexei emerged from his car with his nine-millimeter already in his hand and pointed at them.

FROZEN WITH FEAR, THEY REMAINED in place as he advanced upon them, their eyes glued to his weapon. When he reached them, Alexei slammed the offender's face into the brick wall, and he dropped to the ground. Covering his windpipe with his boot, Alexei kept his gun trained on the other motherfucker who looked ready to pass out. Slowly, he reached down and held his hand out to the woman as she struggled to her feet.

"Are you okay, madam?" he questioned while monitoring the two delinquents.

"Yes, sir!" she responded in a hearty voice. "It'll take more than these wannabe thugs to keep me down. Why don't you go on ahead and let him up, baby?"

Alexei removed his foot from the vagrant's throat, and uncertainly he rose to his feet only to be knocked down again by the woman's uppercut to his jaw.

"There! Now I feel a whole lot better, sir!" she chortled to Alexei, who smiled his admiration. "Why don't you come on with ol' LuLu and let me fix you a plate at my new restaurant?"

She proudly pointed across the street at the small brown building with the sign that read LuLu Belle's. "These fools don't bother me none, baby. I was here before they were born, and I'll be here long after their life of crime finally catches up with them."

"How about I meet you there? I'd like to speak to these gentlemen alone," Alexei suggested smoothly.

She chuckled at the petrified fools. "You gonna learn today, suckas!"

When Alexei finally joined her, she had a plate with blackened salmon topped with crawfish sauce over steamed white rice waiting for him. It was accompanied by a large slice of bourbon-pecan-praline pie and a large sweet tea. He didn't realize how hungry he was until he sat down at the table.

"I appreciate your kindness and generosity," Alexei spoke gruffly, feeling touched by her gesture. The food was delicious. It was something he instinctively knew Vivienne would enjoy. Bracing himself, Alexei absorbed the searing ache that came with that realization. That and the intense longing that always came when he thought of his estranged wife.

"Not more than I appreciate yours!" she cackled. "The name's LuLu, and you're the first person to visit my new restaurant! You come see me whenever you're in the neighborhood, Alexei. You're good with me, and it'll always be on the house!"

"You will not have any more trouble from them or anyone else," he assured her. "Before I go, I will leave my number, and you are to call me if this should ever occur again. I'm Alexei, by the way."

"What you are, is my numero uno VIP! Promise you'll stop in from time to time?"

Alexei did, and they each kept their word to one another. LuLu always refused his money, so Alexei always left the balance equivalent of his meal as a tip. He enjoyed her company and the way she fussed over him. Before he left, she always played a song on her piano for him, and he sang along. Ten years ago, she stopped playing due to health reasons, and her niece took over the singing in the evenings. When LuLu mentioned expanding, Alexei had reached out to her bank to ensure it happened with no issues.

"DOES THAT OFFER APPLY TO all members of Lulu's family, Alexei?"

The question was uttered innocently enough, but there was nothing wrong with Alexei's hearing, and he caught the hidden meaning behind the newcomer's invitation loud and clear as she came to stand between her aunt and Alexei.

"No, it's a private number," he returned coolly to LuLu's niece, Merlene.

"That's a shame," she drawled as she twirled her long black hair around her finger and let it spring loose. "Welcome back, Alexei. What took you so long? Couldn't stay away?"

Covetously, Merlene's eyes swept over the fine-ass Russian and caught her bottom lip between her teeth. From the moment, she'd been introduced him ten years ago, she'd wanted him. Unlike other men Merlene knew, Alexei barely acknowledged her except in greeting, and it drove her *crazy*! Although her aunt tried to assure her he wasn't attempting to play hard to get, Merlene knew better. She could only imagine what a force he was between the sheets.

It was inconceivable to her that Alexei was uninterested in what she was offering him. Her almond shaped sable eyes, full pouty lips, chocolate skin, and curvy body were a combined with her voice was an irresistible package many of her suitors had tried to unwrap. In Merlene's biased opinion, she was the next Whitney Houston, may she rest in paradise. Thinking of her idol gave her inspiration for tonight's song.

"Go on and get on stage, Merlene," LuLu shooed her away with an exasperated motion of her hand.

"I'm going; just know that my song tonight has special meaning, Alexei," Merlene cooed to him, placing her hand on his bicep. She resisted the urge to squeeze and explore the muscles underneath her hand before sashaying away.

"What am I gonna do with her?" LuLu voiced her aggravation aloud. "Where are my manners; let's get you to a table!"

"I'm actually doing takeout tonight," Alexei explained apologetically. "I'm bringing it to my wife—"

"Your wife!" Lulu clapped her hands in excitement. "I'm so happy for you! Please bring her with you the next time you come! I'd love to meet her. Am I getting you the usual?"

"I definitely will, and yes; two orders please," he said with a fully relaxed smile.

"Have a seat at the bar, and I'll get you all squared away. I made some German chocolate cake today that I'll add along with your usual pie, baby."

Alexei followed her request and sat down, checking his emails as the lights dimmed and the music began to play. His body tensed as the spotlight fell on him, and he recognized the strains of the song as Merlene began to sing.

I used to cry myself to sleep at night
But that was all before he came
I thought love had to hurt to turn out right
But now he's here
It's not the same, it's not the same

Irritation began to build at her persistence, and Alexei glanced at his watch impatiently, eager as hell to get out of there. He could feel the eyes of other patrons on him, and he deliberately kept his back to Merlene even as she drew closer.

He's all I've got
He's all I've got in this world
But he's all the man that I need

Alexei felt a certain way about disrespecting women - you just didn't do it. But right now, he didn't feel that applied to Merlene. He'd rebuffed or blatantly ignored every single one of her provocative and wonton attempts, yet still, she paid him no mind, refusing to acknowledge his disinterest.

He saw red when she placed her hand on his back, as if staking her claim. Alexei started to turn around, but then she gave an ear-splitting shriek of pain into the microphone that pierced the eardrums of the club patrons, and they quickly covered them in protection, including him.

Unexpectedly, Vivienne's irritated voice filled the room, and it was pure music to Alexei's ears.

"Trust and believe, this ain't a problem you want, bitch."

VIVIENNE WANTED TO YANK THE wench's arm up higher behind her back until she heard the satisfying snap of her bones breaking. She'd just left her meeting with the Weston cousins in the private dining room. Vivienne was feeling positive about the progress she was making with the baseball player until she saw the heffa touch her husband while passionately singing Whitney Houston's "All The Man That I Need".

What. The. Fuck?!

"You're hurting me!" the formerly confident singer whimpered into the microphone as Alexei shifted out of the way and Vivienne shoved her face down onto the bar.

"Sorry about that, sweetie. I tend to react accordingly when I see some female tryin' to run up on my man," Vivienne explained in a sotto voice that belied her fury, as she deliberately tightened her grip.

With a surly look, she side-eyed her amused husband. "Thought you were getting dinner?"

Alexei leaned over and kissed her forehead in greeting. "I am. This place has the most divine filet mignon in town! Trust me; it's to die for, Vivi! I was just speaking to LuLu, the owner, about you, and she insisted I'd have to bring you in. I think you'll like her -"

"Let go off me!" A terrified Merlene cried out, interrupting them. "My bad! I swear I won't do it again!"

"Damn straight you won't," Vivienne agreed succinctly, reluctantly releasing her. "Now run along, little girl."

Humiliated, Merlene took off for the employee's entrance without looking back at either one of them.

Although she tried to appear calm, Vivienne was boiling on the inside thanks to the sight of the sexpot singer all over her man, complete with a light show. What was worse was that Alexei hadn't tried to discourage her! Insecurities were creeping in the same way they had when she saw him with the blonde woman at The Pink Champagne months ago, in Whiskey Row. Even now, he *still* hadn't really explained who she was.

"Do you always allow yourself to be pawed like that?"

His smile disappeared, and his eyes turned to shards of ice. "Is that what you think you saw?"

"Ain't no thinkin' about it, Lex," she scoffed with a toss of her hair, regarding him with a baleful stare. "I gotta go. You want to discuss shit; bring your ass home."

She walked away from him, only to be stopped by Congressman Stuart Royce as he entered the club with two of his aides. With his blonde hair, blue eyes, Colgate smile, and charm, the politician was a favorite of the people he passionately championed.

"Vivienne! Aren't you a sight for sore eyes! You're not leaving, are you? Come have a drink with me and let's catch up!"

He was one of her firm's clients but had expressed a personal interest in her as well. Since his admission of romantic intentions toward her, Vivienne had deemed it a conflict of interest and passed the handsome politician's account to Ian.

Perversely, she gave him a flirtatious smile and squeezed his hand, knowing Alexei was watching them. "Hello, Stuart; I hope you've been well. Unfortunately, I was just on my way out."

He smiled regretfully. "Well, save me a date in the near future for lunch, please. It's been too long since we got together."

"Have a good night, Stuart."

Vivienne did not bother addressing his last comment because she knew like hell Alexei would allow that to happen. Even now, she could feel his blistering rage like a force blasting her out the door.

Not even the frigid winter wind could protect her from its heat.

WHILE WAITING AT HOME FOR Alexei to arrive with their dinner, Vivienne chided herself for leaving him in anger. She didn't want to spend their time together fighting and was more than ready to smooth things over. To take her mind off the incident, Vivienne called her best friend and business partner, Ian Rusnik.

He greeted her with a droll, "I'm surprised Alexei let you up for air long enough for you to even call me. I thought he would have been 'Bolsheviking' you all over the house by now."

"Hush up, "Gandalf the Grey"! He's not here yet but I'm expecting him shortly. I wanted to let you know that the office Christmas party was a success. How did the New York one go?" Vivienne probed, plopping down on her new luxurious bed.

It had arrived shortly after she and Alexei started cohabitating. He'd upgraded her queen-sized bed to a California king to accommodate his size. In her opinion, they would have been fine with a twin long since he liked for her to sleep on him anyway. Vivienne blushed hotly thinking of the many times she'd woken to cumming from his fingers pleasuring her only for him to slide her down onto his waiting shaft. It was an excellent way to start the day they'd both agreed.

"The party went well; as usual, all the womens' faces and boobs fell when they realized there wouldn't be a Sullivan brother sighting. It's amazing to me, that although they know the boys are deeply in love and completely devoted to their wives, them wenches still think they have a shot. They reek of thirst and desperation, and just like garlic and onions; it's a perfume no woman should ever wear."

Vivienne burst out laughing at his disdain. "Those three have been breaking hearts from the cradle and will continue to do so when they're old and rocking on the front porch. I miss you, boo! When can we expect you home? You stayed away for Thanksgiving, and I know you'd better not come up with any sorry excuses to miss Christmas, Ian."

She hesitated for a moment. "I'm going to visit *her* when I go. Like Jackie, it was too painful for me, but now I think I'm ready. I can wait for you if you'd like to join me?"

"Vivi, I'm not sure I'll be making it to Whiskey Row this year," Ian replied carefully. "I have some personal stuff I need to sort through and don't want to put a damper on the festivities. Don't let my decision stop you from going to visit Moira. I've been a few times, and I always feel better afterward. You need to go and talk to her."

She wished she could tell Ian what had happened, but that was a secret, and like Moira, she'd probably take it to her grave. Except a secret was only a secret if kept between two people, and unfortunately for Vivienne, that wasn't the case. It was also the reason she'd stayed away from her husband.

"Your decision wouldn't have anything to do with a certain dreamy-eyed singer, would it? Because if it does, he won't be here this year. He's spending the holidays with Lucky and Lena before going on tour. I don't think we'll be seeing him until Sid gives birth."

"No, it doesn't have to do with Dominick, Vivienne!" Ian blustered. "Are you trying to imply that because we're both gay, we should hang out and be besties?! Look, I have to go. I'll call you in a few days. Give my love to everyone, kiss the babies, and tell

Moira I love her. You know I feel that way about you too, Diva. Behave yourself or better yet, *don't* with Lex. Ciao."

He disconnected the call before Vivienne could reply, and she was left wondering if she'd touched a nerve by bringing up Dominick Harris. She was tempted to call him back and dig deeper but knew Ian would only send her straight to voicemail. Vivienne prayed he was doing well. She knew he'd been lonely since his longtime partner and Noelle's uncle, Harvey Kramer had passed away. Ian was her oldest friend, and she would not leave him flailing in the wind if he was dealing with problems. They'd get through it together whether he liked her interference or not. The same way they always had.

Come hell or highwater.

IAN CARELESSLY TOSSED HIS PHONE on the dresser where it clattered and knocked his cufflinks and Zenith watch to the carpet. Damn, now he'd have to apologize to Vivi for being rude. It wasn't her fault that he was having a late mid-life crisis.

"Is a tantrum worth that fine piece of jewelry breaking?" the naked man lying in bed inquired softly in his light Scottish brogue.

Ian pulled the pack of emergency cigarettes he kept from the inside pocket of his jacket and caught the lighter his companion tossed his way. He opened the window, and the cold air, dampened from the rain, seeped in. Ian lit the Marlboro up and took a heavy drag from it, loving the taste of the nicotine, which was another bad habit he'd fallen back on. He exhaled slowly.

"What's it to you?"

"You're certainly in a mood. Why is it that every time you talk to your friends, they bring out your terrible disposition? If that's the case, why do you even bother? Just cut your losses and be done."

"You know that sounds like a splendid idea," Ian said giving him a meaningful glance. "Shall I start right this second?"

"Stop being so dramatic! Come back to bed and I'll make you feel better."

Ian held in a mocking laugh and raked a hand through his long silver hair. They'd been doing this dance for several years now, and Bradan seemed to think he was God's gift to men. He was average at best in all areas - looks, bed, dressing, and conversation.

In fact, if he hadn't pursued Ian so hard at a particularly low moment in his life, when he was mourning Harvey, he would have never given him the time of day. The sex was decent and that worked for Ian because he was terrified of ever feeling the way Harvey made him feel again, particularly when he died. Ian had wanted to die right along with him. All he was looking for nowadays was a quick release.

"Your decision wouldn't have anything to do with a certain dreamy-eyed singer, would it?"

Ian closed his eyes and pulled harder on the cigarette. Vivienne hadn't been that far off in her assumption, dammit.

"Fine; be like that. Come back to bed and make *me* feel better then," Bradan cajoled.

Ian rolled his eyes and flicked the bud out into the rain and then pulled another condom from his back pocket. What the hell. He could think of worse things to do on a cold rainy night.

"On your elbows and knees, bitch," he demanded silkily.

ALEXEI COULD HEAR THE SHOWER running when he entered the townhouse. That she knew to wash Royce's touch off her before Alexei saw her again, was a good sign. He set the food on the kitchen counter and strolled through the darkened house. Upstairs, only the bedroom light was on. From the doorway of the master bathroom, he took off his clothes, watching his wife showering through the glass doors. The water slid down her honeyed curves and ran in rivulets between her toned thighs. Her puckered nipples were begging for his attention and Alexei was salivating just looking at them. The more he looked at the masterpiece that was Vivienne Romankov, *his* wife, the angrier, and more ardent he became.

She'd touched another man and smiled her special smile at him just to get back at him, for what she *thought* he'd done. As if two could play that game, but Alexei didn't play games, and clearly, his wife had forgotten that fact. It was time to give her a remedial lesson.

"Are you going to stand there gawking? Or will you be joining me?" she taunted him in a husky purr as she slowly washed between the apex between her thighs. Vivienne pressed her breasts to the glass while the sponge fell from her fingers. Yet her hand remained.

Teasing his imagination...

"You are way overdue for a spanking, Vivienne. I'm just debating if it should be now or later," he mused darkly, stepping forward to join her.

How was it the very thought of being disciplined could send her into a tailspin of lust? Vivienne marveled.

She'd seen firsthand what those large hands were capable of and had to press her lips together to keep her whimper of gratitude in as she watched him approach. *Why was Alexei so everything???* He was arrogant, bossy, opinionated, fine, sexy, and fucked like a God...just watching that muscle between his legs lengthen and expand under her voracious gaze had her dick-drunk and drooling for a taste of him.

"Well, then maybe I'll let you give it to me, Lex," she replied breathlessly.

His eyes darkened and Alexei damn near yanked the shower door off in his haste to join her.

The water pouring over her should have made her look like a drowned rat, but Alexei loved her makeup-free face and the way her hair naturally curled up. She rose on tiptoe, and her sweet mouth brushed his in a feather-light kiss. Alexei exhaled harshly as her hands encircled his cock and stroked him torturously slow from base to tip. Her fingers delicately fondling the broad crown.

"Want me to wash your back?"

"Eventually...right now I want to feel your mouth on me. Get on your knees, Vivi," he ordered thickly.

"Only because I want to," she growled defiantly. Her molasses eyes hot with lust as she obeyed. "Not because you said."

"Bullshit." Alexei's hands sank into her wet curls as her lips kissed the head and she ran her tongue along the underside of it. *"Jesus, Vivi. Open up!"*

"Or what, Wolf?" she teased as her tongue stroked him lovingly. *"You'll huff and puff and..."*

Her hands formed a circle around his shaft and stroked him from head to base and caressed his balls on every down stroke. Precum oozed from the tip, and Vivienne swallowed it as she sucked the broad head into her mouth, swirling her tongue around it as she drew more of him in, inch by inch. Alexei hissed with pleasure and flexed his hips, seeking more of the warm, sumptuous cavern of her mouth. Vivienne slowly relaxed her jaw to receive his full girth until he finally hit the back of her throat. Then she devoured him, loving the salty taste and satiny feel of him against her lips and tongue as she increased the pressure, especially around the sensitive head.

"Just like that, Vivi," Alexei encouraged her as he thrust roughly into her mouth, steadily fucking it and holding her steady by her nape. It was mind blowing the way Vivi did him. Her fingers caressed his balls, gently squeezing and tugging while her tongue showed him no mercy. From beneath heavy lids, Alexei observe her lips inhaling him and thought he would lose it as she moaned and the sensations on his dick drove him perilously close to release.

He flexed deeper, faster, and Vivienne's fisted hands tightened as she stroked him in time to his rhythm and suctioned even harder. She loved the feel of Alexei in her mouth and how out of control she was driving him, as his precum steadily flowed onto her tongue. It was a complete turn on for her, and the slickness between her legs had nothing to do with the water cascading over them.

Alexei fisted her hair and tugged gently. *"Come here, wife."*

Vivienne gave one last pull and released him with a soft *pop*. She rose regally, and Alexei quickly pressed her against the glass wall facing the large mirror. He nudged her legs wider apart and entered her from behind with a deep thrust as he fisted her hair and drew her head back to his chest.

"Watch us, my love," he instructed forcefully as his other hand reached down to tease her clit. Their eyes remained locked in the mirror as Alexei fucked her in slow, intense strokes, biting her shoulder to remind her of whom she belonged to. Vivienne shuddered with rapture, her eyes drifting shut as she enjoyed her

husband's ministrations. The hand in her hair tightened, and Alexei yanked her head back and gave her a bruising kiss. Her eyes flew open to meet his, and she could see the dueling emotions between his anger, love, and desire for her.

"I am the only man who will touch you, Vivi. If you wish for Stuart to die, then continue encouraging him or any other man," he hissed as his thrusts came faster and deeper, causing Vivienne to rise up on her tiptoes and wrap her arms around his, widening her stance to steady herself as her orgasm built. *"Do you understand me?"*

"Yesss," she wailed as her pussy began to spasm. Vivienne whimpered in protest when he suddenly withdrew from her. *"What are you doing?!"*

Smirking at her frustration, Alexei grabbed her hand and led her to the shower bench and sat down. "Come fuck your husband, Vivi. He needs to know that he's the only man for you."

Vivienne pushed at him, urging him to lay back, and she eagerly sank down onto his manhood with a shuddered cry of, "Damn that's good!"

She rocked slow and easy on him, her hips undulating as Alexei cupped her breasts and feasted on them hungrily. Vivienne moaned as he pulsated inside of her. She could feel another orgasm building. She drew Alexei's face to hers and kissed him possessively, her tongue mastering his as his hips controlled their movements, and Vivienne pulled away to whisper in his ear.

Why'd you tell me this
Were you looking for my reaction
What do you need to know
Don't you know I'll always be your girl

"Vivienne!" he hissed as his sac tightened. Her husky voice was driving him insane as she rotated between sucking on his earlobe and biting it.

"I love you, Alexei. It's always been, and always will be you," Vivienne swore, pressing her forehead to his.

"You are my heartbeat, Vivienne," Alexei gritted as she spasmed around him, making his toes curl. *"I do not exist without you, my love."*

They came simultaneously, clinging to each other as they reached the ultimate peak together and shattered in an orgasm that felt like an eternity as they whispered their love of each other over and over.

MUCH LATER IN BED, AFTER their delicious dinner had been consumed, did Vivienne question him about the singer.

"Is she always like *that* with you?" Vivienne queried as Alexei's fingers rubbed her bare back in slow lazy circles.

"She is a bit forward, but per her aunt LuLu, who owns the place, it's just her nature. I believe that after tonight, she will have a new approach with people, thanks to you," he confided with amusement, an involuntary smile on his lips.

"LuLu?" she repeated suspiciously. "How long have you been on a first name basis with the owner?"

"I was her first customer years past when she opened and make it a point to visit her restaurant and check on her whenever I come to town. Was the food not to your liking? She insisted I bring you next time. Had you not run off this evening, I would have made proper introductions," Alexei admonished his wife, and pinched her ass.

Vivienne was silent as she absorbed this newfound information about him. *What else did he do while he was in her city that she didn't know about? Or just in general when they weren't together?*

As if reading her mind, Alexei spoke in a firm voice, "I've never been unfaithful to you, Vivienne. Have I had offers? Plenty of them. Have I ever been tempted? I'm a man whose wife up and left him without warning and ran hot and cold for years before officially checking out, so you tell me?"

"When you put it like that, you would have been well within your rights." Vivienne hated this topic and how bitter she sounded. "And the blonde at Pearl's place?"

Alexei pulled her into his arms and dropped a kiss on her pouting lips. "She's my personal physician and needed my help regarding getting her baby brother out of Russia. He'd gotten into some trouble in Moscow, and it wasn't safe for him to remain. I flew there and arranged for his safety and passage."

"Any of your men could have done that! Why did you have to leave me with no explanation? I was ready to talk, and you just abandoned me-"

"The same way you did me, *da*?! I had to make sure that his transition went smoothly for her. I didn't trust anyone else to do it," Alexei's voice rang with harsh finality, indicating that the subject was closed.

"She means that much to you, then?" Vivienne persisted. Stung by his change, she sat up and pulled away from him, wrapping the bed sheet around her protectively.

Alexei sat up as well and grabbed her hand. He guided her fingers to the small, puckered scar on his back between his shoulder blades. The one he refused to discuss when they were together.

Brusquely he admitted, "I almost didn't make it out alive from an assignment in Switzerland. If it hadn't been for a young medical student that I kidnapped and held at gunpoint to tend to my wound in her apartment, I probably wouldn't have made it. She kept my secret, and I told her if she ever needed anything to reach out to me. I was finally able to repay that debt, and it brings me peace. Anything else?"

Vivienne shook her head then paused with a thoughtful expression. "Actually—"

Alexei grabbed her by her thighs and yanked her to him, landing Vivienne on her back. Swiftly he covered her body with his.

"I would very much like to make love to my wife again, with her permission of course," he added with an expectant look.

Conceding defeat, Vivienne laughed. Looping her arms around his neck, she drew Alexei down to her and kissed him tenderly. "Permission granted, husband."

But their idyllic weekend was not to be.

In the middle of the night, Alexei's phone rang. As he pulled away from his fitfully sleeping wife to answer it, he softly cursed to himself, for it could only mean one thing.

He would have to leave his wife.

"Da???" He curtly answered as Vivienne instinctively snuggled closer to him and his arm automatically curled around her.

"We have a lead in Polonia."

CHAPTER *Three*

PRESENT

SAN FRANCISCO, CALIFORNIA

FRANK MASON THOUGHT HE WOULD have a heart attack as he watched the slow smirk spreading over his adversary Cedric Pembrooke's face when the other man turned to him and held his hand out expectantly.

"Great game, Frank," his nemesis said cordially.

He'd been conned, he furiously realized. Cedric had allowed him to win their last few matches! He'd known that his 'luck' was up when Cedric confidently stepped up to tee off and his smooth, graceful swing sent the golf ball soaring across the green into a perfect hole in one.

"I expect a rematch, Cedric! At least give me a chance to win back the Rolls!" Frank whined unbecomingly as he dropped the keys into the smug bastard's outstretched palm. "It's been in my family for generations! Ginger is going to kill me when she finds out what I've done!"

"Now, didn't I warn you I was feeling lucky today?" Cedric made a tsking noise as he tossed the keys to the Rolls Royce Phantom in the air and did a little shoulder bounce as he caught them. "Surely, you had to know your streak wasn't going to stay hot forever. Every once in a while, the little guy gets a win too! I'll see you next week, Frank. Give my love to Ginger! Deuces!"

As he walked away from Frank, Cedric was almost positive he could hear the other man's teeth gnashing together in anger. He knew if he turned around, Frank's face would be apple red as well. Oh, what the hell! Just for shits and giggles, Cedric turned and waved back at him happily.

Yep, and it was getting redder by the minute.

Take that, you arrogant old fool, he thought to himself smugly as he got into his golf cart and drove back to the club.

In order to obtain Frank's precious car, he'd allowed himself to lose their last ten games for a grand total of twenty-five thousand dollars. It was pocket change to Cedric, but the point was the wins had given his opponent the confidence he needed to keep playing, and he'd started to get cocky. Frank deserved the hustle he'd received. In Cedric's line of work, a cocky fool was a dead one.

As he made his way through the prestigious private club to the valet station, Cedric lit one of his beloved Cuban cigars and affectionately remembered when he and his baby sister Clarissa first started their family business and all the risky chances they'd taken because they believed themselves to be unconquerable and fearless. Yeah, right. It was really like they were just young, cocky, and stupid. They'd run their game with some of Uncle Sam's shadier soldiers and then over the Mexican border and deep into South America. The brother-sister duo had been a force to be reckoned with, and money was pouring in faster than they could count it. Cedric and Clarissa were rich beyond their wildest dreams. With that newfound greenery, they'd bought themselves some respectability.

They'd moved from the brutal streets of Cantona Boulevard in Oakland to San Francisco and into a prestigious district across the bay. One of the most affluent neighborhoods in the city, Sea Cliff was filled with multi-million-dollar homes, gorgeous landscaping, and some of the most coveted views of the city, the Bay, and the Golden Gate Bridge. With their power move, Clarissa hired etiquette teachers, personal stylists, and tutors to educate them. Back then, everyone wanted in on embracing the Black Movement, and they became the toasts of the town and started to believe the lie they perpetrated. That they could be normal and function in mainstream society.

Clarissa even decided to try her hand at marriage with a successful farmer on the east coast. She was bored to tears within a week of moving to his hometown of Baymoor, Maryland. Clarissa managed to stick it out for four months before calling it quits and was glad that her know-it-all big brother managed to refrain from saying "I told you so".

Or it could have been the fact that he was too busy falling head over heels in love with Valencia Malvero, a flamenco dancer that he'd had a tempestuous two-year on-again/ off-again affair with that had resulted in his beloved only daughter being conceived. Cedric had begged Valencia to marry him, but she was too wild a spirit to be contained, not even impending motherhood could make her slow down. In the end, he'd had to bribe her not to have an abortion.

When the baby was born, Valencia walked away without a backward glance, leaving Cedric devastated and a single parent. Her love of freedom stronger than any affection she bore for him. It worked out in the end as Cedric discovered his little girl turned out to be the love of his and Clarissa's life. A year later, he learned that Valencia had been killed running with the bulls in Pamplona. Cedric was relieved that he could tell Vivienne that unfortunate news rather than her mother not wanting her.

Clarissa had insisted they walk the straight and narrow from that point on. They did so for thirteen years until greed pulled them back into the game. Only this time they weren't alone. They taught babygirl the ropes and were proud of the way a reluctant Vivienne quickly caught on. It was only when she was caught in a shoot-out at the age of seventeen and almost took a bullet between her eyes, that they decided to retire for good, unfortunately too late. The damage was done to Cedric and Vivienne's already fragile daddy-daughter relationship was broken, too severely to repair. From that point on, Vivienne had kept an impenetrable wedge between them.

Aside from that, things had been going well until Cedric's membership application was finally approved for this elite golf club. When he'd first joined, all the snooty members had turned their snooty noses so far up at him; Cedric had wondered how they could see where they were going without tripping and falling on their wrinkled, deflated asses. He decided that gentlemanly protocol wasn't going to cut it for him and got his scheming on when Clarissa wasn't looking.

Today's earning had been a con long in the making, and Cedric had felt the time was right to wrap it up. So, he'd started talking about his newly acquired rare wine collection that he'd paid five hundred thousand dollars for and bragged about it being a one of a kind purchase. Frank had eagerly taken the bait and suggested they play for it. A hesitant Cedric agreed, but only if Frank would put his precious car up against it. Confident in his abilities to kick Cedric's ass, the poor bastard never saw the hustle coming.

Cedric reached the glass doors and stood there trying to figure what was wrong. Then it hit him that none of the valet attendants had rushed forward to open the door for him. That was odd. Cedric pushed the door open and saw that there was no staff around.

"Hey, Pete! Joey? Anybody here?" he called out, but his question was met with silence.

He stepped around the valet stand and jumped back when he saw the still form of Pete lying there, blood trickling from his forehead.

"What the hell?!"

Cedric reached into his pocket and pulled out his phone, slowly retreating as he dialed 911. A sharp point pressing into his back made him aware that he was no longer alone.

"I wouldn't do that if I were you, Mr. Pembrooke," an oily accented voice advised him from behind.

"First of all, motherfucker, this cardigan is Gucci, circa 1990! I'll thank you to show it some respect! Now, one, how can I fucking help you, and two, how do you know my gotdamn name?!" Cedric demanded, pulling his cigar out of his mouth. The object, which he assumed was a gun, pressed even harder into his lower back.

"Oh, we know all about you and the Pembrooke family business, sir. Fascinating stuff it is! Tell me, do your privileged golfing cronies who were born with silver spoons in their mouths know anything about the real family business? Perhaps I should tell them?" the voice mused. "We had every intention of staying out of your life, but that daughter of yours doesn't take direction very well. Your son-in-law either, for that matter. So now, you must be made an example of to show her how serious we are."

Cedric narrowed his eyes, and his mouth tightened in response to the cryptic answer, his fingers gripping his cigar until it broke in two. He'd always known that allowing his daughter to marry that big, apple-headed-ass mobster would come back to bite them in the ass. Tea shop owner his ass!

Vivienne, my girl, what have you gotten us into?

PRESENT

WHISKEY ROW, TENNESSEE

"KAT? WHAT ARE YOU DOING out here? We're due at Jackie's house in less than an hour! Everything okay?"

Puffs of air punctuated her words in the icy afternoon air as a shivering Vivienne stepped out onto the balcony of her daughter's suite and joined Katerina at the railing. She wrapped her arms around her only child from behind and held her close as she looked around her at the snow covering the trees and ground surrounding them.

"I remember this working out so much better when my baby was a baby and didn't wear four-inch-high heels. Who you tryin' to impress?"

Kat leaned back in the comforting familiar embrace and rubbed her mother's cool hands. "I'll always be your baby, Mama. You're sure you'll be able to go on our trip next month? By the way, thanks for having my back on that. I hate that it caused static between you and Papa."

"Yes, I am. My schedule is cleared, and Jackie will be going into the office while I'm gone. No need to thank me, love. I will always go to bat for you," Vivienne whispered fiercely as she smoothed the flyaway burnished curls from Kat's face.

As always, the reddish-brown color mystified her. If Cedric and Aunt Clarissa hadn't come to visit Vivienne after Kat's birth she would never have known, it had been her deceased mother's hair color. As there were no pictures of Valencia, Vivienne had no choice but to believe them.

"You always come first for me *and* your stubborn papa and before any relationship that you may have. Never forget it."

With the success of her jewelry line, Vixen and the intentional email scare she'd received not too long ago from her childhood friend Magnus, Kat was going to Europe next month to meet with her buyers and vendors to reassure herself that they're relationships were in good standing. It was against Alexei's and her man, Holton Brammer's wishes, but Kat would not be deterred. Her refusal had caused a small disagreement between her parents before Alexei left two nights ago on a short trip to Poland with Cruz and Holt. Just thinking about it brought a grin to Vivienne's face.

AS SHE LAY IN BED attempting to do a crossword puzzle, an amused Vivienne covertly watched her husband storm from the bedroom to the vast walk-in closet, yanking clothes from hangers and hurling them into his carryon bag on the foot bench at the end of their bed.

Teasingly she asked, "Is there popcorn to go with this show, darling?"

He pinned her in place with a steely glare, index finger pointed accusingly. "I blame you for her stubborn streak, Vivi! That child is nothing but pure defiance! She did not get that from my side of the family!"

Vivienne rolled her eyes and threw her pen at him, which Alexei easily caught and stuffed into his maroon and navy pinstriped bathrobe.

"Lex, your first mistake is thinking she's still a child, made of sugar and spice and everything nice! I've raised her to be a strong, resilient, and independent woman who can take of herself. You have shown her how to take care of herself if a motherfucker gets out of line. Her brothers are ready to beat the shit out of anyone who blinks at her. And the crème de la crème? Her boyfriend is a trained killer!"

Vivienne laughed at him while he remained unconvinced, continuing to glower at her. "Baby, Kat couldn't escape the bubble wrap that surrounds her life even if she wanted to!"

Alexei was only slightly mollified by the truth of her words as he took in the sight of his gorgeous wife lying in his, no, their bed again. For years, it was all he thought about as he got into the cold, lonely bed by himself, longing to roll over and find Vivi there, ready and responsive. Yet even the sight of her clad in an oyster silk, wispy-laced, peignoir could not stop Alexei from worrying about Katerina and the threat hovering above his family.

"She will always be my little girl," he grunted and sat down on the edge of the bed with his back to her, leaning forward with his elbows pressed to his knees. Alexei thought of their daughter's sweet smile and sunny disposition. Of singing Russian lullabies to her when she was little. He'd fallen in love with her upon discovering Vivienne was pregnant. As soon as he saw his newborn daughter, wrinkled and crying, she'd surpassed all of Alexei's expectations. He'd despised co-parenting and missed Katerina fiercely when she was with Vivi. The estate empty without her infectious chatter and giggles. The idea of her traipsing through Europe and out of Alexei's sight did not sit well with him at all, drawing forth his protective instincts in addition to anxiety.

Ominously, he added, "I pray to God nothing bad ever happens to her. Because if it ever did, not even God himself would be able to save the sonofabitch-"

His words were cut off by the soft fall of his wife's lingerie landing on his head and covering his face. Alexei pressed it to his face as always intoxicated by her heady, seductive aroma. The scent of Vivienne's signature jasmine and tuberose perfume stirred his heavy cock to attention. Her soft, seductive laugh that followed caused his blood to heat rapidly.

"Come to bed, Lex," Vivienne summoned him in a throaty whisper from behind, and he did with a low growl as he pivoted and pounced on her naked form. She shrieked with delight, which turned into blissful

whimpers as his lips captured hers skillfully and he filled his palms with her breasts...

HER DAUGHTER'S GAGGING NOISES BROUGHT Vivienne out of her reverie.

"Umm...ewww! Could you *please* stop mentally enjoying whatever it is you and my Papa do that has him whistling so enthusiastically in the morning?! Since you've been home, I've walked into two scandalous incidents that had me calling Dr. Klaus! She assured me that my eyeballs would not be permanently scarred. Also, that I would eventually recover enough to eat at the kitchen nook and swim in the pool again; as long as I find a happy mental place!"

"Pfftt! Chile, please!" Vivienne laughed and hugged her daughter tighter to her. If she tried hard enough, she swore she could detect the faintest scent of baby powder underneath Kat's sophisticated perfume.

"It's a beautiful thing to know that at our age, we've *still* got it and we're gettin' it in while the gettin's good!" She sighed and dropped her chin on Kat's shoulder. "And it is good, you know. Oh, soooo good. So, what did Laura prescribe to you?"

"TMI, Mama!" Kat huffed indignantly. "She requested I either get my own place or invest in soundproof headphones and blinders!"

"I've already ordered you a pair of each for Christmas," Vivienne assured her, ignoring the strangled sound Kat made. "And your father is installing a room entry alarm system next week. Until then, if you could just make a loud announcement before walking into a room that would be great, please and thank you."

"Aaaargh!!! Mother!" Vivienne started laughing again at Kat's appalled tone.

"Sorry, love, it was either that or we'd have to make you wear a set of windchimes or a cowbell. 'Cause we can't stop...and we won't stop..."

"Dear laaawd, what have you done with my mama?!" Kat asked woefully and attempted to cover her ears as Vivienne continued to cackle. "So...do you think everything went smoothly for them?"

Vivienne detected the underlying current of worry in Kat's voice and hoped like hell she was able to conceal hers just a little bit better as she firmly responded.

"Yes, I do, baby. Your father is a professional."

Kat stepped out of her mother's arms and leaned against the railing to face Vivienne, a pleading expression on her lovely face.

"A professional what exactly? That's the million-dollar question that I need answered, and all of you keep avoiding! I'm not a baby!"

Vivienne studied her daughter carefully, wincing as she noticed the shadows, under the molasses eyes so like hers, were darker. These last couple of months had taken a toll on all of them, with Alexei, Cruz, and

Holt flying in and out of the country on a moment's notice every time they received a lead. It was a matter that they'd kept on a need–to-know basis as a safety precautionary, which therefore excluded Ian, Jack, Darby, Casey, their wives, Guy, and Kat. Vivienne vehemently disagreed about leaving Kat in the dark, but it was two against one as Lex and Holt ganged up on her.

Vivienne hadn't grown up coddled, and there were times when she sure as hell could have benefited from it, but she would never regret the skills Cedric had taught her. Most of them had come in handy, such as how to defend herself from unwanted attacks, but skills like smuggling drugs and running guns was not something Katerina Moira Romankov would ever need to do, now or ever. She truly felt they were doing Kat a disservice by not making her aware of the danger, and Vivienne couldn't have that.

Fuck it.

"You want the truth, Kat, then here it is: I'm being blackmailed to stay away from your father, and recently, the extortionist has taken drastic measures to ruin everything I've built. It appears they'll stop at nothing and will resort to whatever means necessary to make sure I'm punished for defying them. That includes using Magnus to threaten my clients."

"What in the hell, Mama?!" Kat's posture was ramrod straight as she jerked off the railing and regarded her mother with a furious expression. "How could you not say something?! Papa would have helped you! You *know* that man loves you beyond all reason!"

Her daughter's eyes flashed dangerously and for the millionth time since giving birth to her, Vivienne was awestruck that she'd created such a perfect person. Kat was fiercely devoted to her loved ones and always ready to lend a helping hand. She had no doubt that if Kat had learned of her predicament a long time ago, she would have foolishly acted on her own to draw the blackmailer out.

Growing up with Cedric and Clarissa Pembrooke had taught Vivienne to fear nothing and to never back down from a confrontation. Not from her schoolmates, co-workers, work adversaries, her husband, and definitely not the bitches who wanted him. She was a brazenly outspoken force to be reckoned with if you dared to tangle with her. Being a mother has a way of maturing and evolving a woman as priorities shifted. She now had to pick and choose the battles worth fighting for and to do what's best for her children.

VIVIENNE SMILED HER THANKS AT the salesgirl holding the dressing room door open while she wheeled Katerina's baby carriage inside. She looked at the wide array of stunning evening gowns she'd selected to try on and prayed like hell that one would fit her post-baby body without needing alterations. Tonight, Vivienne was going to see Alexei for the first time in the three months that they'd been separated. He'd asked instead of ordering her to have dinner with him. Vivienne had been helpless to resist him when he'd humbled himself. Although Alexei kept his tone formal, she could hear all of the same pain, sadness, and longing that she'd kept bottled up inside.

Their last face-to-face encounter had been terribly painful for the two most obstinately, stubborn, and prideful people on the planet as they stormed, raged, and hurled insult after insult at each other nastily. Just another bone added to their rapidly growing pile of contention. It was too overwhelming for the hormonal new mother to handle. Vivienne decided she needed space. With the murder of her best friend Moira and the role Alexei had indirectly played in it, she needed to clear her head.

Call her naïve, but never did she imagine that Alexei would just let her go. Vivienne expected him to come after her. That they would talk and maybe find a resolution. Instead, he sent all of her things to her hotel suite. Devastated and too prideful to call him, Vivienne started house hunting for a space that would suit her, Kat, and her three godsons Jack, Darby, and Casey Sullivan.

Vivienne attempted to softly close the dressing room door, so as not to wake her sleeping baby. Surprisingly, it was shoved back open, and she found herself staring at an evil-looking knife in the hands of a white stranger who held a finger to his lips.

"Not a word, Mrs. Romankov," he whispered, shutting the door quietly with his other hand, leaving

her trapped in the tightly confined space with the baby carriage between them.

Vivienne couldn't speak as her heart was lodged firmly in her throat, and she could only concentrate on his serious gray eyes. He was slender and dressed in a plain light-brown suit with a white shirt and burgundy tie. It registered to Vivienne that she'd seen him folding sweaters in the menswear section on the second floor that she'd passed through to get to the elevator. He'd even had the nerve to smile at her! Vivienne's eyes drifted helplessly to her precious baby.

Dear God, please don't let him...

As if reading her mind, he peered into the carriage and cooed, "Isn't she a beauty! Doesn't she just make your heart melt? I bet you'd die if anything terrible happened to her."

Vivienne almost lost it as he held the knife close to Katerina's plump, rosy cheek. If her child even shifted to get comfortable, she would be pricked or...worse. If only she could get to the gun in her handbag. Except she'd tucked it away under the carriage.

"State your business and get the fuck out of here!" She hissed under her breath.

"Temper! Temper!" he mocked with an easy smile. "I have a message for you. Stay away from your husband."

"W-What are you talking about?" Vivienne demanded, her fear subsiding briefly. "How do you know my husband?!"

"We know everything there is to know about your family, Mrs. Romankov. We can get to you or them anywhere at any time."

He reached into his suit jacket, pulled out a stack of photos, and handed them to her. Vivienne snatched them from him, and her fear came rushing back with a surge of nausea. There were pictures of the inside of her current hotel suite, of her taking Kat to her doctor's appointment, looking at real estate, and pictures of the boys. In Whiskey Row at their school, out and about town with Alexei and also her best friend Ian Rusnik. The pictures were up close and personal, making Vivienne's blood run cold from the knowledge that her children could have come to harm unknowingly at any moment.

"Your husband is a powerful man, but so is my employer," his voice filled with certainty. "If I must pay you another visit, I'll start with this little one right here in front of you. I'd go so slow that you will have died a thousand agonizing deaths before she finally took her last breath..."

"You bastard!" Vivienne forced herself to choke back her sobs of helpless rage as tears filled her eyes.

"Indeed, I am," he agreed with no remorse. "Shall I tell you who would be next? The pretty little blonde boy. I like the look of him...so delicate and fragile. Or maybe I should start with the strapping red-headed man-child? No, definitely the oldest boy. He's quiet, but a leader. I've seen the way they follow his lead without question. The younger two would be devastated to lose him."

He let the impact of his words sink in.

"You'll never get away with it! My husband –"

"Your husband may kill me; but not before I take out a couple of casualties," he finished icily. "My boss won't stop until the streets of Whiskey Row run red with innocent blood. Could you live with yourself if that happened?"

With a cruel smirk on his lips, he faced the dagger downward, directly above Katerina's chest. Vivienne's sharp cry filled the dressing room.

"Please!"

"Last warning: Stay away from him or the end results will not be pretty."

She watched as he quietly opened the dressing room door and felt faint with relief that he was leaving until he turned back at the last minute to appraise her thoughtfully. He reached into his pocket for something, and she collapsed in shocked recognition onto the fitting room chair as he held the item up to the light for her to see.

His compassionate look was accompanied by a rueful shake of his head. "You don't really believe in coincidences, do you? If so, then this should dissuade you of that foolish notion for good. Just remember everything happens for a reason, Mrs. Romankov, and we were always meant to meet. I'll be holding onto this, in case you try anything foolish. Not even the great Alexei Romankov could save you from the authorities."

He left her alone, and Vivienne sat in the dressing room, staring at Katerina as tears silently rolled down her cheeks until after the concerned saleslady's sixth visit, she finally managed to compose herself and left.

When Vivienne arrived back at the hotel, she immediately packed all of their belongings and checked out and into another hotel.

That night, she stood Alexei up and instead, had the maître d present him with a letter that she'd had delivered for him. It stated she no longer wanted to be married and would be filing for divorce. It killed Vivienne to write that she now wanted all forms of communication to go through their attorneys, but this way, everyone was safe and unharmed.

It was the biggest fight that she and Ian ever had, and he'd called her all kinds of fools for not wanting to save her marriage. He informed her of Alexei's rage and heartache, demanding to know why she was doing this.

Vivienne could never reveal her secret to anyone.

"YES, PERHAPS YOUR PAPA COULD'VE helped me, but the price would have been too high to pay, Katerina," Vivienne admitted. Offering her a conciliatory smile, she urged, "Let's not speak of it anymore. It's time to get a move on. Your father and a certain Swede will be arriving soon, and I want to surprise him! You need to finish getting ready."

Vivienne grabbed her daughter's hand and led her in from the cold. She surveyed the bedroom as Kat applied a touch of makeup in her bathroom. The walls of the suite were painted black and covered in family photos. A large sky-lit ceiling and a wooden floor adorned with Kilim rugs. Gold-accented wall sconces, chandelier, and mirrors complimented her white tufted leather furniture.

"You've got a nice cushy setup here. I encourage you to stay and enjoy it with us, baby."

"No problem staying as long as my parents promise to keep their clothes on!" Kat implored her.

"I'm going to make sure all of our dishes are packed," Vivienne called back to her.

"Don't dismiss what I said, Mama. I know you heard me! Mama???"

The sound of her mother's merry laughter floating down the stairs was the only answer Kat received.

CHAPTER *Four*

ALEXEI ROMANKOV THANKED THE CREW of his private plane warmly upon exiting. He zipped up his brown leather bomber before proceeding down the flight of stairs just as two black Hummers pulled up to the airplane hangar, followed by a midnight blue Mercedes-Benz G-Class 63 and then two additional black Hummers. His blood began to simmer as the doors to the Hummers opened and his alert security team quickly surrounded the Benz.

Fyodor, his personal bodyguard that was now assigned to his wife, wore a pained expression as he approached the stairs and waited uneasily for Alexei at the bottom of the stairs.

"Welcome back, sir. I trust your trip went well?"

"What is the meaning of this?" Alexei demanded of his most trusted security member as they came face to face. Fury radiated from every bone in his body as two of the guards opened both the driver and passenger doors of the vehicle.

"She insisted on driving to meet you," Fyodor explained resignedly. "Short of manhandling her and you cutting off my balls, what did you want me to do, sir?"

Alexei started to respond with a scathing retort, but his attention was diverted by the sight of his wife as she stepped from the driver's seat. She wore black knee-length, high-heeled boots, black leather pants that clung to her figure, and a hip-length silver fox fur coat. Atop her head sat a rakish fedora, and from beneath it, he could see her pretty eyes lit up with love for him as her sexy crimson mouth broke into a wide, breathtaking smile.

"Hi, Lex!" she called to him gaily and waved enthusiastically.

"Hello, my love," Alexei acknowledged her with the private smile reserved just for her, despite his fury at her disobedience. The smile was so filled with love, intimacy, and adoration, that it absolutely transformed his stern countenance and made him unrecognizable to his employees. "Stay there, Vivienne! It's icy, so I will come to you."

To Fyodor, he savagely whispered, *"If you ever, in your life, mention manhandling my wife again, I will cut your balls off. Is that understood?"*

"Yes, sir." Fyodor waited until Alexei curtly nodded his dismissal before walking back to Vivienne's car.

"And where exactly are you gonna put them? Hey, maybe you should ask Ms. Vivienne where she put yours; that way, they'll have some company?"

This helpful suggestion came from behind Alexei. The voice belonged to Holton Brammer, his daughter's boyfriend.

Alexei didn't bother looking at the big Swedish motherfucker when he brusquely replied, "Kiss my ass, Brammer."

The lip-smacking sounds came from the third person in their party, Cruz Merada. "I have some Chap Stick if you need it, Holt-"

"Fuck off, Cruz," Holt returned as his eyes fell on his woman standing next to her mother. The shit-talking was quickly forgotten as he drank in the sight of Katerina, or what he could see that wasn't bundled up by her knee-length black parka and boots. Her feline eyes sparkled, and her sculpted cheeks were rosy from the cold air as underneath the fur of her hood, her reddish-brown coils framed her heart-shaped face.

She winked at him and her perfect bow-shaped lips tilted up in an intimate smile. All Holt wanted to do was peel back the layers of clothing that covered her, take her to bed, and explore all of her to his heart's content.

"Do you think you could *try* to restrain yourself when I'm around?" Alexei snarled his disgust as he raked Holt up and down with a surly glare. "I don't need to be a fucking psychic to know how impure your thoughts are right now, asshole! FYI: upgrade your jean size!"

Cruz's eyes followed Alexei's and he raised his eyebrows and spoke with barely contained mirth.

"Sweet Jesuit! Instead of "The Woodsman", I vote that we change his name to Pinocchio."

"Not helping, Merada," Alexei growled to the Spaniard who gave an elegant shrug.

"Can you really blame the man for having a natural reaction to her, Romankov? What's so wrong with that? She's a beautiful woman. Even when she's trussed up like a sacrificial offering, which is kind of ironic, considering your wife has delivered her directly to Brammer's eager -"

"Could you possibly bring any less to the table right now?" Holt interrupted, punching him in the arm.

"Papa, I know what you're doing, and I'm asking you to leave him alone, please!" Kat called to Alexei with exasperated fondness. "We've been over this a million times, and you just need to accept that he's not going anywhere!"

"I am very much aware of that fact, Katerina," Alexei replied drily as they made their way across the icy tarmac. "Trust me; no one knows that better than I."

"I saw the look he gave you," Kat whispered out of the side of her mouth to her mother. "You are so going to get it for not listening to him. Don't say I didn't warn you!"

Vivienne kept her smile fixated as her husband drew closer. Her heart overflowed with love when he trained those gorgeous dark blue eyes on her. Even all these years later, she was still in awe of how much they loved one another. Yes, they argued fiercely, but their love could never be denied. In his middle age,

Alexei was even better looking with the silver running through his jet-black hair and the crinkly laugh lines by his eyes. And that body...goodness...her man was in no danger of letting himself go, and she had no intentions of letting him go.

Ever again.

"Shut it, missy. I am a grown-ass woman, and I'll do whatever the hell I want," Vivienne sniped, tilting her chin defiantly. If she were honest with herself, Alexei's unfathomable expression was causing her to feel a slight twinge of unease.

At her daughter's disbelieving snort, she loftily added, "I'm simply going to explain to my husband that I missed him too much to stay away, and I wanted to ride with my baby for a little quality girl time. Why are you trying to ruin my plans?"

"Oh, you didn't need me for that, Mama," Kat assured her with a laugh that peaked her mother's brow. "Trust me, your plan was conceived with pre-meditated failure. And don't you *even* try to put me in the mix; I refuse to co-sign on this."

"I just want you to know that you are at the top of my list of things I just can't handle right now, brat," Vivienne retorted, affectionately bumping her daughter's hip with her own.

"Love you too, Mama," Kat returned, blowing her a kiss.

Alexei reached them and pulled Kat into his arms for a big hug that she happily returned. It filled Vivienne's eyes with tears of joy to witness the strong and undeniable love they shared. Since the day she was born, Alexei had been putty in Kat's tiny hands.

He kissed her forehead and then held her at arm's length to inspect her with his shrewd gaze. "How are you, *milya moya*?"

"I'm great, Papa. Welcome home!" Kat did some inspecting of her own to make sure that he was okay. Now knowing what she did, her anxiety had increased tenfold about his well-being. "And *you*? How are you doing?"

"I'm fine, Katerina," he said with a comforting smile and kissed her cheek. With a pained expression, he released her, stiffly adding, "I'm sure you and Holton would like to catch up. Why don't you take your mother's car?"

Kat's sweet smile lit up her face as she glanced around him to where Holt was impatiently waiting. "If you insist, Papa."

"Drive carefully," Alexei warned her as Vivienne handed over the keys. To Cruz, he inquired, "Where are we dropping you, Merada?"

"There's no need. My motorcycle is still parked over there." Cruz exchanged meaningful glances with the two men. "I'm sure we'll talk soon. Enjoy the rest of your day, gentlemen."

With a rakish smile, he bowed gallantly to a charmed Vivienne and Kat. "Always a privilege to be in the company of such vibrantly beautiful women. In my country, we have a saying-"

"So do we; it goes like this: Get lost," Holt said rudely, beating Alexei to the punch while Vivienne and Kat rolled their eyes.

Cruz laughed uproariously and saluted them before walking away. "Adios, mi compadres."

"Be careful, Mr. Merada," Vivienne cautioned him as Alexei escorted her to the largest of the custom Hummers and ushered her into the vehicle. Before entering it, he pinned Holt with a deadly gaze.

"I know these roads as well as you do. I also know the allotted time it takes to get to Jack's. No. Detours."

"Papa!" Kat fumed. "Mama, would you please-"

"Alexei darling, let's leave them to it. I want to hear how the trip went!" her mother called from inside of the vehicle.

As soon as they were seated, Alexei pressed the custom divider, and it was barely up before he hauled Vivienne into his arms for a searing kiss. "I missed you, Mrs. Romankov."

"Oooh, the feeling is mutual, Lex," Vivienne purred, framing his face with her hands and tracing the seam of his lips, with her tongue, before helping herself to another kiss. Temptingly, she wiggled her bottom in his lap against his erection, and it managed to expand even more as she tilted her head back to look at him, laughter and desire mingling in her eyes. "I see you brought me back a present. Can I open it now?"

Alexei's laugh was dark and irresistible as he lowered his head and gently suckled the erratically beating pulse at her neck. He loved the way she mewled and her hands fisted locks of his hair as he drew the fragile skin into his mouth and bit. "Actually, that present can wait. I have something else to give you first, Vivi."

Her desire for him reduced Vivienne to a quaking mess, and she pressed herself tightly to Alexei, eager to feel *all* of him. She traced his lips with her fingernail "I can't wait-Ouch!!!"

Her exclamation of pain echoed in the confined space as she furiously grabbed her throbbing ass cheek with one hand and slapped the shit out of her husband with the other. Tears of pain and anger welled in her eyes as she confronted him.

"You, bastard! What the hell was that for?!"

Unfazed by her blow, Alexei caught her flailing hands in one of his and applied two more stinging slaps to her bottom as she viciously cursed him and tried to wiggle away. He grabbed her chin and looked deeply into her eyes, so she would know how serious he was. "*That* is because I distinctly said for you to stay with your detail at all times, and you chose to defy me."

"Let go of me!" Vivienne snarled then stilled as his hand fell to her behind again. Instead of delivering more discipline, Alexei gently massaged her injured area.

"Never again, Mrs. Romankov," he vowed with a grave expression. "The guards are in place to protect all that I hold dear to me while I try to find the person responsible for keeping us apart. Do you think it's easy for me to run a corporation and pack up on a moment's notice to follow up on a lead? What about Holton or

Cruz? They too, have responsibilities that take a back burner due to their pledges in "The Order"."

With a stern and unyielding expression, Alexei continued, "*I* gave the order that you were to be guarded at all times, and you defied it...no, you defied *me*! To my men! I said under no exceptions is that rule to be broken. *Ever!* Vivienne, these men would kill in a heartbeat for me, but I would kill them in less time than that if they ever manhandled you in an attempt to follow my commands. Please, tell me where my honor in that is?"

Despite the stinging blows to her behind and her pride, Vivienne felt duly chastised and remorseful, enough to stop struggling, sit still, and absorb his words.

"I'm sorry, Alexei. I didn't fully think the idea through. I just missed you and couldn't wait to see you. I will apologize to Fyodor, of course."

"You'll do no such thing! Rule number four," he sharply reprimanded her and squeezed her thigh possessively.

"There are so many rules. Refresh my memory please," she teased at his arrogant expression.

Alexei removed her hat and set it down next to him. He grasped the silky strands of her hair and wound them around his fist as he pulled her head back to stare into her eyes, before kissing his wife. He sucked slowly on her bottom lip and reminded her.

"Romankovs apologize to no one."

Vivienne crossed her legs in an attempt to contain the building pressure in her core. "Don't forget women's rule number one, darling."

"And now, you will refresh my memory, Vivi," he insisted huskily.

She unzipped his jacket and pressed her palms to his broad chest. They exchanged languid, teasing kisses with him before her teeth caught his bottom lip and bit down hard. Vivienne laughed as he winced, and she slowly released it before licking away the sting and small drop of blood.

"Always give as good as you get, if not better."

SO SOFT AND SWEET, LIKE ripe peaches, Holt thought as he devoured Kat's mouth. He loved how responsive she was to his touch as she fervently kissed him, silently letting him know she needed more of him. He acquiesced and ruthlessly plundered her mouth as her hand inched up his thigh.

Reluctantly, Holt pulled away, valiantly trying to ignore the pleading look in her eyes as he started the vehicle and they left the hangar.

"You know my terms, Kat."

Katerina bit her lips and looked away from him willing her overheated body to cool down. Of course, she knew the deal. Marry him and she could binge herself on his dick to her heart's content.

"I missed you somethin' fierce, darlin'," Holt drawled, keeping his eyes on the road, careful to steer clear of any patches of ice.

"I'll bet you did," Kat countered coolly, causing Holt to shoot her a speculative glance. "How was Europe?"

"At this time of the year? Cold and unpredictable," was his grim reply as he thought of the frosty reception they'd received in Poland and Romania by the cities' underworld leaders. Neither one had extended a lick of warm hospitality and were eager for them to leave their cities. Not even the rare appearance of "The Wolf" had persuaded them to jump to do his bidding. It was only when Alexei had broken Henryk Kucharski of Warsaw's arm in two places that things began to happen and shocker of all shockers, they'd come up empty-handed.

Again.

"I want to know why you agreed to keep me in the dark about everything, Holton?" Kat demanded. "Did you really think that I couldn't handle the truth? You asked me to be your wife, for God's sake! Am I just supposed to sit blindly in the dark while you flit around the world chasing after bad guys?"

"I did ask you to be my wife, and I meant every word, love," Holt emphasized. "The reason I didn't disclose anythin' to you is because it's not my story to tell. It's your parents, and I respected that. I was simply assistin' where I was needed; it's my...calling."

"Your *calling*? Could you elaborate just a little more for me please?" Kat grouched. "Or better yet put yourself in my position. A woman who's involved with a man she's crazy about and that her father is not so crazy about. Yet, said dream guy drops everything going on in his life to help dear old Dad and expects nothing in return?! Not even a thank you or a little bit of ass from his girlfriend?"

Holt rubbed his heavy beard thoughtfully and tried to vanquish the image of Katerina and her 'little bit of ass' out of his mind. It was to no avail. Nope, the image was there, front and center, making his dick hard enough to pole vault with as he pictured what that particular part of her anatomy might look like. Especially as he bent her over and fucked her. "Hell, I guess when you put it like that, it does sound pretty crazy."

Kat dead-eyed him. "Extremely so, right? Look, there's no need to discuss marriage if you aren't ready to tell me everything. My parents' marriage was not conventional by any means, but my brothers' marriages are. They have no secrets and are completely honest and upfront about everything."

Cautiously, Holt pulled the vehicle over to the side of the road and faced her. "I'll be the first to admit that your brothers have admirable relationships with their wives. I also know they didn't happen overnight. They all had baggage that they had to sort through and trust each other with it to get that point."

He leaned in and pressed a hard kiss to Kat's mouth. "I want no one but you, Katerina Romankov. All of you. There's not a woman alive that shines brighter than you, but I. Want. It. All. There will be no 'I changed my mind' and you run. I don't have a problem lettin' you in and seein' all of me, but if you can't handle all that I am, and accept it, tough shit because there is no goin' back. I need to be able to trust you as well."

Kat wiped her purple gloss from his lips with a confident smile. "That's the kind of relationship I need, Holton Brammer! Because the bottom line is: if we can't even trust each other, then what are we even doing, boo?"

He grabbed her hand and kissed her knuckles, relieved by her answer.

"Us, love. We're doin' us."

CHAPTER *Five*

"DAAADDDY! GET JACKIE!"

Ruby Sullivan's plaintive cry was shrill and demanding as she pushed her little brother off of her and rolled away, shaking snow off her bright blue snowsuit. Her gray eyes were irate, and her expression, mutinous as she shook her small, hot pink-gloved fists at him.

"Bad, Jackie! Bad!"

Taken off guard by his sister's shove, baby Jack went tumbling sideways into the snow and he landed on his back, where he began to whine piteously. Large crocodile tears sprang from his distressed hazel eyes and rolled down his fat, cherry stained cheeks as his whine turned into full on bawling.

He held his arms out to his big sister, pleading his case. "Wuweeee! Wuweee!"

Bristling with indignation, Ruby refused to give in to him. With a flip of her black French braids over her shoulder, she crossed her arms and turned away from baby Jack, allowing his distraught cries to fall on deaf ears.

Jack Sullivan placed the garland he'd been decorating the back porch railings with on the ground and went to pick his devastated namesake up, gently wiping his cold tears away. He made soothing sounds as the sniffling baby consoled himself by playing with his beard.

"It's okay, Zilla. I don't think your sissy liked the way you demolished her snowman."

Baby Jack's eyes lit up when he heard his nickname that was short for "Godzilla". He raised his mitten covered hands into claws and growled at his father.

"Raaahr! Raaahr!"

As always, the baby's zest for life was contagious. Jack barely managed to suppress a smile as he bent down to address his seriously pissed-off daughter.

"Hey, babygirl, you know that your brother was only tryin' to help you, right? He didn't mean to knock down your snowman," he said solemnly. "It was an accident, Ruby, I promise."

Jack held his breath, hoping the terror in his arms would stay quiet and docile long enough for Ruby to make an informed decision. Her big gray eyes, so like her mother's, slid suspiciously from him to her little brother, who blinked his curly eyelashes at her innocently and smiled his gummy grin, revealing two incoming teeth. However, she wasn't having it today.

"No! Jackie is wude, Daddy! Fix him!" Ruby insisted stubbornly just as baby Jack lunged at her again and his father quickly pulled him back.

"Raaahr!"

"Ahhhh!" she screamed, jumping away as the baby fell back in Jack's arms, chortling uncontrollably with mirth.

Ruby's lip wobbled, and Jack knew the waterworks were coming full blast at any second. He tried to pull her close, but she refused to be coddled with 'wude Jackie'.

"Don't let him get to you, Rubes."

The encouraging words came from her older cousin D.J. who came around the corner of the house, pulling her pink sleigh.

"Baby Jack can't help himself."

Ruby launched herself at him, and he gave her a big hug. She gave him an affectionate smile.

"Hiiiii D.J.!" She turned her back on her brother and loudly whispered, "Jackie sooooo wude!"

"I think he just wants to be your friend and doesn't know how to show it," D.J. placated her. "I brought the sleigh just for you. Do you wanna ride around the yard? Or I can help you rebuild your snowman?"

Her braids flapped around as she nodded her head vigorously, and pointed to the sleigh. "Wide please."

"Okay, have a seat, and I'll get you buckled in."

"Thanks, nephew." Jack was grateful that World War Umpteenth had been prevented between his children as he fist bumped his nephew. "I really appreciate you helpin' out."

"Ain't no thang, Uncle J. You might wanna get with Uncle Casey and see if he's got any more of his special medicine and maybe put some in baby Jack's milk," D.J. suggested helpfully as he carefully buckled Ruby in. "He said it works wonders for Aunt Sid."

"It does?" Jack asked curiously as he tossed his unruly son in the air and the baby squealed with joy. "Well, it must be good if it works on your aunt. Tell me more about this miracle drug."

"I heard him tell Daddy that he gives Aunt Sid a large dose of it before gettin' outta bed in the mornin'. It helps to calm her butt down. Accordin' to him, it makes her really happy and mellow. Vitamin D is what he called it. I figured it couldn't hurt for baby Jack to try some, right?"

He was for sure going to kill Casey this time, was Jack's only thought as his mouth flapped open and closed and he struggled for something to say. Would that idiot ever learn??

Finally, he settled for, "Thanks for the helpful suggestion, D.J. I'll make sure to take it up with your uncle as soon as I see him."

"Sounds good to me. Let's go, Ruby!" D.J. slowly pulled the sleigh around the back yard as his little cousin giggled and clapped her hands. "Any idea what you want Santa to bring you, Rubes?"

Her answer, loud and clear, rang across the yard to reach her daddy.

"NO BWUZZER!"

"Thank you, God, for sendin' us that little boy," Jack murmured the heartfelt sincerity as he looked up at the sky.

It was hard to believe how far they'd come from the shocking day they'd come to know about his existence. D. J. was no longer the angry kid who challenged everything anyone said to him. With the love of the Sullivans, their friends, and extended family, he'd turned into a happy, well-adjusted, charming, and respectful child who loved to learn and try new things. Everyone loved D.J., especially Ruby.

"Dadadaaa!" Baby Jack sang as he wiped his drool all over Jack's vest, trying to to gnaw at the puffy nylon fabric.

"I'm gonna go check on the cocoa!" Jack called to the children as he shifted the baby in his arms and headed up the steps of the back porch. D.J. gave him a thumbs up signal of acknowledgment. "Come on, bud. Let's go tell mama what your sissy *really* wants for Christmas."

He opened the back door and stepped into the warmth of the kitchen, breathing in the delicious smells of whatever his wife was cooking. Jack stopped short at the sight of his beloved Noelle bustling about in her element. She was the heart and soul of not just their home, but of his life and their family's as well. In addition to being a wonderful wife, mother of two very active children, and co-owner of a successful event planning business, Noelle insisted on hosting their large family gatherings.

"Our house is overflowing with love and we have so much to give! The doors should be opened for us to share great times, laughter, and to create wonderful memories. Family is what it's all about, Jack."

He watched the gentle sway of her curved hips and ass as she moved around, and it was still like seeing her for the first time all those years ago, at her twenty-first birthday party, when he'd fallen in love at first sight.

"Cat got your tongue, Jackson?" she teased without looking up from the tray of skirt steaks. He loved watching the bangs of her new hairstyle fall into her eyes and how she pursed those luscious lips and blew them out of the way.

In attempt to freshen up her image, Noelle had recently gotten her haircut in a shoulder-length, layered shag with long bangs that emphasized her wide gray eyes. True to her word, she hadn't turned into a jazzercised bunny in an attempt to lose the remaining baby weight, and Jack couldn't get enough of the changes. There was just more for him to cherish. The plum turtleneck sweater dress she wore emphasized and hugged those curves he was forever addicted to.

It was almost too easy, he mused with a grin as she realized what she'd said and raised her head to pin him in place with narrowed eyes. "Oh, darlin, I wish I had some-"

He chuckled as she dashed across the room and pressed her finger to his lips, her eyes shining with love and laughter.

"Don't you dare say it! And in front of our impressionable son, too?! You're incorrigible, husband of mine," she cooed as he opened his arm and drew her close to him and a wiggling baby Jack.

"Hardly, love; I'm just a man who is head over heels in love with his wife," he confessed and kissed her tenderly.

"Maaaaa!" the baby shouted as he pumped his legs and aggressively tried to navigate his way into Noelle's arms.

"Is all of the garland hung up?" Noelle asked, stealing another kiss from him. Not that stealing was needed as kissing his wife was one of Jack's very favorite things to do with her.

"No, I had to stop what I was doin' to play peacemaker between our kiddos. By the way, I just got Ruby's wish list," he drawled holding on tight to his son, who was vehemently protesting and looking longingly at Noelle.

"Does it have anything to do with getting rid of this precious butter bean? Or her new idea of a brand-new sibling? It changes from day to day. Indulge me."

Noelle kissed baby Jack's cheek and rubbed noses with him, loving the way he squealed with joy.

"Not right now, baby. Mama's hands are dirty. We'll play as soon as I finish cooking, sweetheart."

"You knew about her diabolical plot to rid the world of my son?!" Jack's horrified voice made Noelle roll her eyes at him.

"Man, get a grip! Who hasn't thought that at one time or another about their siblings, Jack?" Noelle inquired as she straightened up and moved back to her task. "At least she's going about it in a pragmatic matter and asking Santa to do her dirty work, which if you think about it, it's pretty ingenious! Who's going to suspect the jolly fat guy that brings gifts to take something, instead? This way her hands stay clean. It's brilliant."

She shook her head with admiration. "*Mmph!* That girl is slick! I think we have a future politician on our hands. My father will be proud to hear it."

"Except that, there is no Santa. What kind of monster have I married?" Jack wondered eyeing Noelle warily.

"Did you know that most female sharks conceive more than one baby in their belly?" she countered with relish. "Or that the strongest one eats the others? How gruesome is that? Now, aren't you glad she went the violence and cruelty-free route?"

"Please; there was no other route for her to go! If it came to physical strength, Jackie woulda had her! Hell, even I don't wanna meet this big fella in the octagon ring. Isn't that right, Zilla?" Jack growled at the baby who scrunched his face as he threw his arms up and roared mightily.

"Raaahhhr!"

If she lived to be a hundred years old, Noelle would never tire of the sight of her gorgeous husband, who was even sexier than the day they met now that he was a father. His beard was freshly trimmed, but he continued to let his black hair grow, and it now brushed past his shoulders in black waves and curls.

Right now, all that hair was tucked under a black beanie, and he wore a red and black plaid vest over a black turtleneck with his jeans and black boots.

She laughed as Jack roared with him. Never had she thought her life would be so fulfilled with the man of her dreams who adored her and their children as much as they did him.

"You keep lookin' at me like that, love, and you and I are goin' half on another baby," Jack warned as he carefully placed baby Jack in his playpen and headed her way with a purposeful look.

Noelle smiled as he caged her in against the counter from behind and nuzzled her neck. "You wanna hear something *really* crazy?"

"Because "Operation Santa Kidnap Baby Jack" talk was so *normal*?" he whispered into her ear, causing her to tremble and lean back against him as his tongue slowly stroked her lobe.

"Hush! I honestly wouldn't mind another baby."

Noelle turned to him but kept her stained hands on the counter as he teased her jaw with whisper-soft kisses. She turned her head slightly, and their lips met in a steamy kiss that had her gripping the counter as Jack's arms encircled her waist, and their bodies melded together seamlessly.

"Touch your man, darlin'." His growl held a pleading note because Jack yearned to feel his wife's hands laying claim to him. "I was made to get dirty with you and vice versa, baby."

Noelle smiled against his lips framed his face with her hands carefully. "I love you, husband."

"And I love you. So very much, Noelle," he rasped before helping himself to another taste of his husbandly dessert. The kiss turned hotter as he backed her against the counter.

"Ahem...should we come back?" Avery's tone was laced with good humor as she hovered at the kitchen entrance. "I knocked but didn't get an answer..."

"Hell yes, come back," Jack grunted, unwillingly pulling away from his wife. "Or better yet, stay and babysit, and *we'll* leave."

"Well, seein' as how y'all gave us a night off and let our son spend the night, it'd be the proper thing to do, I suppose," Darby generously agreed as he discreetly pinched his wife's bottom and propelled her into the kitchen with a gentle swat.

"Quit actin' like y'all didn't just get outta bed yourselves," Jack scoffed, leaning down to kiss Avery's cheek then hug his brother.

Darby wiped seasoning off his cheek and held it to his nose, Jack wasn't surprised to see his green eyes light up deviously as he gave a soft whistle. "Oh, y'all are on a whole other level of kink, using steak rub in your foreplay! Ms. Avery, we got to up our game! I can't have my older, sleepless-with-two-kids' brother bein' more creative than me!"

"Quit cuttin' up before I call Sister Mary on you," Jack threatened, wiping his own face clean with a grin.

Darby chuckled and leaned down to kiss Noelle's offered cheek. "Go on ahead. Shoot, ever since I married this angel, me and the good Lord have been straight! Got me a table in the V.I.P. section of heaven with a bottle of holy water on chill."

Avery hugged Noelle before heading straight for her eager nephew. She picked him up with a little bit of effort and addressed her husband with an intimate smile and wink.

"Darby Sullivan, there's nothing wrong with your game and you know it." She walked over to inspect the stove, sniffing appreciatively. "It smells good in here, doll. What are we eating?"

"Your son requested poutine steak and frites," Noelle replied dryly. She pulled out a large cast iron skillet and set it on a burner of her new stainless-steel Verona 5-burner double oven range. Cooking was essential to her as was having the best products to feed their family. "*Then* he called his Nana up and requested crème brûlée sweet potato bars and French apple cake with maple icing."

"Yeah, that sounds about right," Darby confirmed as he wrapped his arms around his wife and the baby. "Where is he by the way?"

Jack grabbed a plate and loaded it with the iced gingerbread cookies the children had made with Noelle this morning. Then he grabbed two mugs and filled them with hot cocoa from the crockpot. "He's out back with Ruby. Wanna let them know their snack is ready?"

"Sounds like a plan." Darby hoisted baby Jack into his arms and grabbed Avery's hand. "He's comin' with us. Ain't that right, Zilla?"

"Raaahr!"

CHAPTER *Six*

"WATCH YOUR STEP, MRS. SULLIVAN," Darby cautioned his wife as she held onto the railing and took the first porch step into the yard. "Actually, hold on one second, love. I'm goin' to sweep the snow and ice off the steps. Just have a seat on the porch while I do it-"

"Is this how the next nine months are going to be, Mr. Sullivan?" Avery interrupted him with an amused smile. "I'm pregnant, darling, not an invalid."

"Hell yeah! This is exactly how it's going to be!" Darby established, and Avery couldn't help but laugh at his determination. "I still can't believe it! Are you sure you're feelin' okay, baby? I don't want you to overdo it. Why don't you go lay down in the family room and put your feet up?"

Avery reached up and cupped his nape, and Darby lowered his head. Their lips met in a lingering kiss that was interrupted by their nephew's joyous shriek at seeing his big sister again.

"Wuweee!"

"Hey, Daddy! Hey, Mama!" D.J. waved as he turned the sleigh around and headed toward them.

"Hi, Uncle Darbeee and Aunt Aireee!" Ruby greeted them as well, keeping her hands on the reigns. With narrowed eyes and a mulish expression, she pointed at her brother and ordered, "Put him back!!!"

"Hi, my babies!" Avery called.

She walked down the steps with Darby glued to her side and his arm around her waist. Under her breath, she chided softly, "You're being a helicopter. Stop hovering before you give the surprise away."

He groaned his dismay. "Cryin' all night, darlin', I can't help it! Why are you wearin' them high-heeled boots anyway?! From now on, you wear those in the bedroom only!"

Avery rolled her eyes at the love of her life and gave his hand a firm, reassuring squeeze. His emerald green eyes were filled with consternation as he stared at her footwear, and aside from the children, his worried expression was the most adorable thing she'd seen today. Life with Darby "Wild Child Turned Sin Bin" Sullivan was never dull, and she felt blessed to be sharing it with him. It was a constant adventure filled with love, laughter, and lovemaking steamy enough to peel paint. And now they were adding a new chapter to their love story.

Avery had been feeling overly tired lately. Yesterday when she woke, she'd mentioned it to Darby. Her attentive husband insisted Avery stay in bed while he took D.J. to school. Later, before picking him and Mai Ling up from Tae Kwon Do class, she'd gone into town and made a stop at Care For Me Apothecary and picked up two different pregnancy tests. Then Avery had taken them to Hooligan s to have supper with Darby before dropping Mai Ling off, and then D.J. for his weekly sleepover with his cousins.

When Darby arrived home later that night, she'd nervously presented him with the tests, and he'd practically shoved her into the bathroom. Hands clasped tight together, they'd anxiously waited for the results, silently praying even while reassuring each other everything would be fine if the results were negative.

When the plus sign appeared, Avery began to cry, hands pressed to her mouth and a stunned Darby sank to his knees in front of her. With tears in his eyes, he gathered her in his arms, bending to press reverent kisses on her belly as she held him close to her heart.

"I KNEW ALL THAT MISTLETOE would pay off, baby," he hoarsely joked on a strangled laugh.

He carried Avery into the bedroom and gently placed her on their bed. That night, instead of ravishing each other, no holds barred, the way they normally would, if kid-free, Darby and Avery lay awake and discussed their future that now seemed impossibly bright. He had to talk his wife out of going to get D.J. so they could share the news with him. Just knowing their family would be expanding made Avery long for their baby boy.

"Don't tip our hand, Mrs. Sullivan," Darby advised her, pressing a kiss to her forehead. "We show up at damn near midnight tryin' to claim our kid, and that pair of bloodhounds will know somethin' is up. Hell, Noelle is so fertile, she can probably smell it on you right now from her damn house! Let's tell them after our first doctor's visit."

"WHY DO YOU TWO LOOK like a couple of cats that ate a canary?" D.J. asked with a toothy grin. He hugged his father first and kissed his mama's cheek loudly.

"Oh, no reason," Darby replied innocently. He grunted when baby Jack's feet kicked him solidly in the stomach in a desperate effort to be put down. "Hey, Ms. Ruby! Got some sugar for your uncle?"

"Kisses, Uncle Darbeee!" Ruby exaggerated the pucker of her lips, and Darby complied while trying to keep her brother from getting to her.

"Wuweee!" he whined sadly and held out his arms to his sister who refused to be conned again.

"Oh dear," Avery tsked sympathetically. She took him from Darby and took Ruby's hand. "Come along. It's time to go back inside and get your snack. Don't be too long, family."

Father and son watched the woman who was their entire world walk away with the tumultuous siblings.

"I don't envy the boy who gets outta pocket with that one," D.J. informed his father sagely. "Ruby is gonna have every boy she comes across wrapped around her fingers. But don't let 'em cross her because baby Jack is givin' her some serious trust issues. At this point, there ain't a forgivin' bone in her body, Daddy."

"And me, her daddy, all her other uncles, *and* papa will be ready and waitin' on them fools," Darby vowed, bending to pull his son's beanie down to cover his red ears. "However, her hissy fits oughta keep 'em in line. Whatcha know good, buddy?"

"I'm good, Daddy. Everythin' okay with you and Mama?"

The flicker of worry across his face immediately triggered guilt in Darby. Ever since D.J. had come to live with him, making sure he was well-adjusted had been Darby's, and then Avery's, number one priority. It was the main reason that they'd decided to wait to have other children.

"Everythin' is perfect," Darby smiled, looping an arm around his son's small shoulders. Life couldn't be better. He was married to his best friend, and Avery was his complete match in every way. Never in a million years did Darby ever dream he could be so happy and fulfilled with one woman, but from day one of their meeting, she'd put blinders on him for everyone else.

Avery always insisted that he loved her just right, no extra effort was needed, but she did so much more for him. Other women hadn't been able to look past Darby's physicality and taken the time to get to know the real him. Not his woman, though. With her warm smile and sparkling brown eyes, Avery had looked past all the bullshit and touched his carefully guarded heart. With her special brand of loving, she'd nurtured it, and treated it as if it were her most valued possession.

"Almost perfect," D.J. corrected him, and Darby glanced down at him in surprise.

"Care to elaborate, Red?" he asked, curiosity piqued.

"Said the pot to the kettle," was D.J.'s quick reply. "I love our life, but don't you think it's time you and Mama thought about addin' on to it? Camille says that her parents are havin' a baby-"

"Boy, I am not about to give you a little sister or brother because your girlfriend is gettin' one," Darby interrupted, picking him up and heading to the house. It still amazed him that his body was able to handle all the love he felt whenever he looked into this little-freckled face. And now there would be another child, and he just prayed to God to be as good a father as Lex and Jackie were.

"Quit tryin' to keep up with the Joneses and let's make a deal. How about me and your mama add on to our family when God sends us a baby, because He knows our family's love keeps growin' and growin', and we have so much of it to give?"

D.J. held his hand out, and Darby shook it firmly.

Solemnly the little boy agreed, "Sounds like a blessed plan to me, Daddy."

"Yes, sir, it does." Darby kissed his son's cheek. "From your lips to God's ears."

"BABY, PLEASE PASS ME THE pickle board," Sidra requested of her husband, Casey, as she cut into her steak with gusto. "I have to say that was awfully sweet of Max to send it to us."

"Darlin', I don't believe he had a choice after you cleaned him out of his own inventory, and then followed him around, demandin' he make you more." Casey placed the cutting board with containers of pickled beets, dill pickles, spicy carrots, bleu cheese, and sharp cheddar wedges in front of his ecstatic wife.

"Now, you know good and well that it's not really me being this crazy, Casey! *It's the baby,*" she finished in a loud whisper, pointing to her protruding stomach with her fork.

All conversation at the table stopped as everyone stared at her with such blatant disbelief, that Sidra drew herself up defensively. "It's true! She's made me totally unbalanced and impulsive. I'm sure once I give birth, I'll be back to my normal, sane self."

Vivienne coughed delicately. "You're blaming your "extra" enthusiasm for life on your unborn child who can't even defend itself?" She eyed Sidra compassionately. "Oh honey, check your email when you get home. I'm pretty sure Karma just sent a message to your inbox, subject line: I'll deal with you soon."

Sidra stuck her tongue out at her and simultaneously grabbed her husband's wrist as Casey attempted to pull the tray away. Squeezing until he winced, she sweetly requested, "Please don't poke the bear, hon."

From the other side of the table, an incensed Guy glanced around the table for support, tapping his fingers on the table top impatiently. "You do realize that he sent the extra-large board for all of us, don't you?"

"Somethin' on your mind, Pip?" Holt inquired mildly. "Feel free to hold back on us. I can tell from the slightly psychotic look in your eyes, that once you get started, there's no off switch."

"As a matter of fact, there is! I gotta say I'm not likin' the changes around here!" Guy pointed at D.J. who was sitting at the other end of the table between his parents, minding his own business.

"Ever since "Mr. Steal Your Girl" hit the scene, battin' his big brown eyes, I've had to beg to get my favorite meals made around here! Do I get them? No! Then Sidra gets pregnant, and she gets her favorite meals and then some! It's like I don't even exist around here anymore! I feel violated...and not in a good way!" he finished with a self-righteous huff.

"Is there really a good way to be violated?" Casey pondered with a doubtful look.

"Pip, I think I might have a solution to your problem," Jack said helpfully. "I heard that Ms. Fern is an excellent cook. Maybe you could guilt trip her into makin' you some meals."

"So, now I have to drive to another state to get a homecooked meal?!" Guy yelped his outrage. "What kind of animal are you?"

"Or you could go home and cook one," Avery teased, laughing at the reproachful look he shot her.

"Not you too, Ms. Avery? Say it ain't so?" he mourned and took a long drink from his water glass.

"I heard a good meal can be found at The Pink Champagne," Sidra added with a sly grin, causing Guy to choke and spew his drink into an unsuspecting baby Jack's face.

"My baby!" Noelle cried in dismay as Guy grabbed his napkin and attempted to wipe down the startled little boy whose sister was now laughing at him.

"I got it, sis." Kat picked him up and smacked Guy upside his head on her way out.

"What are you talking about, Sid?" Darby peered at his friend suspiciously. "Is there somethin' we should know about, Pip?"

"No!" Guy yelled, drawing the attention of everyone seated. He scowled across the table at a smug Sidra. "Fine! You and your crazy-greedy, unborn baby can keep the pickle board! I believe Karma just sent you another email titled: What Goes Around, Comes Around."

"This is all very fascinating, children, however, Vivienne and I have an announcement to make," Alexei revealed, ignoring his wife's surprised look. All heads swiveled toward them expectantly, as Kat reentered the dining room with a freshly cleaned baby Jack. "We will be hosting a Christmas party this year and would be honored if all of you could attend."

As excitement buzzed about the news, Vivienne addressed her husband through clenched teeth. "What a surprise. I don't believe we discussed this yet, dear."

"What is there to discuss? Will we not be together this Christmas?" he challenged her in a low undertone, the warmth receding from his eyes. "Do you remember our last Christmas together in the house? Just the two of us?" At the flash of regret on her lovely face, Alexei bit out, "It was the year before you left, correct?"

THEY LAY NAKED ON THE mink rug in front of the roaring fireplace in their bedroom. The amber glow reflected the sheen of perspiration on their skin from their recent bout of lovemaking. Alexei drew her back against him and kissed her shoulder.

"Happy, my dear?"

"Unbelievably so," Vivienne stifled a yawn and snuggled closer to him.

"There will be no sleep tonight, Vivi," he promised wickedly, sitting up and grabbing her hand.

"What are you doing?" she asked sleepily as she felt a cool heavy weight on her wrist.

Her eyes flickered open suspiciously when he remained silent, then Vivienne sat up as well. She looked down at her wrist to see an exquisitely breathtaking wide, braided-gold bracelet with diamonds interwoven through them. 'All my love, Alexei' was engraved on the clasp.

"Do you like it?"

Vivienne's vision was blurry as she gently ran her finger over the intricate piece of jewelry. "It's gorgeous, Alexei, you shouldn't have! You've already given me so much!"

Alexei gently pushed her down by her shoulders and covered her body with his. His eyes were serious as he kissed the corner of her mouth, the tip of her nose, and then finally, her parted waiting lips.

"Merry Christmas, Vivi. All that I give you pales in comparison to the invaluable gift that I have already received. You giving yourself to me, Mrs. Romankov. YOU are the only gift I will ever want. Never doubt that. Now, open for me..."

"IT WAS A BEAUTIFUL DAY *and* bracelet, Lex," Vivienne said with a tremulous smile.

Alexei grunted. "Good, so you do remember it. That is the last Christmas that I truly celebrated, Vivienne. For more than two decades, I've clung to that memory as I celebrated them your way. *Apart from one another.* I decorated my house for the children, but my heart was never in it. I refuse to do that anymore."

Vivienne's heart wrenched at his words and she could not have hated herself more as she reached for his hand, her fingers running along the thick, platinum wedding band, he'd never taken off.

"It wasn't easy for me either, Lex."

"Wasn't it?" he murmured caustically. "A dear, mutual friend of ours once told me that "Life isn't complicated; it's people that make it so." I'm certainly inclined to agree with him."

"Don't you dare try to quote Ian-isms to me!" she retorted. Vivienne tried to withdraw her hand, but her husband held fast. "Where is he, by the way? Have you heard from him?"

"I believe he's now vacationing in Malta. It was always his favorite place to visit with Harvey, he mentioned." Alexei studied the ten-carat, emerald-cut wedding ring Vivienne now wore again. "This is the only jewelry item from me that you wear. I would like to see you wearing the bracelet again. Or any of the other pieces, but *especially* the locket I gave you, Vivienne."

His expression was fierce as touched his forehead to hers. "If you wear nothing else, always wear the locket! It's always been very important to me, and I don't believe that fact has ever escaped your memory, my love."

He was referring to the heart-shaped platinum pendant with the pave diamonds that he'd given to Vivienne a week after they'd become lovers. The lavish gift triggered their first argument as she refused to accept it.

"I DON'T NEED YOU TO give me things like this!" Vivienne stiffly informed Alexei as she closed the velvet box and shoved it back at him.

Calmly her lover reopened the box again and took the pendant out. Alexei unclasped it and moved to stand behind her and put it around her neck. "You are my woman, and as such, a necklace like this is a necessity. It will deter anyone foolish enough to bother you. They will know you belong to me."

"Why don't we just go to the vet and have a collar engraved for me instead that says 'Property of Alexei Romankov!'" she replied tartly, raising her hands to take the stunning but offending item off, but his hands knocked hers out of the way.

"Or better yet, check out the new tattoo shop in Fillmore and have that bullshit inked on my forehead! Fuck you, Alexei! I have my own money and can buy my own things. I will not accept this gift!"

Alexei gripped her chin and tilted her head back. Defiantly she met his icy eyes.

"Indulge me, Vivienne."

He lowered his head and the bruising kiss that followed obliterated her protests.

Soon the argument was forgotten, and Vivienne was wearing the locket.

A KNOCK ON THE FRONT door startled them all. Alexei's eyes met Holt's. Noticing the silent interaction, Darby rose simultaneously with them. Whoever was at the door had passed through security with flying colors.

Or taken them all out.

Darby motioned for Jack to stay seated. "I'll get the door."

"Goin' to the restroom," Holt mumbled.

"It would appear Guy needs a new drink. I could use a beer myself." Alexei gently shut the double doors behind them as Vivienne and Kat engaged everyone in an enthusiastic discussion, attempting to distract them.

"I've got the front door," Darby said grimly. "And then I want y'all to tell me exactly what the hell is goin' on."

"Take the back door, Holton." Alexei withdrew his pistol from his ankle holster. "I'll cover him."

Darby radioed his second-in-command.

"Who's the guest, Tuck?"

"Some Samuel Jackson, loud-mouth wannabe. He refers to himself as your Pop-Pop." The radio cackled a bit. "Says he's Ms. Vivienne's daddy."

"Damn straight he is!" Darby co-signed eagerly while Alexei gritted his teeth and tried to fight the instant headache he received with that aggravating tidbit of information. "Well, if that don't beat all! I haven't seen him in years.

Knowing how Alexei felt about him, Darby shot him a mischievous smirk.

"Shit just got *real* interestin' around here."

He laughed diabolically at the aggrieved expression on his father's face.

THE REST OF LUNCH PASSED without incident. It was a boisterous affair as Cedric charmed them all effortlessly except Alexei and Vivienne. If anyone noticed the tension between the married couple and her father, no one commented on it as Cedric, who held baby Jack in one arm and Ruby and D.J. sat next to him, regaled them with tales of his celebrity neighbors and their outrageous behavior.

When lunch was officially over, he addressed Alexei and Vivienne. "May I please have a word with you both outside?"

Alexei bared his teeth in a semblance of a smile. "There's nothing I'd like more."

As soon as they were out of earshot, Holt asked Kat, "What's the deal with your dad and Cedric?"

"Pop-Pop has never thought my dad was good enough for my mom," Kat said with a shrug. "I'm not surprised he showed up here now that they've reconciled. I'm assuming he's here to "C.B. and C.J." them, which is not necessarily a bad thing," she finished with a shudder.

"C.B. and C.J.?" Jack prompted as everyone leaned forward in fascination.

"Ears," Kat reminded them, and all the adults closest to a child quickly covered them. "Cock-Block and Clam Jam."

Jack looked extremely queasy as the women burst into laughter,

"*Aaaand* there goes my appetite," Casey mumbled, eyes closed in disgust as he put his head on the table, and Sidra rubbed his back consolingly. "I couldn't care less for this topic."

"Don't worry babe. I'm curious enough for the both of us!" she said excitedly. "You better dish, Kat!"

"I'm outta here," Darby said hastily and picked up a sleeping baby Jack, holding him in front of him like a protective shield.

"Thanks a lot, guys!" Kat fumed to her brothers. "How do you think I feel when all those packages from Feminine Intuition arrive at the house and my papa looks like a kid on Christmas morning?!"

"Wait a second...and not one of them is for you? They're all for your mama?" Guy rubbed his hands together appreciatively as an unholy light shone in his eyes. "Ooohwee! Well, bless Ms. Vivienne's heart for keepin' it sexy in the bedroom."

"You're so overdue, Pippy," the Sullivan brothers growled in unison, each of them shooting him a look of deadly intent.

"Whaaat?" he blinked innocently. "Can't Ms. Vivienne live a little? I say we just go on ahead and let her be great!"

"Not a one is for me," Kat assured them sorrowfully. "They're all for Mama."

"Do you not like Georgie's designs?" Avery inquired. "She's extremely talented. Or I'm sure that Fern could custom design something-"

"Stop right there, Ms. Avery," Darby warned with a frown. "The last thing I need is our good friend Holton here gettin' all hot and bothered thinkin' of our kid sister in some risqué lacy underwear."

"I think you just did that instead," Noelle pointed out wryly, indicating Holt's cherry stained cheeks.

He put his elbows on the table and rubbed his face, trying to get that enticing vision out of his mind. When that didn't work, he pressed the cold beer bottle a helpful Sidra provided for him to his face with a muttered, "Thanks."

"My ears are goin' numb!" D.J. reminded his Uncle Jack loudly.

"One more second, buddy," Jack replied, shooting Holt a dirty look.

"Relax; You've got nothing to worry about," Kat confidently assured her brothers.

She stood up and cleared away some of the dishes from the table and put them on the rolling tray.

"Thank the Lord," Casey groaned from the tabletop, finally lifting his head as Jack and Darby exhaled a relieved sigh.

Kat paused at the doorway and winked at Holt.

"I don't wear any," she purred.

"Jesus, Kat!" the brothers howled collectively while the women laughed, and Guy sent up a heartfelt prayer of thanks for wild women everywhere.

She laughed even as she felt Holt's lustful gaze scorching a hole into her back.

Good. If she had to suffer, then so did he.

Score one for me, Kat smiled gleefully.

"WHAT ARE YOU DOING HERE, Cedric?" Vivienne demanded without preamble as they exited the house and moved away from the security detail.

At his insistence, she'd started to address him by his first name when he pulled her into the family business.

"It's not good for our reputation if these fools see me as having a kid, babygirl," Cedric explained to his innocent, wide-eyed daughter. "It makes me look like I have a weakness, and in my line of work, I just can't have that."

Her father pulled a cigar out of his festive tartan plaid jacket and lit it. Cedric removed his black Kangol hat and ran a hand over the low white waves covering the top of his head with agitation before replacing the hat. Even after all these years, whenever Cedric looked at his beautiful Vivienne, he was assailed with memories of the gorgeous Valencia and how she'd broken his heart.

The pain from his moment of weakness still lived within him, and he was reminded each time he saw his fiery daughter. Cedric couldn't undo the fact that it was the very reason he'd always kept her at arm's length and tried not to love her as much. All he'd ever wanted to do was love, protect, and teach her how to stand on her own two feet without needing anybody.

But what did she do instead?

She got involved with the first motherfucker she slept with and married the sonofabitch! He'd tried to talk her out of it, warned her about the pain that being in love would bring, but Vivienne's hard-headed ass hadn't listened. He still wasn't sure what had happened between them, but as long as Alexei was out of her life, then Cedric was done interfering.

Until now.

"The better question, daughter dear, is what in the hell are you doing *here* again?" Puffing on his cigar, Cedric assessed his surroundings with disdain. "Now, don't get me wrong, I'm always happy to see you and all the kids. The boys have done well for themselves and seemed to have developed a severe sweet tooth for chocolate, which I ain't mad at, but this place ain't you, Viv. Never has been and never will be. By the way, your Aunt Clarissa says to tell you hello and to quit actin' like a stranger."

Alexei took a step forward, wanting to wrap his hands around this worm of a man, who'd added his fare of strife to his already strained marriage. "As usual, you have managed to overstay your welcome in such a short time. It would be in your best interests to leave. *Now.*"

Vivienne flinched at the underlying menace in his voice and savagery on his face. She stepped between the two men. Although Alexei towered over her father by a foot and a half and was solid muscle, she was fairly certain that Cedric was packing heat, which more than evened the score.

"I've got it, Lex." She placed her hand on his elbow and shivered, feeling the violence rumbling underneath her hand, itching to break free. Vivienne shot her father an irate look. "You don't speak for me. My place is with my husband and children, and it's where I'll be staying. Now again, what are you doing here? And please give Aunt Clarissa my love on your way back."

Cedric tossed his cigar into the snow with aggravation. "What can this hick town offer you? Tell me that, Vivienne! *What?* A lesson in churning butter or maybe how to cobble your own shoes?"

"Get to the point!" Alexei snarled, stepping toward him.

"Lex!"

"Fine, I will." Cedric clicked the unlock button on his car key, and the trunk popped open slightly. "I heard that the match made in hell had reconciled and decided to bring them a gift."

He lifted the trunk lid and inside was a badly beaten tied up white man with cigar burn marks all around his swollen eyes. One side of his face was scarred by burn marks.

"I believe this belongs to y'all. Merry Fucking Christmas."

CHAPTER *Seven*

"NICE DIGS YOU HAVE HERE," Cedric grudgingly commented as he stood in the vast, opulent foyer of the Romankov estate and appraised the luxurious setting. The pale silk walls provided the perfect background for the eclectic combination of vivid abstract artwork and the soft pastel hues of the still-life paintings that adorned them.

"I'm so relieved it meets your approval," Alexei jeered. He deliberately ignored Vivienne's warning glance. "I can now die happy."

"I guess that means we'll both be happy then," Cedric rebutted.

The already thick tension between the two men escalated, making it hard for Vivienne to relax. It didn't help, either, that all of her husband's men were taking their cue from their leader. They regarded Cedric with open hostility, ready to decimate him if Alexei gave the order.

"It's been a long day, and you must be tired from your trip, Cedric," Vivienne interjected. Looping her arm through her father's, she pulled him away from the stare-down he and his son-in-law were currently engaged in. "Let me see you to your room."

Once out of earshot, she whirled on her father, confronting him with her wrath.

"Do you think you can manage to keep your mouth shut while you're under his roof?!" Vivienne hissed. "Because that would go a long way in ensuring you live to see daylight, Cedric! My husband has offered you his home for the night! I'm demanding that you show him the respect that he deserves!"

"I didn't start it; he did," Cedric groused with an affronted sniff. "All I did was compliment the damn house! It hasn't escaped my notice that you still haven't said that you're happy to see me, Viv. My precious granddaughter and the boys have been over the moon, but not my only child. That's straight-up cold, babygirl."

"Of course, I'm always happy to see you! However, you could have given me a warning, Cedric," Vivienne fumed.

He continued speaking as though she hadn't spoken a word as they walked up the long staircase. "I wonder why that is? Does it have to do with the gift I brought you? Don't bother denying it because I know it does. You know, any other person would have freaked the fuck out at seeing a man trussed up like a turkey. You didn't even react; if I didn't know any better, I would have thought it was an everyday occurrence for you, Vivienne."

"Would you be quiet?!"

"Not until you tell me why that fool tried to run up on me," Cedric glowered. "I had to fake a damn heart attack on him! He leaned over to pick me up and I shoved my cigar into his eyes! Then I used his pistol on him, before burning him some more, just on principal! What kind of trouble are you in? And does it have anything to do with 'apple-head'?"

They reached the guest bedroom, and Vivienne shoved him inside and closed the door carefully.

"This is your last warning, Cedric! Do not disrespect my husband or try to come between us. If you even attempt to, I will allow him to show you what he's capable off! Are. We. Clear?"

Seeing the fury in her face brought Clarissa's advice from their last phone call to mind. Cedric managed to catch her before she boarded her cruise ship for a month-long adventure and complain at length about his daughter and her husband. His sister was the calm and rational one between the two of them and always had been, even under fire. Clarissa had patiently listened to his ranting about Alexei and how he had to save his babygirl. When he finally paused to take a breath, she offered him some advice.

"Now, don't you go down there startin' shit, thinkin' you some Captain Save A Ho, Cedric! Vivienne doesn't need you like that. If you don't like that fact or can't accept it, that's too damn bad! You have no one to blame except yourself when it comes back to bite you in the ass, brother dear."

"You don't have to shout at me, Vivienne." With a wounded expression, Cedric sat down on the settee by the window and dejectedly stared at his shoes. "I know something is going on with you, and all I want to do is *help*. Hell, I know we're not close, and I take full responsibility for that, but I'm here for you now and always will be. Please believe that."

He glanced out the window. "I know you always wanted normalcy and stability; Clarissa and I wanted it for you as well, but we'd been doing our thang for way too long to just change overnight."

Cedric gestured toward his clothing with a disapproving frown. "I tried to tell her that no matter how much we tried to look the part, we weren't born to fit in with 'normal' people. I did try to settle down for you, Vivienne, but I just couldn't let it go, and for that, I'm truly sorry. That's why we didn't stand in your way when you left for school and didn't return home afterward."

He observed his daughter in consternation. "That's why this situation with Romankov is hard for me to understand! You were supposedly searching for 'normalcy'. A full-time, nine-to-five and maybe marrying a regular guy. Instead, you married a killer! And not just any killer; no, my daughter had to always have the best, so she got herself "The Wolf" of all people!"

Alexei's deadly reputation was legendary and definitely preceded him. No matter where he went, people tended to give him a wider berth because of it.

"There's nothing wrong with a man who has ambition and is good at his job," Vivienne pointed out feebly, knowing he spoke the truth. "And for the record, Alexei got out of that business a long time ago."

"Chile, you and I both know that you can never quit any business that you don't need a W-2 for! Once you're in, you stay in—*for life*. If you believe otherwise, you're a damn fool, and I know I didn't raise no fool," Cedric retorted bluntly.

Yet Alexei had come damn close to normal for her, Vivienne knew. She would never forget him leaving her small San Francisco apartment after informing her that he was returning home to speak to his father. They'd spent two crazy weeks getting to know each other and making love every waking moment that they weren't speaking or eating. He didn't elaborate on why he was going, but Vivienne knew from his fierce kiss and the way he searched her face as if memorizing every detail, it had everything to do with her.

Alexei didn't expect the outcome to be pretty.

"I KNOW THAT WE HAVEN'T known each other long, but I just thought you should know that I love you!"

Vivienne's face stung with mortification at the admission she'd just blurted out, but Alexei did not appear to be surprised in the least by it.

Infuriated when he remained silent, Vivienne punched him as hard as she could in his stomach. Wincing when her throbbing fist connected with solid muscle, she shook it and waspishly snapped, "It was a shitty thing to make me do if you had no intentions of staying, asshole! So, now you can go! Bye and good riddance!"

Satisfaction and tenderness filled his eyes as his index finger traced from her forehead to her cheekbone, and then along her jawline. In his heavily accented voice, Alexei gruffly responded, "Of course, you do, Vivi. What did you think we were all about? That this was?"

The kiss that he gave her was the forever kind, a quality one that spoke of a lifetime of promises she knew he'd see through. Alexei's eyes glittered with undefined emotion, and resolutely he declared, "I'll be back, Vivi. Never doubt that you and our relationship are my number one priority."

Unnerving, nail-biting silence was her nerve-wracking companion for the next two weeks. By the time the quiet knock came at her front door, Vivienne was ready to snap. She flew to it and flung it open without looking, ready to let Alexei have a piece of her mind for keeping her on pins and needles. His shocking appearance was the only thing that saved him from a severe pimp-slapping with a complimentary tongue-lashing.

His face was a stomach-churning mixture of black, purple, and blue bruises, fading into yellow that trailed down his neck and disappeared underneath his white-dress shirt.

"What in the hell happened to you?!" Vivienne sobbed hysterically as she pulled him into the apartment and then her living room.

"You should see the other guys," he joked, trying to lighten the mood.

Guys??? Vivienne wondered.

His attempt at a smile, with his busted lip, looked more like a grimace. "Unfortunately, you will have to visit most of them at their gravesites."

Alexei winced but allowed her to take charge as he stiffly sat down on her sofa. Vivienne kneeled in front of him and unbuttoned his shirt and her stomach plummeted, then ricocheted back up. She swallowed hard, fighting to keep the uprising bile down her throat as the gruesome myriad color pattern continued, only to end where the large gauze bandage wrapped around his middle started.

Their eyes met and locked, a wealth of understanding was conveyed with what he said next.

"I have three more assignments that are my sole responsibility. After that, I am done, Vivienne. I will be out of that side of my family's business. That is what you wanted, is it not?"

He'd taken a brutally, vicious beating that would have killed a lesser man.

All because of her.

Softly, she pressed her lips to his, tears spilling when Alexei inhaled sharply at the gentle contact.

"Had I known the results, I would have handcuffed you to my bed in order to prevent you from leaving to meet this hellish fate, Lex. I'm so fucking sorry. If I could; I would take the pain for you," she vowed in a raw whisper, meaning it to the depths of her soul.

She'd been raised to be independent and detached, and thus far successful until Alexei's claiming. Now Vivienne couldn't imagine life without this man.

Alexei's eyes closed briefly, her declaration all the healing balm needed. Her words of love had gotten him through the most difficult time of his life as lines were drawn and loyalties rescinded.

"Why do you act like the use of handcuffs in bed is so reprehensive, Vivi?" he teased. "Remind me when I am better to show you how good it can be."

"Kinky bastard!" Vivienne laughed tearfully. "I'll make sure to hold you to it."

Alexei ignored the pain as his lips brushed hers, before he set her back. "You must wrap your business up in San Francisco, before we leave for Tennessee. But first we will get married."

"Say what?! Boy, I am not leaving the Bay area! This is my home! I'm building a career here!" Vivienne protested with an uneasy laugh in the face of his stoic face. "You're so crazy! Besides, I can't marry you; it's too soon!"

Alexei raised an eyebrow at her, and the laughter died on her lips.

"You're fucking serious, aren't you?! About marriage and moving across the country???"

"I will work alongside my uncles at Romankov Industries, the legitimate side of the family business, and we will reside in Whiskey Row, the town they founded in the Smoky Mountains." Alexei hesitated for a brief moment, and his indigo eyes were clouded, an indication that his thoughts were troubling him.

"I cannot ever go back, Vivi, so we will go forward together, da?"

He'd changed his life for her – no – for them and she loved him all the more for it.

"Da," Vivienne agreed softly.

Later, Vivienne would discover that Boris Romankov had disowned his beloved son but could not bring himself to ban him completely from the family. She'd also learn that Alexei's uncles had also forbidden the shunning and insisted he work alongside them. That as his mother screamed her protests until she was locked in her room, Alexei had to fight his own cousins and men that he'd known from childhood, whom he'd considered his brothers. All to have a life with her. Too many had died in the process for him ever to be forgiven. And when Alexei's parents died in a gas explosion in their home months later, he had to mourn them from afar as he was not allowed to attend the funeral. Whilst he did not get to pay his respects, Alexei did inherit their mass fortune, which he found no comfort in.

WITH A LONG EXHALE, VIVIENNE sat down next to her father and put her head on his shoulder, smelling his familiar fragrance of expensive cologne and cigars. She smiled when Cedric put a comforting arm around her. They were not a demonstrative or affectionate pair, and hugs were rare. Vivienne fondly recalled the days when she was little and searched his coat pockets for hidden candy. Unfortunately, she'd had to mature quickly, which resulted in drastic changes to their relationship.

"I know you mean well, and I *do* appreciate your offer to help. Just...let me handle this, okay? Should anything change, I'll let you know."

She patted his knee and stood up. "Yuri is the manservant on duty, and he'll be coming by with your nightcap. Please let him know if you need anything, Cedric."

Vivienne headed for the door, but his next words stopped her in her tracks. "I'd give anything to hear you call me 'Daddy' like you used to. Makes me wish I'd been a better man to make better choices."

She glanced over her shoulder with a pensive smile, eyes reflecting her wistfulness.

"Don't we all? Goodnight."

Vivienne walked down the hall to the master wing, and impulsively made a right turn, heading to what was once a familiar area of the estate. She went down another corridor to a set of large double doors. Vivienne grasped the handle and turned it, but it would not budge. Only when she leaned her shoulder into it and gave a hearty push, did it open with a creak. Vivienne pushed the heavy door open with both hands and stepped inside.

Her anguished gasp echoed in the suite.

It was as if time had stood still. The huge bed was still made up, but the bedding and drapes were faded and outdated as was the heavy cherry oak furniture. She stepped further inside and dust rose from the thick gray carpet that the bossy interior designer had called Winter White and insisted would be perfect for the room. Vivienne choked on the thick particle swirl, and it quickly turned into a coughing fit.

When she was finally able to regain some control, the exploration of the rooms continued. The closet doors were hanging off their hinges, and there were holes in them as well as the walls, and shattered bathroom mirrors. Vivienne knew that only Alexei's wrath could have wreaked a havoc of this magnitude. Her eyes welled up with tears, and she pressed her back to the wall and slowly slid down to the floor with her face in her palms, breathing deeply, struggling desperately to remain composed as the memories came rushing back.

Alexei sitting in his Mercedes outside of her new D.C. residence, staring up at her darkened bedroom window as if he knew which room was hers while she hid behind the curtains and watched, longing to let him in or go to him.

He'd rejected her divorce proceedings with the explanation that his bloodthirsty relatives would deny Kat, Jack, Darby, and Casey their rightful inheritance if they were not married at the time of his death.

Vivienne had insisted that they would be fine without it and begged him to sign the papers.

"Nyet! We shall remain married. Unlike some people I know, I can keep my word! I did not marry only to get divorced. I suppose I shouldn't be surprised at your level of selfishness, Vivienne. You've been on a roll

lately, thinking you know what's best for everyone," Alexei spat venomously.

Vivienne clasped a hand to her chest, anxiety kicking in at the savage rage sizzling down the phone line, directed solely at her.

"This is madness! I'm starting the proceedings –"

That was all she was able to get out.

"If you attempt to divorce me again, I will fight you for sole custody of the children. After I win, and I will, destroying everything you hold dear and making your life a living hell will be my main objective. Do you understand what I am saying? You will never win against me, Vivienne."

What a terrible fool she'd been...

Another memory popped into her mind. It included the man her father had brought here. She'd never expected to see him again, but she definitely planned to be there when Alexei interrogated him.

Vivienne had questions of her own that needed answering.

CHAPTER *Eight*

IT WAS ONE IN THE morning when Alexei finally finished sorting through the pile of paperwork on his desk. There were contracts to be renewed and proposals to peruse for Romankov Industries. These items needed reviewing before his impromptu trip to Europe, yet he'd put it all on the back burner to obtain information regarding his wife's blackmailer.

There were too many dead ends lately. The kind that weren't coincidences and could only be created by a greater power at work. The kind of power that rivaled the Romankovs. There were only six other families in the world that were on their level. His mind drifted back to Glasgow and the small-time thug who thought he could rise above his status.

Ermines McNally insisted that he was only following orders from an unidentified mastermind and was paid handsomely for his troubles. The only reason he knew about Magnus and his brilliant skills was because he'd kept a spy from Scotland Yard on retainer.

THEY STOOD NEAR THE EDGE of the rocky cliff as the brutal Scotland winds howled wildly around them, and the dark, turbulent sea crashed against the jagged rocks below.

The badly beaten, blubbering Scotsman crawled to Alexei's booted feet, groveling. Clutching at his pants leg Ermines begged, "Forgive me, Romankov! I truly dinna mean to cross ye! I was told ye and yer wife were separated, but no harm would come ta 'er! Ye have ta believe I-"

"Was it not you who came up with the idea to ruin her business?" Alexei interrupted in an uninterested tone, that belied the menace in his eyes. "It was you who spoke those words, correct?"

"Aye, but I dinna mean-"

Ermines stopped and shrank back as Alexei suddenly squatted down to his level and trapped him with those glowing blue eyes. The Russian smiled thoughtfully.

"Perhaps it is just me, but I find that every time you open your mouth, more bad intentions than good ones spill from your tongue, hmmm?"

Alexei's fist slammed into his mouth, and Ermines fell back with a yelp of pain. The larger man took advantage of his position and jumped on top of him, pinning his arms down with his knees as he pried his mouth open. Ermines' eyes filled with terror as Alexei produced a switchblade in his other hand and with one swift motion cut his tongue out.

Ermines thrashed around on the ground clutching at his mouth as blood spewed forth from it.

"We'll need to wrap it up," Holt called from the edge of the cliff watching the sun disappear behind the roiling clouds. "The storm is heading in quickly."

"Why must you try to rush the masterpiece he is creating?" Cruz admonished, handing him a wrapped package. "Let his art guide him-"

Holt gave a derisive snort. "You are such a bloodthirsty-"

"Gentlemen, if you don't mind?" Alexei inquired politely, slightly turning his head to address them. "A little respect would be appreciated while I work. Don't get me started on the lack of work you did, Merada. Wasp injection knives? Really? Your blatant disrespect for our craft-"

Holt snickered as Cruz vehemently cut Alexei off, "I had pussy ready and waiting for me and didn't bring a change of clothes! I was not going to show up for my date bloodstained and still expecting some ass!"

""I had pussy ready and waiting for me"," Holt mimicked him in an accented falsetto. "It's not dinner for chrissake!"

"Oh, I beg to differ," Cruz said with a salacious laugh. "I ate quite well that night."

There was a pause before he continued delicately. "Do you not have erm-DINNER waiting for you when you returned? Is that why you're always so grouchy, Brammer?"

"Asshole."

"Mother of God! Would the two of you cut it out?!" Alexei shouted.

Impatiently he grabbed Ermines' arm and twisted until it snapped. Amidst his moans of anguish, Alexei did the same to the other arm as well, rendering them both useless. Ermines attempted to kick Alexei, but his leg was caught and twisted until he heard and felt the sickening snap. Efficiently, the Russian repeated the action on the other leg. His pain was so excruciating that Ermines passed out, only to regain consciousness shortly after when Alexei grabbed him by his hair and dragged him to the edge of the cliff where Holt and Cruz were waiting.

"Good news, Ermines. I'm not going to kill you," Alexei remarked cheerfully.

He dropped him in a crumpled heap at Holt's feet.

The broken and bloodied Irishman's face was a grotesque caricature of excruciating agony as the Swede clutched him by his nape then lowered Ermines over the side of the cliff. Meanwhile "The Butcher" was unwrapping the necessary tools. Once finished, Cruz grabbed one of Ermines' limp arms, took his hand, and placed it five inches from the edge. Whistling A-Ha's "Take On Me" under his breath, he took the large wooden mallet and drove a metal stake through the back of Ermines' hand.

Jerking with pain as tears streamed down his face and blood trickled from his mouth, he looked at Holt, eyes silently pleading with him to end his misery.

Except there was no mercy in "The Woodsman" as the congenial tone of his words belied his unsympathetic, wintry gaze.

"Magnus sends his regards, McNally."

Cruz did the other injured arm, and Holt lowered him so that his useless body hung over the edge of the cliff. The only thing that stopped him from going over were the strong metal stakes in his hands as excruciating pain flooded his entire being.

Death would not come soon; no matter how much he wished for it, Ermines knew as he stared up at the three devils staring down at him with stoic expressions. The brutal, blustering Highland winds increased, and the gray clouds darkened and gathered quickly in the sky, promising a great Scottish storm to come. Ermines' only consolation as the men walked away and left him to his hellish fate was that the bastard who hired him had it coming to him ten times worse.

UNFORTUNATELY, THEIR RECENT TRIP COULD only be called a waste of time instead of a success as they met with another dead end. Their search in Poland for Douglas McNall, Ermines cousin who took control of the Scottish gang after he was banned was nowhere to be found. It was rumored that he was hiding out there and was last sighted two days prior to their arrival. But they soon learned their source was in the wind and Douglas would not be divulging any information ever again.

His body was fished out of the Tisza River near Ukraine two days later.

And now Cedric Pembrooke had shown up here with a stranger who added another element of surprise to Vivienne's mystery. Alexei grimaced at the thought of his condescending, jackass of a father-in-law. From day one of their meeting, he'd made his disapproval of their relationship known. An extremely vocal and brash man, Cedric had been adamant in expressing his opinion. Alexei distinctly remembered them going to the mansion he shared with his sister, Clarissa, to announce their plans to marry.

"WHAT IN THE HELL IS wrong with you, girl?!" Cedric bellowed at his only daughter. Anger and disapproval stamped all over his face as he regarded Vivienne. "I thought I taught you better than this! You claimed not to want the life we lived, yet with this man, you've proved how stupid you are!"

In a flash, a livid Alexei had risen from his seat next to Vivienne and crossed the room to grab Cedric by his tie. He twisted it around his hand and jerked until the older man was before him on his knees. "You forbid it?! If you ever, in your life, speak to my fiancée like that-"

"Alexei, it's fine!" Vivienne shouted as she ran across the room to yank on his arm while her father

glared at him and reached into his coat pocket. "Don't you dare, Cedric!"

Realizing his intent, Alexei knocked his hand away and reached into the suit jacket and withdrew the nine-millimeter. With a sneer at his future father-in-law, he swiftly dismantled the weapon.

"Cedric, where are your manners?" Clarissa questioned her brother sharply as she reentered the room with a tray of coffee and pastries. She carefully set it down, before dropping all pretenses of civility as she twisted her neck and sucked her teeth at Cedric, uncaring of his precarious position. "Don't be harassin' Viv's young man! He's obviously here because they care deeply for one another. Now quit actin' a damn fool and let them speak!"

With a gracious smile to her aunt, Vivienne addressed her father, who was just recovering from his near date with death. Her words were spoken in a strong, confident, and unwavering voice that made Alexei's heart sing as much as the meaning behind them.

"Alexei has asked me to marry him, and I have accepted. I would very much like for you to get to know him and was certain that you would come to think highly of the man who has made your daughter unbelievably happy. Of course, I will understand if it's not possible due to your ignorant and narrow-minded ways, Cedric. You will understand if a wedding invitation is not forthcoming, won't you?"

Vivienne approached her aunt and hugged her. "Aunt Clarissa, if you'll excuse us, we have better ways to utilize our time than allow our love to be insulted."

ALEXEI SMILED, RECALLING HOW TURNED on he'd been by her defense that rendered Cedric speechless as they left together. Eventually, he'd conceded defeat and shown up tight-lipped to walk his only child down the aisle at their small ceremony.

A delicious aroma wafted into the room and he rose from his chair. After locking his study, Alexei headed toward the kitchen. Kat was staying with Ian at Noelle and Jack's guesthouse while he was in town. Alexei was still unused to the silence of the household now that Vivienne had returned. The staff now clocked out by six in the evening unless they were entertaining. Security was kept to the outside as well. Alexei and Vivienne enjoyed and valued their privacy greatly as they got reacquainted and grew accustomed to each other's quirks. For instance, when Vivi couldn't sleep, she could be found in the kitchen, cooking or baking, to take her mind off of things.

When Alexei entered the kitchen, she was removing a copper Bundt pan from the oven. He quietly observed as Vivienne carefully examined it before placing it on the large marble island counter to cool. Her cranberry silk robe was wrapped tightly around her slender body, and her black hair was twisted in a loose topknot. Vivienne emitted a small yawn as she turned the oven off.

"Penny for your thoughts?" Vivienne queried without glancing his way.

"As my thoughts are regarding you, they are certainly worth far more than a penny," Alexei replied smoothly, approaching her. He smiled faintly at the sight of her bare feet. "Is everything okay, Vivi?"

"Yeah, everything is fine," she spoke listlessly moving to the sink in the center of the island. "I was just thinking of recipes for the Christmas shindig you sprung on me at the last minute and remembered an oldie but goodie that I wanted to try."

"What's the recipe?" he inquired, sliding behind Vivienne as she turned on the faucet and washed her hands.

"Cinnamon ricotta pound cake,"

Alexei whistled softly, peering into the Bundt pan and admiring the buttery golden-colored cake. "I'm impressed. You've come a long way in the kitchen."

She turned to face him and rolled her eyes and gave him a playful flick of her wet hands.

"What exactly is that supposed to mean, Lex? I've always been good!"

"Yes...at reservations and takeout," he teased, lifting her onto the counter.

"All lies, sir! Thank you for letting Cedric stay the night." Vivienne brushed the hair back from Alexei's forehead. "I know he can be very difficult, but I did talk to him, and he's promised to behave himself, babe."

There was silence as Alexei raised an eyebrow at her skeptically, and Vivienne smiled winningly at him. *Hmm.* He still didn't look convinced. She glanced away and looked around the state-of-the-art kitchen as the silence stretched even further and her husband's eyes remained unwaveringly on her. Finally, Vivienne could stand it no more.

"Alright! So, he didn't *exactly* promise anything," she grouchily admitted, to his amusement. "But I did threaten him with you if he didn't behave. Cool?"

"Sounds fair enough," Alexei agreed as he leaned in and kissed her briefly. Her eyes shone with interest, and his gaze dropped to her luscious mouth as she smiled invitingly at him.

"I thought you might like that, babe." She released a sigh of pleasure as Alexei kissed the other corner of her mouth. Vivienne laughed softly against his firm lips and wound her arms around his neck, needing him closer. Her fingers playing with the black and silver streaked waves that graced his broad shoulders while his fingers tugged on the tie of her robe. "What do you think you're doing, Romankov?"

Alexei kissed her deeply, his tongue gliding and meshing with hers as his cock sprang to life and pushed against the front of his pants, demanding attention. He gripped Vivienne's hips and yanked her to the edge of the counter, spreading her thighs wider to accommodate him. The bottom of her robe opened and exposed her smooth thighs and bare pussy. "You have no slippers on, so I thought I'd keep you warm."

"You're too good to me, Lex, but my toes are down there." She curled them around his pant-clad calves.

"Do not doubt that I will get to them before we're done, my love," Alexei vowed, his dark blue eyes full of sensual promise before he trailed kisses down the slender column of her neck.

As he was a man of his word, Vivienne had no cause to doubt him.

CHAPTER *Nine*

ALEXEI PULLED THE RUBBER BAND from her hair, and it cascaded in soft waves around her shoulders. He opened her robe, and his body throbbed with lust, and primal satisfaction at the sight of Vivienne's full, pert breasts and their dark brown, puckered areolas, the cherries on top of the perfect dessert. Under the kitchen lights, he could see a strand here and there of silver and white in her hair and knew Vivienne would *kill* him if he even mentioned it to her before she went back for her next hair appointment. Or he would die if she found out he knew about it and said nothing. He was damned either way, but he didn't care because he adored every inch of Vivienne, from those strands as well as the faint crow's feet at the corners of her eyes, her sharp mind, and smart-ass mouth. Like a fine wine, his graceful spitfire of a wife was aging beautifully.

Alexei cupped her breasts, loving the weight of them in his callused palms, and the way his wife trembled at his touch as he rolled the plump nipples between his fingers slowly. "Have I told you how much I love your body, Mrs. Romankov?"

"You'd better, mister, because you're not ever trading me in for a newer model," Vivienne replied tartly, trying not to be distracted at the way her clit hummed in response to his touch. She unbuttoned his shirt and exposed his muscled chest and the light sprinkling of salt and pepper hair that trailed down his washboard abs. Vivienne reveled in the way the bulge in his pants expanded further as she raked her fingernails through the fine hairs. In response, he squeezed her nipples, causing her sex to flood with excited anticipation.

He narrowed his eyes at her in disbelief. "You should know by now that I've no use for another woman, young or old."

Alexei released one of her breasts to palm her pussy, his fingers slipping between the voluptuous folds. He smirked knowingly at her wetness, and her head lolling back in ecstasy. "This is the only pussy I want. Now release me, Vivienne."

Alexei gripped her chin, and her swollen lips met his again, as with shaking hands, she hastily obeyed his command and unbuckled his belt. He swallowed her moans as he thrust his fingers into her silken heat and stroked the core of her pleasure while thumbing her clit.

I am going to cum so fucking hard, Vivienne thought dazedly as she spread her thighs wider and rocked urgently into his thrusts. Alexei fed her deep strokes of his tongue as he plundered her mouth.

Finally, she was able to get his pants undone, and she pulled his boxers down to take his tumescent erection into her hands and possessively stroked it, just the way he was stroking her.

Alexei growled feral and low at the back of his throat as Vivienne drew on his tongue and moved her small hand up and down his cock, pausing to draw from the heavily weeping slit at the top. He could feel her gushing around his fingers and thrust harder, to push her off the edge. Vivienne wrenched her mouth away from his and shoved her fingers into her mouth, sucking them clean of his sticky pearlescent precum as she came with a muffled hoarse cry.

Alexei gripped her thighs and lowered his head to bury his tongue in her pussy as her release flowed uncontrollably and he greedily lapped up every drop of the creamy nectar.

Vivienne's hands clenched Alexei's hair rigidly as her hips rose and fell repeatedly, seeking more of his masterful tongue. He sucked her sensitized clit into his mouth, and a second orgasm quickly chased the first. Vivienne saw stars beneath her closed lids as her body arched off the counter.

"Gawd, Lex, yessss, just like that!"

He couldn't wait any longer, Alexei rose up majestically, lined his cock up with her dripping center and shoved into her sweet, tight pussy with a hiss, loving the way Vivienne clamped down around him as she climaxed for a third time. He leaned over her, and his arms slipped under hers to hold her in place by the shoulders as he captured a turgid nipple with his lips, relishing the way it turned even harder as he laved it with his tongue and drew it deeply into his mouth. He then buried his face between her breasts and licked the fine trail of perspiration as he fucked her harder mightily. She mewled with pleasure as she gripped his shoulders.

"Oh, shit, Lex...Lex!"

So fucking addicting, was the only way to describe making love with Vivi. Alexei watched the myriad of expressions play across her face, loving the way she shut her glazed eyes tightly and bit down on her lips when he went deep, or her dreamy expression when he slowed it down to languorous strokes and paid homage to her nipples with slow licks and sharp nips of his teeth.

"Who do you belong to, Vivi?" he gutturally demanded, loving the way her panting increased and she wrapped her arms around his neck to draw him closer to her. Despite their size difference, they fit together perfectly and always had. The ache in his balls increased, and sweat dripped from his forehead and glistened on his back as he put in work, owning her pussy.

Vivienne clung to her husband, loving the way he thoroughly dominated her. There was no one in the world like Alexei, and she couldn't get enough of him as he painstakingly dicked her down. Her juices were sliding between her ass cheeks, and the wicked glint in his eye let her know what his next move would be. He raised an eyebrow at her and she dazedly nodded her consent as his thumb moved between them to play with her French star.

"I belong to you, Alexei. Just as you belong to me, baby."

"It has always been so and will continue to be until the end of time, Vivi."

Slowly he pushed his thumb forward, and Vivienne clung to him as he filled her ass. Gripping her throat with his other hand, Alexei fucked her harder.

"You're not leaving me again!" he declared fiercely, the words bursting from within him. He closed his eyes and struggled for control. Damn! He hadn't meant to voice his insecurities aloud. Alexei opened them again and stared deeply into her soft eyes as his forehead pressed against hers. *"I don't give a damn what story your father has waltzed in here with! It does not change things between you and me! You will stay put! We belong together!"*

Vivienne thought she would faint from being incredibly full as she moved with him. The orgasm tore through her, a raging inferno that rendered her speechless and brought tears to her eyes, shuddering as tiny ripples that started in her toes, spread like wildfire. The ripples increased tenfold until her body was wracked with tremors.

"I'm not going anywhere, Lex. I...can't wait any longer! Please baby!"

"Christ! Vivi!"

As he could never deny her anything, Alexei had no choice but to obey Vivienne. Succumbing to the unbearable rapture of her sex milking him tightly, he emptied his seed into her convulsing warmth.

It was several minutes later when they finally caught their breaths. Alexei rose off of Vivienne and reluctantly withdrew from her heat. He reached over and grabbed a dishtowel from the drawer next to him and gently cleaned between his wife's thighs.

Vivienne gave a heartfelt groan as she sat up gingerly, took the cloth from him, and finished cleaning herself. "Dammit, I'm going to need a spa day at the Miramar Resort tomorrow just to recover. I'm getting too old for this impulsive, acrobatic shit, Lex!"

"You should get used to it because I don't plan on stopping," he informed her arrogantly as he tucked himself back into his boxers. He pulled her robe closed and tied it before lifting her from the island.

Vivienne bent down and opened the cabinet underneath the sink and pulled out the bleach. She made quick work of cleaning the counter while Alexei washed his hands. Then he picked her up again and cradled her close to his chest.

"It's anytime, and anyplace with you as far as I'm concerned, Mrs. Romankov. Now let's go to bed so that I can tend to your pretty little toes."

"Whatever you say, babe," Vivienne agreed happily as she raised her head and bit his chin lightly. She laughed when he growled and squeezed her ass.

"As it should be, wife."

In their room, Vivienne removed her robe and slid into bed waiting for Alexei to shed his clothes as well and join her. When he finally got into bed, he immediately rolled her on top of him and cupped her face in his hands and regarded her somberly.

"Vivienne, you know this man that your father has brought to us, don't you?"

The only sound in the room was their breathing as she searched his serious eyes. Although Vivienne had great faith in her husband and the shadowed world he'd lived in, the fear that she'd lived with for so long was too strong to disregard. Everyone she loved had been threatened, and that was not something to take lightly. Except the time for being fearful had come and gone.

Vivienne could no longer be without Alexei.

How she'd been able to live without this man for so long was a miracle to her. Then again, she hadn't really been living, no matter how many clubs, charities, and classes she signed herself up for to fill the Alexei void in her life. To everyone else, it probably seemed like Vivienne had it all, but it had been the farthest thing from the truth.

Licking her lips nervously, she confessed, "I've only seen him once before, and that was enough for me."

"When?" Alexei's jaw locked as he thought of the man and his menacing features.

Had she ever been alone with him? Worse, had he ever tried anything with her?

"At Moira's laundromat," Vivienne admitted softly. "The day I was going to meet you for dinner in D.C. after our split, I brought Kat to the department store with me to buy a dress for the evening. An associate of his slipped into the dressing room right before I shut it. He held a knife to our sleeping baby and threatened me to stay away from you. There were pictures of the boys, also."

All Alexei saw and felt the red haze he was suddenly engulfed in from his fury. Someone had threatened his beloved family, and the man in their basement was somehow connected. *They* were the reason his wife had stayed away, and their long, torturous separation. Vivienne cried out and a startled Alexei released her. His hands gently massaged the sides of her face that he'd accidentally squeezed.

"*Jesus!* Forgive me, love! I would never-"

"There's nothing to forgive! Lex?"

"Yes?"

"No mercy, right?"

"For those who cross a Romankov? I think not, my love."

He rolled them over so that he was on top, and his mouth seized hers in a torrid kiss.

"But we need to discuss your meeting at Moira's laundromat."

"Right *now*?"

"Hell no."

HE HAD TO MOVE FAST.

There was changing of the guard everywhere except the basement. It was the perfect opportunity to turn the hallway and basement cameras off in addition to the electric fence system. He slipped into the basement and waited patiently for the burly guard to turn his back. As soon as he did, he jumped on him, twisting his neck sharply. He caught the body as it crumbled and pressed the code on the heavy metal door.

"'Bout time you got here," was the greeting he received for his troubles.

"Shut up! We don't have much time! Switch clothes with him so you can go! We need to stick to the plan."

Once that was done, they dragged the body to the cot, and placed it, facing away from the camera. Next, the soon to be free captive received a phone.

"Burner, of course. I'll be in touch tomorrow. I've already lowered the alarm. When you exit, stick to the shadows and trees and jump the fence at the south end. A mile down the road is a black truck hidden by a cluster of maple trees. Currently, the dogs are at the north end of the property. Go now!"

CHAPTER *Ten*

AS SHE STEPPED OUT OF the car, Vivienne smiled apologetically at Fyodor who was holding the door open for her. "I realize that I was a pain in your ass the other day, but I would appreciate it if I could have just a little bit of privacy please."

The burly Russian nodded respectfully while sharply scanning the perimeter. "As you wish, madam. Please, all I would ask of you, Madam, is that you understand that I cannot stray too far."

"Yes, of course," Vivienne agreed.

She accepted the large floral arrangement that Bruno, Fyodor's second-in-command and brother-in-law, handed to her, while he fired off directives to the remaining six guards.

Patiently Vivienne watched the circus show unfold in front of her and the eight men took their positions surrounding her. They began to walk in unison. She proceeded carefully in her stiletto boots through the icy patches of grass to her destination. A freezing gust of wind whipped her long, velvet, emerald paisley-printed dress around her body, and with a shiver, she tucked her chin deeper into her fur coat.

Today's visit had been impulsive but long overdue. As Vivienne was leaving Miramar's spa, she'd noticed there was a wedding reception being set up in the ballroom. The centerpieces of lush pale pink roses were complemented by deep red and light green berry sprigs, surrounded by olive branches, and the entire arrangement was set in a rustic, bark container.

As soon as she laid eyes on the stunning floral assembly, Vivienne knew she had to have it and exactly where it should go. She requested to speak with the father of the bride and offered him six hundred dollars on the spot for it, which despite his wife's protests, he readily agreed to. On her way to her destination, she'd called her husband from the road and informed him of her change of plans. As always, Alexei was incredibly supportive of her decisions.

Yeah, right.

"YOU ARE SORELY TRYING MY patience, Vivi," he rumbled. His thicker than usual accent was a sure sign that he was irritated by her spontaneity. "I like to think that I am an extremely reasonable man-"

She quickly interrupted him with a light laugh. "That is sooo not the word or words I would use to describe you, babe. I would have gone with 'demanding pain in my ass', or maybe 'bossy as hell' rather than 'reasonable'."

There was a moment of silence before he mused aloud, "I do believe that I neglected the other side of your delectable ass the other day in the car. I'll make sure to rectify my mistake as soon as you get home, my dear."

Laawwd, this man could make her hot without even trying, Vivienne thought with longing and exasperation as she shifted in her seat at his words, her bottom already aching for his touch.

"Promises, promises, Lex," she taunted, knowing that despite his annoyance, he loved their wordplay as much as she did.

"When have you ever known me not to be a man of my word where you're concerned, Vivi?" he questioned silkily. "I look forward to seeing you...hurry home."

"As I do you, husband," she said softly. "I love you, Lex."

"Not more than I love you, Vivienne. Be careful," he cautioned gruffly.

Then he was gone, leaving her fighting the impulse to have the driver turn the car around and rush home to her husband.

VIVIENNE REACHED HER DESTINATION, AND as promised, the men spread out a little more than usual to give her the privacy she requested. She set the arrangement down carefully before leaning forward and placing her cheek against the icy granite heart-shaped tombstone. Vivienne closed her eyes and spread her arms wide, encircling it as much of it as she could.

She could still remember the first time she met Moira Sullivan as clear as day in the waiting room of her OBGYN office. Vivienne had gone to renew her birth control prescription, and Moira was there to terminate her third pregnancy, something that she'd only confessed to Vivienne because she needed someone to talk to. According to Moira, Vivienne had the kindest eyes she'd seen in a long time. Alexei's sudden appearance was the only reason Casey was alive today. Divine intervention is what Vivienne called it whenever she looked at her youngest son.

What kind of world would this be without the baby of the Sullivan brothers?

"Hey, Mar," she said, referring to her friend by the nickname she'd long ago given her. Tears blurred her eyes, and with a sniffle, she blinked them away and laughed. "You're lookin' good, lady! I'm sorry that I haven't come by sooner to catch up. Something tells me that you already know everything that's going on in our lives. But just in case you've finally met James Dean and the two of you are too busy making goo-goo eyes at each other, I'll fill you in, okay?"

"Let's see…they brought the Muppets back, and Ms. Piggy and that little pussy Kermit finally got together, only for him to break up with her," Vivienne huffed with a disgusted shake of her head.

"She deserves better because we all know he couldn't handle all that ass she was throwin' at him. Oh, and girl, we *finally* got a black president! Barack Obama and his lovely wife Michelle, our gorgeous First Lady, and their two equally gorgeous daughters, Sasha and Malia have brought a new level of class and grace to our nation. You would have loved them! Educated, accomplished, kind, and compassionate. They're the true definition of family values and goodness. A lot of people talked shit about him, but nowadays, it's hard to come across a politician who doesn't have a scandal swirling around them. Mar honey, this man had none. I see them every now and then at political functions in D.C.. They've even attended two of the boys' fundraisers for the Take A Stand foundation!"

As always, when she thought of their sons, Vivienne's tone was affectionate. "You'd be so honored by our boys, hon. They've turned out phenomenally, and I'm just incredibly proud of them, and I know you are too. Handsome, kind, smart, and hardworking! You know they got it honest— that's all you, Mar. The incredible love they have for their wives and children makes my heart sing! Ruby and baby Jack are going through it right now. My poor lil' mama doesn't even know what to do with that butterball who just adores her. However, I'm confident that in time, they'll be just fine."

Vivienne rubbed her hands together with excitement. "The next baby coming is going to be hell on wheels, and I'm *sooo* here for her arrival! I'm hoping that she has her parents' temperament and keeps them on their toes, especially her mama's feistiness. No doubt, she'll be a junior Sidra, even though she is your namesake."

Vivienne reached out and touched the heart again. "I know that he's not your flesh and blood, however I know *you*. You would be proud to call D.J. your grandson as much as I am. That boy is pure goodness personified, Mar! There's not a mean bone in his body. D.J.'s heart is so big and open to love, that I know the world could benefit from more angels like him in it. I was shocked to discover his existence and that of his biological father. It made me wonder if you knew anything about it. Even from the grave, that sonofabitch still managed to wreak havoc, but the joke was on him once again because that boy is a Sullivan *man* through and through, being raised up right by our boys, and following fast in their footsteps.

Now, let's talk about your goddaughter, Katerina! She's setting the world on fire with her jewelry line. You would love her, Mar! Everyone does...*especially* Holton Brammer. Do you remember Holt? Quiet, blonde Swedish kid? Well, he's all grown up, and Kat's taken notice." Vivienne gave a rueful chuckle. "I'm afraid she's a lot like her mother and has fallen in love with a special type of man, that's just like her father. As she's the apple of his eye, Alexei is fit to be tied about the situation, but as you and I both know, there are far worse choices out there. The boys have promised me that if he breaks her heart, they'll fuck 'em up something awful. Or at least, whatever is left of Holt after Lex gets through with him."

A discreet cough from Fyodor let her know that time was up, and they needed to get back on the road. Vivienne found herself in no hurry to go. It'd been so long since she was here, and despite being surrounded by the dead, the graveyard felt cozy as she talked with her old friend. *Dammit, she still had so much to say!* Except Vivienne knew that if she didn't go now, Alexei would rip Fyodor's head off and stuff it up the bodyguard's ass.

"Ian is doing well. Right now, he's traveling, but I suspect he's also avoiding a second chance at happiness that's been hovering right in front of him." Vivienne smiled good-naturedly thinking of their mutual silver-haired friend and Sidra's half-brother and rock star, Dominick Harris, possibly getting together. "Don't worry, I'm going to stir the pot and see what I can get cooking. He's long overdue for some happiness and romance. Come to think of it, they both are."

Vivienne placed her cheek against the granite heart once more. "I have to get going, but I wanted you to know that Alexei and I are back together and working things out. It's time for me to tell him and the boys our story, Mar. In order to fully embrace a future with Lex, I must, since I refuse to be without him any longer and also because an unexpected visitor showed up."

Again, tears blurred her vision, but this time Vivienne allowed them to run unchecked down her face. Fiercely, she clutched the heart tighter.

"Dammit, I miss you so much, Mar! Not a single day has passed where I haven't thought about you. I hope you're happy up there in heaven and dancing your heart away because even though I know it's selfish, I would give anything for one more conversation in your laundromat as we had coffee breaks and you tried to teach me Gaelic. I could never retain it for shit, but the boyos have taught me the most important words, and they've stuck with me ever since. You should know them because they live in my heart for you, dear friend; **Mo ghrá, go deo agus i gcónaí ag** (My love forever and always). Until next time, Mar."

The group started down the small hill as a light flurry of snow began to fall and Vivienne liked to think it was Moira speaking to her. A memory flashed in her mind and brought a smile to her lips.

VIVIENNE'S EYES WERE WIDE WITH wonder as she entered the laundromat. Proudly she held out her hand to Moira and exuberantly announced, "Look what I've got!"

Moira peered into her gloved hands and looked up at her friend curiously. Her soft Irish brogue was one of the many things Vivienne adored about her good friend.

"Tis a snowball, Viv."

"It's not just any snowball, Mar! It's the first one of the season!" Vivienne explained enthusiastically. "I cannot wait until we're knee deep in it!"

Moira pulled back, her hazel eyes filled with suspicion as she regarded her best friend.

"Are ye mad?! You dinna by chance happen to fall and bump yer head all the way down yer big fancy staircase, did ye? Now, thanks to ye, we'll be covered in the stuff fer months to come!"

"Yeah, starting with you!" Vivienne grinned mischievously.

She smashed the melting ball of ice into her friend's shiny black tresses. Moira squealed with laughter and ran outside to gather some arsenal of her own and a ten-minute snowball fight ensued.

THEY REACHED THE CARS, AND Fyodor held the door open for her. The seatbelt fell out and before she could reach for it, he stepped in front of her to pick it up. It was the briefest of noises, a soft whizzing sound, yet Vivienne recalled it vividly from her days of working with Cedric and Clarissa as gunrunners. Automatically she grabbed Fyodor as he fell back into her arms, a crimson stain spreading horrifyingly fast across his white dress.

He'd been killed instantly by the shot.

Vivienne hit the ground with him on top of her, and for a moment, heart slamming chaotically, she lay staring at the back of his dark head as men screamed in Russian around her, a hail of bullets followed by choked cries as the guards were picked off. Vivienne shoved Fyodor's body off of her and rolled over, crouching against the side of the car and frantically survey her surroundings. Everything moved in slow motion. Three more men fell while Bruno and the remaining other guard, Zander, took aim and fired into ...nothing. Their shooter was so carefully blended into the scenery that she knew they'd never be able to find him.

Or was there more than one?

"Get down!" she screamed to them as Zander's head exploded like a firecracker. Blood sprayed everywhere as his body collapsed onto the icy road.

"Madam, are you alright?!" Bruno demanded urgently, grabbing his phone and placed a call.

Vivienne tried to hear what he was saying, but another barrage of bullets riddled the other side of the caravan in quick succession, causing the tires to rapidly deflate. She attempted to crawl inside the bullet-ridden car to get to her phone, from inside of her purse, but another quick procession of bullets hit the car and thwarted her efforts.

Vivienne was suddenly struck by another memory. "We're going over the bridge!"

She ripped Fyodor's shirt open and, tears in her eyes, Vivienne dipped her fingers into the wound that had killed him and placed her wet fingers to his face. Then she shoved him into a sitting position, head first into the car before turning back to Bruno. Vivienne grabbed Fyodor's gun from his concealed ankle holster and held onto it.

"I'm fine, but we have to move!" Vivienne crawled over to him. "We're sitting ducks if we stay any longer. They could try to blow the gas tank, Bruno!"

She pointed to Zander's fallen body. "Grab it and use it as a shield! On the count of three, we run for it!"

"Madam, that's easily a hundred-foot drop!"

"I know a place that we'll be safe! We'll run down the road toward the tunnel, but at the last minute, we veer left and go over. We move together, but not in a straight line! Let's go! One...two..."

Bruno grabbed the dead man's body and carried it on one shoulder and wrapped the other around Vivienne and gave the final count, "Three!"

They began to run the twenty-five feet to the tunnel, and those few moments in time were the scariest of Vivienne's life as she held onto Bruno and they weaved as bullets whizzed around them. Her heels were killing her, and she was trying hard not to slip on the now wet road, but Vivienne knew she'd not only be damned but dead if she stopped running.

Five feet...ten feet...fifteen feet...twenty feet...

"Here!" She yanked on Bruno's hand, and they swerved left and to the railing as another round of bullets were fired.

The guard flung his fallen comrade's body aside and spun Vivienne around quickly. Startled by the motion, she dropped the gun. Before she could retrieve it, Bruno picked her up as he leaped onto the railing and used it as a springboard. In a flash, they were free-falling as snow swirled and danced around them and the wind gripped them in its bitter embrace.

Her terror-filled eyes met Bruno's determined brown ones, and she began to pray and he joined in.

"Our father, who art in heaven..."

The roaring rapids below them drowned out their voices, and they could only read each other's lips as they plunged into the freezing waters, instantly submerged in the icy depths.

They were instantly separated upon impact by the powerful current, and Vivienne struggled to kick to the surface but the heavy velvet fabric of her dress and coat weighed her down. Immediately she shed the coat. Suddenly, Vivienne felt a life-saving grip on her hand and was being propelled upward as Bruno held onto her, and together, they kicked toward the surface. But at the last-minute, Vivienne unexpectedly jerked on his hand.

Bruno looked back at her, and she motioned toward the waterfall, gesturing that they swim there. He nodded in understanding, and valiantly they swam against the current as the waves threatened to sweep them away.

Vivienne's lungs were on fire and felt like they would explode at any second. The little energy she had was rapidly waning, but they were too close for her to give up now. Bruno gestured to use the rocks to help them further advance, and Vivienne blinked her understanding. Her freshly manicured fingers were numb, and her body was freezing as the wet fabric adhered to her frame, but she clung to Bruno's jacket as he hugged the rocks. They made the painstaking journey and gradually the current lessened. Only when they'd passed through the waterfall did they shoot to the surface, gasping.

Freezing, Vivienne released Bruno's jacket and collapsed, shivering, against a large flat rock with a groan. She was alive! *Thank you, God!* Her entire body ached, especially her feet in those fucking designer boots that Vivienne had been convinced her dumbass just had to have. Her chest burned from holding her breath for what felt like a Guinness world record.

They had to keep moving, though.

Vivienne wanted to scream as she stumbled to her feet and needles of pain shot through her arches. With a weak gesture, she motioned to the bodyguard.

"Follow me, Bruno!"

She turned her back and pain detonated in the back of her head.

Then everything went dark.

CHAPTER *Eleven*

TWO HOURS EARLIER

HE DISCREETLY WATCHED HER FROM two balconies above as she moved with her security detail through the Miramar Resort. He could easily understand why Romankov was so smitten with her. She was an extremely stunning woman, and he wasn't surprised to see men, young and old, blatantly checking her out—something he knew they wouldn't dare indulge in if her husband was anywhere in the vicinity.

She tilted her head, and he was finally able to see all of her face. He grasped the opportunity to quickly snap a picture with his phone. Pleased that it had come out to his satisfaction, he texted it to his employer. Within minutes his phone rang, and he answered the call.

"That was quick."

"You are still with her?"

"Has my assignment changed and I wasn't informed?"

"Don't be flip with me. I can assure you that when we next meet, I will remember this conversation."

The man rolled his eyes and frowned into the phone. "You have my sincerest apologies."

"She looks just the same. I can't wait to finally see her again! It's been such a long time. We have much to catch up on...especially why she just couldn't follow directions."

"It will not be easy. She is always heavily guarded. Her husband would have it no other way."

"A man who loves that fiercely is a danger to himself and those around him. It makes one blind and careless. I'd hate to see him meet with an accident because of it..."

The man froze in place. "What exactly are you saying?"

"Whatever do you mean? I'm not saying anything at all. Just making an observation."

"Alexei Romankov is a problem no one wants if you are contemplating it," he warned the caller sharply as Vivienne exited through the revolving glass entry. "That was never part of our deal. She's on the move. What would you like me to do now?"

"What you do best, of course. Don't keep me waiting too long for the next picture."

"I'll be in touch, then."

"WOULD YOU PLEASE EXPLAIN TO me why in the hell we're freezing our asses off out here in this disrespectful weather instead of gettin' down to business and handlin' the fool in your basement?"

Shivering, Cedric bundled deeper into his gray cashmere coat. He continued to smile cordially and acknowledge people who stopped to speak and thank his son-in-law as they passed through the gates of McClusky's Tree Farm.

"And why are all these people fallin' all over you like you're the next damn Messiah?"

Alexei paid his disgruntled father-in-law no mind as he warmly greeted people, shaking hands, and handing out gift bags filled with holiday treats to the children. Cedric had insisted on coming with him and thinking of the pleasurable way he'd passed his early morning hours with his wife had put him in a lenient mood. Not to mention he liked staying in Vivienne's good graces. Now, he wished he'd made a quick stop and tossed Cedric's complaining ass down the steep ravine just outside of town. Alexei was convinced no one would miss him.

"This is a Romankov family tradition," Kat informed him as she and Holt joined them with a tray of steaming cups of holiday treats. "Papa has made sure that families in need of a Christmas tree have had one for more than twenty ears."

Cedric noted the procession line as the Sullivan brothers handed out multi-colored and clear string lights, Ruby and Guy passed out wood-carved tree toppers, and Jenny Colloway and D.J. oversaw the ornaments.

"Every year? Why do you do all of this? This has to cost a fortune!"

"Not everything is about money," Kat replied seriously as she linked her arm through her father's while Holt passed out the drinks. "Papa, we got you a gingerbread latte. Pop-Pop, you have the red velvet hot chocolate."

"I'm supposed to believe that you do this out of the goodness of your bleeding heart?" Cedric scoffed derisively. "I've heard many things about you, Romankov, but having a heart ain't one of them!"

Kat responded before Alexei could.

"You are way out of line, Pop-Pop!" She scolded him. "I don't know what your problem is, but you need to correct it! *Now.* My father is the finest man I know. You don't have to believe it, and that's your right, but you should probably keep your mouth shut while staying under his roof! If you're interested in keeping a relationship with me; don't disrespect him again."

Alexei hid his smile behind his cup. With those molasses eyes brimming with fire, her lips pressed into a tight line, and chin tiled stubbornly, Katerina looked exactly like Vivienne.

"It's fine, *milya moya*. Your grandfather's opinion of me doesn't bother me in the least."

Except that, it did, just a tiny bit. With his own father disowning him, he'd hoped to find a place within his wife's family. Clarissa was very gracious, warm, and hospitable, but Cedric, on a good day, was intolerable and always had been toward him. He'd tried to be the best husband that he could be to Vivi, and this event had been one of his attempts. The concept of helping those in need with no strings attached had been a foreign one to Alexei before his wife entered his life.

"LEX, WHY WON'T ANYONE SPEAK to us?" Vivienne fumed as they strolled along Main Street. "I feel like they're just looking right through me! Is it because they're not used to seeing an interracial couple?!"

"No, my dear, that has nothing to do with it."

Alexei guided her into Wok This Way, a new Chinese restaurant that Vivienne mentioned wanting to try. He pretended not to notice the way that all conversation stopped as they entered the establishment. The hostess nervously greeted them at the podium then scurried away to get the manager.

"Do you see what I mean?" Vivienne placed a hand on her hip and tapped her foot impatiently. She'd been so excited to go out tonight and looked forward to seeing more of the town that they'd moved to a month ago. With Lex working long hours at the office and her flying back and forth between Whiskey Row and San Francisco for business, they hadn't really spent that much quality time together. "I knew it! They don't like black people!"

"Have you looked around this place, Vivi? For a small town, there is plenty of diversity here."

The manager came to greet them with a stiff smile and bow. He introduced himself as Bao Huang before leading them to a table in the center of the dining room. As Vivienne sat down in her chair and picked up the menu, she was acutely aware that conversation had not resumed, and it was painfully awkward. Everywhere she looked, people promptly avoided her gaze.

"I think I'll have the Spicy Honey Garlic Chicken over steamed white rice," Alexei stated as he loosened his tie. "Have you decided, Vivi?"

She wasn't listening to him. In the corner of the room, Vivienne watched a woman lean over the table and whisper to her companion before discreetly nodding her head in their direction.

That did it!

Vivienne flung her menu on the table and stood up so fast, her chair turned over. She clapped her hands loudly. "Alright, everyone! I'm going to need your undivided attention for a few minutes!

"This is not necessary-"

"I got this, Alexei!" Vivienne cut him off, her hand thrust into his face. "I will not have anyone treating us a certain way because they have a problem with US being a couple!"

She glared around the room, making sure to meet each shocked face with a sneer. "If anyone has a problem with our relationship, you can kiss my black ass! This is the eighties, not the sixties; it's perfectly fine for us to be with each other without people freaking out and judging us like they've never seen two people of different nationalities in love!"

The manager hustled over with a fretful expression. "May I be of some assistance, Mrs. Romankov? What seems to be the problem?"

"The problem is that everyone can't, or won't, stop staring at us!"

Alexei leaned forward, enthralled by the sight of his wife getting worked up on their behalf. Her nostrils flared as she looked down her nose at the other patrons, and her hands were balled into fists. The poor manager looked like he wanted to faint as Vivienne got revved up. He decided to take pity on everyone.

"Vivienne, they don't have a problem with us being a couple or even with your race. It's me that they are unsure of," Alexei explained to her patiently.

"Whaaat?!" She appeared disconcerted by his reasoning. "Why would they feel like that about you?"

"Because I am a Romankov." He said that as if it explained everything as he picked up his menu again and continued to observe it. "Now, please sit down so that we may continue with this fascinating dinner."

Aware that everyone was still staring at them, a bewildered Vivienne remained standing over her husband and addressed his bent head. "That's your explanation?! "Because I am a Romankov"?! What does that even mean? I'm afraid you'll have to do better than that, Alexei!"

"I believe Mr. Romankov is trying to inform you that the Romankovs aren't really seen in town," the manager said carefully as he watched the big Russian

remain perfectly still. Taking Alexei's silence as an approval to keep talking, Bao continued with his explanation.

"They're not a very social group. So, to see the two of you enjoying Whiskey Row is a rarity for us. Please forgive our appalling manners. We are so very sorry to have offended you both. Your dinner tonight will be on the house."

"That won't be necessary, Mr. Huang," Vivienne replied as he fixed her chair and she sat back down, hoping she didn't look as mortified as she felt. "Tonight, everyone's dinner is on us, so please encourage them to eat, and drink responsibly."

"Thank you, Madam!"

She waited until he was gone to confront her grinning husband.

"Happy with yourself?" Vivienne huffed.

His deep chuckle further incensed her. "I did tell you to leave it alone, but as stubborn as you are, I knew you'd persist."

"I'm glad you enjoyed yourself," she retorted. "Now that I've provided you with your daily dose of amusement, you can tell me why your family disassociates themselves from the very town they put so much money into?"

Alexei rubbed his jaw as he looked at his lovely wife. People were drawn not just to her looks but to her vibrant personality as well. They didn't run the other way as they did with him.

"My family's fortune was earned in blood. For a long time, it was all we Romankovs knew. Shedding it

afforded you power and wealth. My uncles, Petr, Ivan, and Sergei came here to start a new way of life, away from the violence, but it wasn't to be. My Uncle Ivan became greedy when they discovered gold and, and he wanted more of it. He attempted to demolish a whole side of the mountain to get deeper into the mine, but his brothers stopped him. Unfortunately, a small cluster of dynamite ignited, and the explosion caused the mine to collapse. The other two were lucky to make it out alive.To them, this town has now been tainted by blood money, and they feel cursed by it, so they stay away."

Alexei glanced around the restaurant and noted the faces were more approachable, so he nodded, accepting the tentative smiles directed their way.

"I do not necessarily feel that way, so if you wish to spend a little time here, we will do so, my love."

Vivienne reached across the table and grasped his hand in hers. She squeezed it encouragingly.

"We'll have to do better than that, Lex! If you want me to live here, we will immerse ourselves into our community. Since Christmas is next month, I've got the perfect way to do it..."

"I JUST CAN'T STOP PUTTING my feet in my mouth," Cedric apologized roughly. "I'm sorry, Romankov, but I'm concerned about my daughter. I wasn't the best father to her, and she wound up with you, a man with an unusual skill set. As a father, why wouldn't I be worried? Then you guys had a big falling out, but the reason behind it is still a mystery, and then you get back together. On top of all of that, someone shows up in my territory, threatening me to get to her! Naturally, I have grave concerns about your reconciliation! Can you blame me?"

"No; from one father to another, I understand your concerns," Alexei conceded. His eyes met Holt's and held. "Eventually you'll have to trust that she made an excellent choice and that the man she loves would give his last breath protecting her. It may not be what you want to hear because that's supposed to be your job as her father, yet eventually, you'll need to take a step back. Allow room for the man her heart chose to do that job instead."

Cedric noticed the silent exchange between the two men and relaxed. "I can see that you do get it...Alexei."

Kat smiled at her father with understanding. She untangled her arm from his to link it with her grandfather's and kissed Cedric's cheek.

"Come on, Pop-Pop, let me treat you to a cheese-stuffed corn dog."

As she led him away, Kat blew Holt a kiss before calling to Ruby who was attempting to tangle herself in the Christmas lights despite her father and uncles' best efforts to keep her out of them.

"Rubes, come with us to get some snacks for everyone!"

Alexei affectionately watched his granddaughter readily drop the lights and run toward her aunt as Holt spoke for the first time.

"Excuse me, sir!"

"Yes, young man?" Cedric inquired, turning back with a raised eyebrow.

"The reason he hasn't done anythin' with his 'guest' is because he wants him to regain all of his strength beforehand," Holt offered. "Durin' your trip to get here, you starved him. It's made him weak and disoriented. We don't do it that way in 'The Row'. In prime condition and alert is how we'd like you to be for whatever we have planned."

Cedric's eyes met Alexei's arctic blue ones, and the chill that he experienced had nothing to do with the thirty-degree weather.

"I…see. Well, I'll trust your judgment then."

As Cedric walk away, Holt said, "I like him. I can tell he's got a real hard-on for you. That, and he really loves his daughter. Bet he's made your life hell on occasion?"

"I'll buy you an island if you get rid of him in a freak accident," Alexei bribed. "Or how about money? Five million dollars sound good?"

"Nope."

"I'll let you do the interrogation?"

"Tempting, but hell no. After that touchin' speech you gave dear ol' Dad, you know what I want, Romankov."

There was silence as Alexei stubbornly refused to speak. Holt pulled a small piece of wood from his pocket and his pocket knife. He stared at Kat while the smooth strokes of the knife glided over the oak. When Holt was done whittling, he handed the piece to Alexei without looking.

Like the jewelry box Holt had made Kat the previous year for Christmas, the details were painstakingly vivid in detail. The bastard had brought the wood to life with Katerina's lovely face.

Fucking showoff.

"Fine! Ask your question but be quick about it!" Alexei groused.

Holt smiled victoriously. "I'll wait. I would like Ms. Vivienne to be there as well when I ask."

Alexei breathed a little easier at the reprieve he'd been granted, but he knew the question would be coming all too soon. His phone rang and his anger faded when he saw Vivienne's name.

"Excuse me while I take this call."

"No problem. Think I'll go get you a fresh drink. I'm pretty sure the one you've got has been watered down by your tears."

"Jackass."

"Yes, sir."

CHAPTER *Twelve*

EVERYTHING HURT.

Specifically, her head.

Eyes still closed, Vivienne winced. The throbbing at her nape caused the nausea in her stomach to roil. The ground below her was hard and unforgiving, and Vivienne longed for the cozy comfort of her bed and Alexei's warm body wrapped around hers with the satin sheets. The sounds of the waterfall surrounded her, but the air around her was unnaturally still. Vivienne knew that danger was near. It was why she hadn't opened her eyes yet. She could smell it, and as her body gave an involuntary shiver, she *heard* it.

It was a deep-bellied menacing growl that was followed by a man's harsh laugh as he hacked and spit. Vivienne heard the crunch of boots approaching until they stopped right next to her.

"Ain't no sense in playin' dead, gal. You'll have plenty of time for that when ya meet your maker shortly."

Still, she kept her eyes closed, trying to assess what just happened. And where was Bruno? Had he been killed as well? All Vivienne recalled was trying to get them to the shelter of the cave, and then...pain. Obviously, they'd made it to the cave-

Vivienne's train of thought was shattered as pain exploded in her ribs. Her breath left her in a whoosh as it radiated along her side, and she curled into a fetal position to protect herself. Wheezing, her eyes flew open.

Somewhere above her, Bruno spoke. "You are not to hurt her! That was not part of the agreement!"

"Boy, you ain't runnin' this show, no more!" The man who'd kicked Vivienne spat. "Just in case you ain't noticed, yer outnumbered! I take my orders from the man payin' me, and that ain't you!"

When the pain finally subsided, Vivienne dragged herself into a sitting position and came face-to-face with a pair of unblinking amber eyes on the squat face of a heavily muscled beast. The pit bull was black everywhere except for the large white spot on its chest, and despite its absolute stillness as it stared her down, it screamed "killer" loud and clear.

Then Vivienne focused on the two-legged animal. She was stupefied, recognizing the scarred man from her past. Rumsford. *How was he here?* He smiled at her confusion.

"You seem real surprised to see me, gal!"

"How did you get free?!"

Had Alexei's estate been invaded?

"Why, my good pal Bruno let me out! Ain't that right, buddy?"

Vivienne relaxed slightly, knowing Alexei was okay. Until she realized the implications of his statement.

"Would you shut up?! She doesn't need to know any more than necessary!" Bruno shouted, refusing to meet Vivienne's glare.

Rumsford paid him no heed.

"I went and got you a babysitter while we wait to complete our mission."

He gestured to the dog that was still staring at her. "Yer babysitter's name is Bessie. She's the only bitch I'll tolerate, so ya better behave yourself. I don't take no lip from any woman, but especially from the likes of you, Ms. High and Mighty."

"Why did you do it? You had the money; why didn't you complete the job?!" Vivienne screamed at him.

Rumsford laughed at her, and Vivienne vowed that if she did nothing else in this world she would ensure he met his maker.

"Bitch, you still don't get it do ya? *She was the job*!" He tapped the scarred side of his face and rolled his eyes. "Why don't you use that big fancy brain of yours to figure it out! All I had to do was let ol' Patty know what y'all was up to. Easiest job I ever had. It was like takin' candy from a baby. Pity that dumb fuck thought he'd make it out alive once he killed his Irish bitch. I entered through the back door and slipped up them stairs. I seen she was dead and then I knocked Patty out from behind. Puttin' the gun in his hand and pullin' the trigger for a murder-suicide effect. I call that a 'twofer'." He snickered nastily. "I guess I did do the job after all! You're welcome."

A 'twofer'.

Vivienne laughed. Not because shit was amusing but because if she didn't, the overwhelming guilt over her beloved friend's death would break her.

The eerie musical sound bounced off the cave walls and echoed around and around like a Ferris wheel.

Rumsford kicked her legs viciously. "Bitch! What the fuck is so funny?"

Vivienne's laughter trailed off eventually, ending on a sigh. "I'm sorry. I was just thinking about something that tickled me, but you wouldn't understand it due to your handicap."

"Bitch, I ain't handicap! Where the hell did you hear that? Whoever told you that is a gotdamn liar!" Rumsford's scarred, bloated face was florid with anger as he bent closer to her.

"I'm sorry. I forgot that in this part of the country, being inbred is considered an honor instead of a disability."

He raised his brawny hand, and calmly, Vivienne watched it swing down toward her face. Stars imploded her vision as his fist connected with her jaw, flinging her face down upon impact. Face throbbing and dizzy from fatigue and pain, Vivienne finally lost the battle. She dropped, then rose on all fours and vomited. Her hand went to her throat, and she tugged the high collar of her dress down. Clutching at her throat as she gagged the last remnants of the upset away.

Needles stabbed her scalp when Rumsford lifted Vivienne by her wet hair. She was turned around to face the odious man, whose eyes blazed with hatred for her as she dangled limply from his meaty fist.

Still Vivienne didn't fight back.

"When I get done with you, I'm gonna kill your Daddy for what he did to my face."

"I was laughing because I was thinking about how much I would enjoy killing you," she whispered.

"Put her down, Rumsford!"

In the background, she heard Bruno running toward them. Bessie's growled ferally as she rushed to confront him. The traitor's screams and the pit bull's growls were a violent symphony that echoed throughout the cave, distracting Rumsford. Vivienne used it to her advantage.

Click.

It was the most joyous sound she'd heard today. Vivienne grabbed him by the back of his neck to steady herself and slit his throat from ear to ear. She graced him with a brilliant smile as he realized what she'd done. A gunshot sounded, and then Bessie's mournful whimper filled the air, followed by a heavy thud.

The stunned bastard released her hair. Vivienne landed on her feet as he gurgled, blood running in rivulets down his neck. Rumsford dropped to his knees, clutching at his throat desperately trying to stop the uncontrollable bleeding, but to no avail. He was dead before his face hit the ground.

Vivienne looked at the petite, bloodied blade and laughed again, this time with a grateful heart. She lifted the skirt of her damp dress and wiped it free of varmint blood before pressing the side of the locket and retracting the blade. Vivienne almost wanted to stay put thinking about how Alexei would gloat when he found her. Thank God, she'd worn it today. She'd only had to use it one other time and had also derived just as much pleasure then...

"WHY DO WE HAVE TO dine with them?" Vivienne complained, sitting down at her vanity table to do her makeup. She applied moisturizer to her face and watched in her mirror as her husband walked by in only a towel that encircled his waist. His chiseled muscles rippled with each step he took, and Vivienne gave a sigh of appreciation at the creation God had seen fit to bless her with.

Now, what was she saying?

"I don't like Olav or whatever hooker he shows up with! They always try to speak in Russian and exclude me, while the over-made-up woman eye-fucks you! Your friend smacks and slurps, and I can't even eat after hearing it!"

Alexei regarded his wife patiently. "We will go and have a drink, and pay our respects, Vivienne. If you don't think you can handle dinner, then we will leave after an hour. It's very important to me to stay on good terms with associates from my old occupation. You never know when they may come in handy. Please grant me this favor."

"What I can handle?!"

Vivienne threw her blush brush down and swiveled around in her seat, rolling her neck as she snapped at Alexei. "You seriously think I can't handle some "Krusty the Clown" lookin' bitch?! Please don't insult me! I stay in my seat for you, dear husband, when I get dragged to these things! I know it's important to you! Forgive me for not wanting to embarrass you. "

Alexei glowered exasperatedly. "Then get out of your seat if you feel you have to! Whatever will make you happy, Vivi! It is not my intention to smother you where you feel the need to hide your true reaction. I admire your candor and honesty! Do not worry-I will let you know when you've gone too far."

"You'll do what!" she shrieked at him with outrage.

He approached her with those predatory blue eyes and a telltale bulge pressing against the front of the towel, letting her know how aroused he was by their exchange. Despite her anger at his overbearing attitude, excitement flowed through Vivienne's body, and she acknowledged her weakness to herself. Alexei was her addiction, and she needed him like she needed oxygen and water. Her love for him overwhelmed her, and sometimes she wanted to pull back because the intensity of it frightened her.

"Oh, no you don't, Lex! Do not try to distract me by—"

The towel hit the floor as he snatched her into his arms with a sinful laugh. There was no talk for the next hour, and because they were late, Alexei said they'd do dinner instead of drinks. By then, Vivienne was feeling way too relaxed to put up a fight.

Her good feeling evaporated ten minutes into their dinner. Afterward, all she could do was thank God that they were in a private room.

Olav's latest companion had brought a friend, and neither woman was interested in conversing with Vivienne. As usual, Olav was loud and boorish in only the way a man who thinks he is God's gift can be. Alexei tried to include her in the conversation by speaking English, but they refused to. The dark-haired wench on his other side had leaned into him one too many times in Vivienne's opinion. Each time exposing more of her cleavage in an attempt to entice him. Alexei paid her no mind as he conversed with his associate and Vivienne.

From across the table, her eyes met Olav's leering ones and then his blonde companion's malicious brown ones. Both of them wore superior expressions as if their being Russian made them better than her. Fired up with anger at their blatant disrespect, Vivienne removed her locket and placed it in her hand.

It was only when she saw the brunette's hand move to her husband's thigh that Vivienne reacted. Alexei grabbed it quickly and squeezed it hard before flinging it away from him. As if reading his enraged wife's mind, he pushed his chair back, and Vivienne lunged over him as she pressed down on the locket, exposing the hidden blade. She grabbed the bitch's hand and stabbed it to the table. Then punched her in the face, knocked her unconscious.

The bitch fell sideways out of her chair, and her friend screamed as Vivienne stomped her in the stomach and face several times, only stopping to address her husband with a raised eyebrow.

"Alexei, are you done here because I've been done since before we got in the car. Frankly, I'm annoyed that I've wasted twenty minutes of my life that I'll never get back, dealing with these rude motherfuckers," Vivienne informed him tartly.

She pulled her weapon from the woman's hand and the table and wiped it clean on the tablecloth.

"Yes, my love, let's go," Alexei spoke calmly. His eyes were full of love as he pressed a kiss to her cheek and whispered admiringly, "Well done, Vivi."

"Thank you, sir," she curtsied. "I thought you'd enjoy it."

"I did. I can't wait to show you just how much," he crooned into her ear.

Olav stood up, blustering, "What is the meaning of this disrespect? Control your whore, Alexei!"

"And now I believe it is my turn," he added in a silky tone. "Give me one second, my love."

Alexei approached his old business associate, radiating with deadly intent.

"What did you call my wife, Olav?"

The other man held his hands up placatingly, backing away from him with an uneasy laugh. "Surely, you can see her attack was unwarranted, Alexei! Her lack of manners-"

He squealed like a pig when Alexei grabbed him by the back of his neck and applied pressure to it. "I beg of you, Romankov! Think of our friendship-"

Alexei shoved him face first against the wall. "I have put up with you for years because I respected our previous business dealings. Yet tonight, you came here full of malicious intent. You and your companions disrespected my wife, and you had the nerve to bring a whore for me! Why would you deliberately try to hurt my wife in this manner? Very spiteful of you, I must say. The Americans have a saying about spite, don't they, Vivi?"

"I believe you're referring to the one about cutting off his nose to spite his face," Vivienne said helpfully as she handed him her locket. Rising on tiptoe, she kissed the back of his neck. "Okay, I just want you to know that I am so incredibly turned on right now; I seriously think we're going to make a baby tonight."

Alexei looked up from his wiggling target with interest. "A baby? We have not really discussed children, Vivi. How many would you like? Eight is a good number, wouldn't you say?"

Vivienne rolled her eyes at him, and he laughed then dug his fingers deeper into Olav's neck, forcing the squirming man to stay still.

"Um, no, I would not say! Are you crazy?! This pussy is for play, not working overtime, Lex!" she replied firmly and held up her index finger. "One is a nice strong number."

"One is a lonely number, my love," Alexei countered with a frown. "Six then."

Vivienne did some frowning of her own. "Yeah, when you can give birth –"

"Are you people crazy?!" This came from Olav's tearful companion, cowering in the corner with mascara streaks down her face.

"Oh, so now you wanna talk to me, bitch? You sure you want my attention?" Vivienne inquired sweetly.

"Alexei, I beg of you! Do not do this!" Olav cried into the wall as he tried again to get away. His plea fell on deaf ears as Alexei reached around and cut two inches off the end of his nose off.

He admired his handiwork as blood spurted onto the pale blue drapes and wall as the small piece of cartilage fell to the floor.

"Ah! That's much better!" he praised with satisfaction, though his eyes remained chilly. "Your face now reveals your true character. Know this, Olav; If you ever disrespect my wife again or feel compelled to discuss her with other people, I will come for you and cut off something far more precious to you, da?"

He released the blubbering man, who quickly stumbled to the table and grabbed a cloth napkin, holding it to what was left of his profusely bleeding nose.

Alexei held his wife's hand, kissing it as they left the private dining room.

"Are you not glad you wore the locket?"

"I am," Vivienne readily replied with a cheerful smile. "I don't think I've had this much fun in years! Thank you for my gift."

Alexei pulled her into his arms and his expression was solemn as he gave her a lingering kiss.

"Always wear the locket, Vivi. You never know when it will come in handy."

"H-HELP ME."

Bruno's broken plea brought Vivienne back to the present. She staggered toward him, averting her eyes from Bessie's inert form. Although she was sure the pit bull would have decimated her on command, it bothered Vivienne that its life had been taken. Her foot kicked something, and she looked down to see Bruno's bloody hand with his revolver still in it. Unfortunately, for him, or rather, *fortunately* for Vivienne, it wasn't attached to Bruno. She pressed her boot on the hand and pried the gun out of it, then walked over to where he sat in a pool of blood, against the cave wall.

One of his thighs had been ripped open.

"Please, kill me now," he begged weakly. Bruno's stark face was drained of color, and against his raven-black hair, he resembled a vampire. "I know Romankov's way will be inhumane. Just make it quick, I beg of you!"

Vivienne's hard tone matched her unsympathetic expression. "I'll consider it, but first, I have questions that need answering. I want you to tell me *why* you did it! How could you do that to Fyodor and your friends?

To my husband? What will you tell your wife, Fyodor's sister?!"

The helpless look fell away from his face as did his usual polite façade. With his lips curled in hatred, vitriol spewed from his mouth. "As if I could forget that fat, useless bitch! I don't give a damn about her or any of them! If it wasn't for Fyodor, I would have never married her in the first place!"

He laughed mirthlessly. "The only one I do care about is "Alexei The Great"! If it wasn't for him, I wouldn't even be in this predicament!"

"What predicament is that exactly, Bruno?" Vivienne interrogated him dispassionately, as she battled the urge to put a bullet through his eyes. This man that she'd been so concerned for had tried to take her from the love of her life. She was done with people trying to keep them apart, and he was about to be the second person to learn that fact. "You were paid well for your services, and my husband always rewards loyalty. Your family lacked for nothing as far as I know."

"Only a rightful firstborn son and a baby sister!" he shot back at her. At her puzzled look, Bruno nodded his head as if she was confirming exactly what he thought. "Your confusion is understandable, madam. "The Wolf" has killed too many men in this lifetime for anyone to keep track of, including my oldest brother Taras Boykov! The bastard is not above killing children also."

Vivienne reached down and backhanded him with the butt of his gun. "You've now been officially warned that I don't take kindly to people lying on my husband, Bruno! Alexei would *never* kill a child!"

Bruno cradled his split open cheek and spit on her shoes contemptuously. "That is exactly what he did. You're a fool to think he has a conscience!"

Vivienne noted his anguish was real as she racked her brain, trying to recall the name, he'd given to no avail. She was drawing a blank. She cocked the gun and aimed it at his face. "If Alexei killed your brother, I'm sure it was because he deserved it. Now you're going to tell me everything, because if you don't, I'll make sure that my husband pays a visit to your remaining family members," she smiled, watching his eyes widen with understanding.

"Go to hell, bitch!" Bruno tried to reach for her, and Vivienne calmly sidestepped him.

"He was a good brother and always sent money home to take care of us! Romankov killed him because he felt threatened that my brother was an exceptional soldier! Without the money, we were thrown out in the street. Do you know what it's like to be homeless in Russia's brutal winter? My little sister, Sasha, died sleeping inside of a slide in a park! We had to leave her there because we were too poor to bury her. It wasn't until my mother was lucky enough to remarry that our lives changed, and her new husband adopted us."

Tears started to fall from his eyes, and exhausted by his tirade and injuries, he leaned his head back against the wall again. "For years, revenge was all I dreamed about, but my mother begged me not to go up against the great Romankovs. She claimed I would not win, that more blood would be shed, but I had to try! Especially when the gentleman made it sound so easy with his offer."

"Judging from how things turned out here today, your mama sounded like a smart lady. It's too bad you were too damn hardheaded to listen to her," Vivienne remarked unsympathetically. "Tell me about the offer."

"I was studying at Uni when I was approached by…" he swallowed hard and mumbled something inaudible.

Vivienne stepped on his bleeding wrist, and he jerked, screaming his agony.

"Tick, tock, motherfucker." She smiled icily.

"I should have let that man do what he wanted with you!"

His face was dripping with sweat, and his eyes were starting to glaze over. Vivienne raised her foot again.

"*Nyet!* Alright! I was approached by a man. I don't know his name, I swear! Just that he was Irish, I think. He gave me ten thousand dollars the first time I met him and asked if I was interested in exacting revenge against Alexei Romankov. He knew all about what happened with Taras and said his employer would make it worth my while. Our first step would be for me to adopt a new identity, court Fyodor's sister, and get her to marry me."

"Enabling you to get chummy with him and secure a position with Alexei's security detail,"

Vivienne concluded grimly. "Tell me about the man and his boss."

"I don't know anything about the man or his boss. My only duty was to report if you and Romankov were meeting up. I was assured vengeance would be mine when we finally destroyed him."

"But your contact has been compromised," Vivienne argued. "What is supposed to happen now?"

"Rumsford was sent to kill your father but failed. I released him late last night and he reached out to me this morning and explained what was going on yesterday when he arrived at his house. A plan has already been set in motion; I just don't know what it is. I was only to notify him of our locations so that he could plan where the ambush would occur and then take you to the airport, but I figured it would be too hot and the first place Alexei looked, so I called Rumsford and arranged for him to come get us. But then you started talking about going over the bridge-"

"And you deliberately knocked the gun from my hand to give him a clue about where we'd gone," Vivienne guessed.

She wasn't surprised to see him smile mockingly.

"Gold star for Mrs. Romankov!" Bruno held up his handless arm. "I wasn't planning on this happening, of course. It's not important, though, because I've been assured of a favorable outcome. *Your husband won't win.* He may be very good at war, but his enemy is a master at strategy. Every moment in our lives has been because of him thus far. We're all pawns in the making of the downfall of "Alexei The Great"."

Vivienne shoved the gun in his mouth. "Yours first, motherfucker! I'll be-"

"VIVIENNE!!!"

The thunderous roar caused Bruno to blanch and tremble. Vivienne smiled with relief at her husband's voice. Except it didn't really sound like Alexei; the raw, crazy fury in his voice was animalistic. She withdrew the gun from Bruno's mouth.

"It looks like the cavalry has arrived. Pity."

She cupped her hands and screamed, "I'M IN THE CAVE, LEX!!!"

"Please! You said you'd kill me!" Bruno pleaded, visibly distraught as they heard the deafening footsteps of what sounded like an army. "I'm begging you to kill me!"

"And deny my bloodthirsty husband his vicious and ingenious revenge at your expense?" She placed her hand against her chest and gave him a wounded look. "Honey, how cruel do you think I am?"

Vivienne stared him down. "When Judgment Day comes, may God be merciless on your soul."

CHAPTER *Thirteen*

ONE HOUR EARLIER

"OUR MYSTERY MAN'S NAME IS...." Magnus Carlisle paused for dramatic effect as he perfected a drum roll on the wooden desk and met the un-amused gazes of Alexei, Holt, Cruz, and Cedric. "Yeesh, you guys are a rough crowd. Fine! His real name is Buchanan Rumsford, and he's from Gatlinburg, Tennessee."

Magnus apprised the men gathered around his laptop in the Romankov library. "An only child, he was born and raised there. Mother died of natural causes five years ago, and father left when he was but a wee lad. I can personally confirm that he is definitely not the man who broke into my place and instructed me to obtain information on Mrs. Romankov's clients."

"Dig deeper!" Alexei bit out, heading for the door. "I think it's time for me to have a talk with Rumsford."

"Man, you guys always think violence is the answer to everything," Magnus said disapprovingly, making his employer pause then head back his way with a grim look. "Surely, ya ken have a conversation without blood being shed, can't ya?"

"So *you* say. In our line of work, we find it adds a nice touch as a conversation starter and to keep it flowin'," Holt disputed with a feral grin.

Cruz challenged Magnus. "What would you suggest, geekboy? We buy him a bouquet of flowers then wine and dine him? I'm damn good at that but not willing to try. Pull up his room. Let's see if he's up to a visit."

Magnus did as requested, showing them the feed of Rumsford's basement prison.

Alexei stared hard at the gangly young man with bad skin, whom he'd often wanted to strangle with his bare hands when he was a young child mooning after Kat. His father, Richard Carlisle, had died in a freak accident at one of Romankov Industries plants in Glasgow, and Alexei had ensured the Carlisle family received a generous care package. Although he was an obnoxious twat most of the time, Alexei was willing to overlook it for the most part because of his aptitude with a computer and insightful moments like these.

"Thank you for the information, Magnus." Alexei finally said before heading toward the door again. "That will be all for now. Sorry to pull you from your vacation, you may now return to Bora Bora. Should I need more information from you, please be available."

"Wait!" Cedric shouted with alarm. "That's not the man I brought here!"

Tension skyrocketed as the group huddled around the laptop. Alexei called down to the basement on his cell, barking orders in Russian to the guard. On the screen, they watched as he cautiously entered the room with his gun drawn and turned the still form over.

It was Dimitri Noyelov, an eight-year veteran of Alexei's team.

Alexei was filled with a terror he'd never known as he comprehended what this meant. He took off running with Holt and Cruz right behind him. He pulled his phone out and dialed Vivienne's number as he shouted orders to his men. The terror was spreading, and he tried to push it back to think clearly, knowing his Vivi's life depended on it. Dear God...

Holt grabbed his arm. "My truck is right here! Let's go!"

Back at the house, Cedric's fear matched his son-in law's, and he reacted on anger. He grabbed a scared Magnus by the front of his hooded sweatshirt and shook him until his glasses fell off.

"What's happening?! Someone tell me what this means!" Cedric hollered

"It means that there's a traitor among us, sir," Magnus whispered numbly.

THE CARNAGE THAT GREETED THEM as they arrived at the cemetery was an inhuman sight to behold. The bloodied, bullet-ridden bodies of his men caused grief and fury to tear at Alexei's soul, especially Fyodor's, who'd been with him for twenty years. He had been a great man, and Alexei had trusted him implicitly with his family's lives.

"Spread out!" he ordered his men. "Get a cleanup crew here now!"

What terrified him most was there was no sign of Vivienne.

Her purse was still in the car and appeared untouched. Alexei grabbed it and tore it open, searching for a clue. Her phone showed twelve missed calls from him and that he was the last person she'd spoken to.

"They were picked off from over there," Cruz announced grimly, pointing high into the forest. All of the bullets are on this side of the car. They never saw it coming."

Holt surveyed the men carefully. "We've only got seven! They left today with eight, Alexei. Who are we missing?"

Alexei went from man to man and studied their faces or what was left of them. Finally, he was able to determine the guard. He faced them, his face a savage mask.

"Bruno is missing. I think he and Vivienne are together. Vivienne wouldn't just leave without a clue for me. She would *know* to do this!"

Holt walked down the road toward the tunnel, studying the ground as he went, while Cruz moved into the forest. Alexei tried to remain calm in the face of what this could all mean.

What would he tell the children if something had happened to their mother?

How would he go on without her??? He'd only just gotten her back goddammit!

Focus, Alexei! he instructed himself sternly.

The killer would have picked off whoever was closest to Vivi first. Alexei crouched down over Fyodor's lifeless body and slowly twisted his head left and right. His shirt was soaked in blood from the gunshot wound to his chest. At first, Alexei saw nothing out of the ordinary and thought Fyodor just had blood smeared on his cheek. Until he looked more closely and made out the letters someone wrote in his blood.

"Whoever was up there is long gone. The tracks are covered by the snow," Cruz said heavily when he returned. "Did you find anything?"

"Maybe..." Alexei replied slowly, trying to understand the clue she'd left.

"I've got a gun!!!" Holt shouted.

Alexei shot to his feet, his heart racing once more as he saw the Swede standing near the bridge railing. Understanding dawned on him, and he fought back relieved tears with the newfound realization.

"I know where she is! Let's go!" Alexei motioned to his men. He pointed to three of the twenty men he'd brought along. "Get this scene secured!"

"Where is she?!" Cruz anxiously demanded.

"The waterfall!"

Dear God, please let her be alive, Alexei silently begged.

"BABY, HOW DOES THIS JACKET fit me?" Casey called to his wife from the three-way dressing room mirror, trying to inspect the black tuxedo jacket from all sides.

"I like it, boo. It fits you just right." Sidra waddled up behind him and tried to wrap her arms around his middle.

Casey laughed at her efforts and pulled her by her hand in front of him in the mirror to wrap his arms around her and nuzzle her neck. "Better?"

Sidra sighed with pleasure as he gently massaged the top of her large belly where baby Moira loved to kick her vigorously. "Much better. You look damn good, while I'm gonna look big as hell in my dress!"

Casey kissed away her pout then continued to kiss her just because he couldn't get enough of Sidra Jane Sullivan.

"Cut it out, Sid. You'll be gorgeous as always. Is my baby behavin' today?"

Jack snorted as he walked by them carrying his own tux and into a fitting room. "Which one?! And if they are behavin' as your wife once told me, the day is still early."

"Yeah, well you should just respect the unexpected and roll with it!" Sidra called after him playfully.

Casey kissed her cheek. "Come on. I'll help you to your chair and get you some tea."

They held hands, with Sidra leaning into him adoringly as Casey escorted her down the long dressing room hallway to the sitting area of the men's boutique, Pour Homme. Guy, Darby, Avery, and Noelle were already waiting there. On the table before them was a tea service and little sandwiches and scones that they shared while Ruby and baby Jack slept peacefully in a double stroller. D.J. was at Mai Ling's for the afternoon.

"Lookin' good, brother. How's it fit?" Guy put some sandwiches and scones on a plate and handed it to Sidra while Noelle passed her an apple juice.

"Nice and tight. Think this one's the winner." Casey kissed Sidra once more and took a bite of the herbed chicken salad sandwich she offered. "Like it?"

"If it fits you nice and tight, then it's definitely the one for you. Kinda sounds like a straight jacket. Your crazy ass should feel right at home in it," Guy drawled.

Casey gave him the finger while the others laughed. Suddenly, he gave Guy a speculative glance. "Say, isn't that Ms. Pearl over there by the cashmere sweaters? I wonder who she's shoppin' for?"

His pointed look at Guy's chocolate brown cashmere turtleneck sweater had his friend tugging at his neck uncomfortably.

Guy's cheeks were stained red as he slouched down lower in the leather chair, clearly not wanting to be seen by the owner of The Pink Champagne. Pearl was blowing his phone up and stopping by Americana Traditions, ordering stuff with an evening delivery. Irritated by her persistence, Guy passed the deliveries to his employees and paid them the overtime to avoid having to interact with Pearl personally. Luckily, Holt and Jack were busy dealing with other things to pay closer attention, but it was getting harder to avoid the Creole beauty.

He mumbled, "I wouldn't know. I do believe it's time for me to go and try on my tux."

Noelle pinned him in place with a steely-eyed stare. "Not until you tell us what happened between the two of you! Spill it!"

"It's a long story." Guy looked pained by the admission.

"Y'all fucked and she just can't quit you?" Darby fathomed as he shifted to make Avery more comfortable in his lap.

"Okay, so it's a short story!" Guy blustered at his accuracy.

"You put it on her like that?" Avery's look was doubtful, and everyone turned to look at her with mixed versions of amusement and disbelief.

"Correct me if I'm wrong, but didn't your own husband once school you on the men from 'The Row'?" an offended Guy sat up straighter in his chair. "I'm more than just a pretty face, you know."

"I just meant that...well, you're..." she looked helplessly at Noelle and Sidra. "Help me out here!"

"I believe Avery is trying to say that she sees you as our dear, sweet, good friend, wonderful uncle, and businessman rather than "Pippy the Pipe-Laying Piper"," Noelle finished dryly.

"Yeah, and we sure as hell didn't have you pegged as a "Mr. Ho and Go", you little tease," Sidra added happily as she munched away on her cranberry-lime scones. "So, it wasn't good or what?"

"I don't like to kiss and tell," Guy said piously. He yelped when Noelle plucked his ear. "I'm tellin' Jackie on you!"

"If you don't dish, I won't cook for you anymore," she threatened. "Which would be a shame, considering how bad I was feeling about the guilt trip you gave me..."

"I expected this type of behavior from the soulless one!" Guy pointed at Sidra who shrugged unconcernedly, "not the sweet mother of two, impressionable, young children who are watchin' her every move-"

"Details and make them good!" Noelle scooted closer to him with an expectant smile.

"This seems right to y'all?!" Guy gave his friends a beseeching look.

"Yeah, I'm good with it," Darby answered. "The last time you brought up your sex life, you mentioned being very cozy with your hand, so all of this is a pleasant surprise, and we want to know."

"Well, it was obviously more than a one-night thing. Why didn't you just keep it to that? Don't you know your limits?" This came from Avery, who was discreetly trying to catch a glimpse of the other woman from across the store. "I like her! Look at how she's bundled up appropriately. She must have *some* class and home trainin'. Everyone knows hoes never get cold."

"Of course, I know my limits!" Guy muttered indignantly. "I just don't always pay attention to them is all."

Surprisingly, his defense came from Casey, who normally loved giving him shit. "Y'all leave him alone! If she ain't the one, then that's it. When he finds her, he'll stop playin' games."

"Ain't no game-playin'!" Guy insisted quietly. "I told her that we should stop because I had other things goin' on. I didn't lie to her and have no plans to pick up where we left off. There ain't a damn thing honorable in that."

"When you say 'other things', do you mean *Fern*?" Darby probed. "We all saw you with her at Max and Georgie's weddin'. I thought I was gonna have to hose your thot ass off! Won't she be here for Christmas?"

Guy thought of Fern's large onyx eyes and her satiny dark skin and the way her close-cropped natural enhanced her beauty. He'd just seen her at Thanksgiving in Baymoor and was convinced that she grew more beautiful each time he laid eyes on her. Fern had him thinking unmanly shit like what pretty, dainty clavicles she had. *The fuck?* Then his thoughts took a turn into deeper, darker desires to how she would look in his bed.

Or taking his dick wherever he liked...

"Pervert alert!" Noelle smacked his leg, and everyone laughed. "You're a damn dream tramp!"

"You can do and be whatever you want in your dreams!" Guy's expression grew sly. "Or are you just mad because dirty minds think alike, Mrs. Sullivan?"

This time, the smack landed on the back of his head and knocked his cognac Brixton hat off.

"Have I mentioned you're overdue, Pip?" Jack reminded him from behind and joined the group, sitting on the arm of his wife's chair. "We gotta get goin'. Vivienne just texted me a mandatory order to get to their house.

His severe expression had them all on their feet and heading toward the door.

Casey noticed how Guy used his pregnant wife as a shield to hide from Pearl, and kicked the back of his knee, causing him to stumble forward.

"Chickenshit."

"Bite me, Beauty Queen!"

"T.L.C., MAMA? REALLY?" KAT JOKED tearfully as she held onto Vivienne's hand and kissed her mother's forehead. Since her arrival home, Kat had refused to let Vivienne out of her sight. Even when she took a long soak in the tub, her daughter had sat on a footstool and refused to leave. Currently, she was holding tightly to Vivienne whose head lay against her bosom. "You honestly thought that Papa would know an R&B song from a nineties girl group?! He's still listening to Fleetwood Mac and Carly Simon!"

"It was the only thing I could think of! I couldn't get to my phone, and it's not like I could write a letter complete with instructions, baby." Vivienne gave a big yawn and turned her head to smile tiredly at Alexei who was stretched out on the other side of her. "I knew your father would figure it out. I had complete faith in him coming for me."

"And Bruno?"

Kat's voice matched her expression - hard and unrelenting. She'd been raised in love and kindness and was generally a perpetually happy person. Yet Kat had no problem walking into darkness if you fucked with her family on any level and expected to come out unscathed.

"Will be well fed and cared for until it is time," Alexei guaranteed his daughter.

Kat appeared satisfied and leaned against her mother, trying to be mindful of her injuries. Now that she had her in her arms, it was hard to stop the tears from falling. If anything had happened to her...

Alexei knew exactly how Kat was feeling. Today had taken a hundred years off of his life. As long as he lived, Alexei would never forget how he felt when he realized his Vivienne was missing. The mystery of her clue was solved when he saw Holt standing by the railing. Suddenly the song Harvey Kramer used to always sing about waterfalls, came to him.

Years ago, after he and Vivienne had a particularly vicious fight about lack of time together and her growing friendship with Moira, Alexei had taken her to have a picnic by the river, hoping to reconnect.

"WHAT ARE WE DOING HERE, Alexei?" Vivienne inquired irritably as she followed him, trying to navigate the soft ground in her heels. "Dammit! I wish you would have told me where we were going! I could have worn appropriate footwear."

Alexei, already weary of her griping, had set the basket down and tossed his wife's complaining ass over his shoulder before picking the basket up and resuming his trek.

"You're an asshole!" Vivienne screeched but to no avail.

Once they got to the waterfall, Alexei set her down and ignored her to lay out the blanket and picnic spread. Vivienne tried to stay mad at him, but she was secretly impressed by the trouble he'd gone to for her. So, she sat down and, soon, they were sharing pate, cheese, crackers, fruit, and wine. Afterward, Alexei lay his head in her lap and read to her aloud from the dictionary. It was his way of trying to lessen his accent. She was proud of his determination, but the thought of him losing the accent made Vivienne sad. It was one of the things she found most attractive about him. Especially when they were making love.

"We should go for a swim," Alexei impulsively suggested. He tossed the book aside and rolled to his feet. "Come along, Vivi!"

"I didn't bring a suit, Lex," she pointed out reasonably.

Alexei surveyed their surroundings before turning back to her with a wicked grin. "I believe I can solve that problem. Come with me!"

They packed up the basket and Vivienne followed him closer to the waterfall where they shed their clothes and readily stepped into the cool waters behind the fall. Vivienne squealed happily.

"Lex, this was a great idea! Thank you for this day!" She launched herself into his arms and kissed him hungrily. All the tension of their fighting was gone, and they were both relieved and happy to be with one another.

Alexei's hands lowered to her bottom, and he hitched her up where her legs encircled his waist; as always, he was hard for her. With a wiggle of his eyebrows, he huskily murmured, "And now, you will show me just how thankful you are, my love."

Vivienne kissed down the strong column of his throat before rising up to bite his chin. "Oh, will I?"

"Please do not doubt yourself," he teased her as he positioned himself at her opening. "I have faith in your talents, my beautiful wife."

After that first round in the water, they'd noticed the cave and went to explore it. That's where rounds two and three took place.

"Today was a fantastic day. One that I'll remember forever," Vivienne announced as Alexei positioned her to lay on him so she wouldn't have to be uncomfortable on the cave's hard floor.

"You and me both, Vivi. It was very much needed. We should do this again in the near future." Alexei's arms tightened around her, happy that they were not fighting. Perhaps, they could discuss having a baby. They hadn't mentioned it in at least a year.

However, it would be their first and only time going to the waterfall together.

By the next year, their lives would be forever changed.

THE BUZZER ANNOUNCED A CALL from the security gate. Alexei's men were aware of what had happened, and after Bruno's betrayal, everyone was on high alert.

"Sir, your family is here to see you. They said Mrs. Romankov has requested their presence."

Vivienne called out, "Please send them in."

"Absolutely not, Vivienne!" Alexei growled at her. "I want you to rest and get some sleep. It has been a long day for you. This can wait until tomorrow!"

"No! It. Is. Time, Alexei." Vivienne sat up with her daughter's assistance. "Especially after what happened today! Kat, please help me out of bed."

"Yes, Mama." She shot her father a censorious look, which he ignored as his phone rang.

"What, Magnus?!" Alexei barked into the phone.

"Sorry to bother you, sir," Magnus cleared his throat noisily; "I just thought you'd want to know that Buchanan Rumsford has been to Whiskey Row before."

A cold premonition slithered down Alexei's back as he watched his wife and daughter through narrowed eyes.

"When?"

"The week prior and the week that Moira Sullivan was murdered, sir."

CHAPTER *Fourteen*

"WHAT IN THE HELL HAPPENED to you?!" Jack snarled as soon as he saw Vivienne's bruised, scratched up face. His face was apoplectic with rage as he noticed how small and fragile she looked in Alexei's arms, and it scared the hell out of him.

Ruby started to whimper at her father's anger, and it quickly turned to full on sobbing at the sight of her Nana's face. She raised her arms to Noelle as a startled baby Jack woke up crying as well.

Guy took the little boy out of his stroller and consoled him by rubbing his back while Noelle picked Ruby up and tried to reassure her that Daddy was okay.

"Calm yourself, Yakov," Alexei spoke sharply as Vivienne winced at the volume of her oldest son's voice. "You will not speak to your mother in that manner ever again!"

Darby placed a hand on his oldest brother's shoulder, struggling for composure himself as he spoke to him and Casey, who was fuming with clenched fists, his pregnant wife held him back by placing her body in front of his.

"Then give us the answers needed to reassure us so that we don't fly off the handle again, Lex!"

Kat and Holt locked eyes, and she could tell that he was torn between his duty to her father and that of being her brothers' friend. From the way they didn't question his presence, she knew the guys automatically assumed he was there for her, though Darby was now observing him suspiciously.

"It would seem your mother has all of the answers, and we are all now waiting to hear them," Alexei bitterly told him as he placed Vivienne on the large leather sofa in the study.

"Everyone, please calm down!" Vivienne said soothingly. "I feel fine, and it's really important that I speak to the three of you and your sister. Would everyone excuse us for a little bit? I had Marta prepare refreshments and would appreciate it if the children were not present while I spoke with them."

After shooting the brothers and Kat concerned looks, everyone begrudgingly left the room. As the last one out, Holt closed the door behind them.

He overheard Guy casually ask Cruz, "Any particular reason you're here at this gatherin'?"

"I was making a delivery and waiting for a signature," "The Butcher" smoothly replied. "Still am as a matter of fact."

"Uh-huh."

Oh shit, Holt thought with grim amusement.

Guy loved to give the impression of being an affable jokester, but Holt knew his friend didn't miss a damn thing around him. He was just selective in what he chose to address, and Cruz was officially now on his radar. Holt's mind drifted back to Kat and his friends. Shit was definitely about to hit the fan. He hoped they would be able to weather the storm that was about to be unleashed. It was definitely time to finish this quest.

"LET ME START BY SAYING that your mother was my very best friend in the world. I loved Moira because she was the nicest and sweetest person I'd ever met. Despite any troubles she may have been experiencing, she always kept that beautiful smile in place. Even on the day we met, when she was obviously struggling with an enormous decision in the OBGYN office, she greeted me with that smile and said, "So what are ye in fer?"."

Vivienne's smile disappeared with her next words. "As wonderful as your mother was, your father was the exact opposite, but I'm not saying anything you didn't already know firsthand. Your mother was very good at keeping secrets about his atrocious behavior. I just didn't know the extent of it until he intentionally broke Casey's arm."

She gestured to Darby helplessly. "I didn't know about your beatings and fighting for money or her being continuously raped by him until you boys went to therapy. I found out about Casey's arm, not from my husband who broke Patrick's leg when he found out, but because your mother decided to take actions into her own hands and be rid of the bastard once and for all."

The room was silent enough to hear a fly's heartbeat.

"I would have never known if she hadn't run into a monetary obstacle."

"What are you sayin'?" Jack's lips barely moved as he uttered the question that he knew his brothers were dying to ask. "What did she do?"

Vivienne's eyes were shadowed with concern for their reaction to her answer. "Moira hired someone to kill him."

Casey shot to his feet with an untamed expression. "Then how did he wind up killin' her? What went wrong, Vivienne? Tell us!"

Alexei was stunned by her admission as well, but his questions could wait until the boys were settled, especially Casey, who'd only recently come to grips with the cruel words he'd spoken to Moira on the day she died.

Their pain tore at Vivienne's heart, and she wished to God she didn't have to tell them all that had transpired. "I went to see your mother at the laundromat for our standard morning meeting, and she had company..."

"I HOPE YOU'RE HUNGRY, I'VCE got bear claws and coffee!" Vivienne trilled as she entered the laundromat. "Why do you think they're called bear claws? It's not a very attractive name. I can honestly say that if they weren't so good I would totally pass."

Her comment was met with silence from her friend, and immediately, she was overcome with concern for her. If that fucking husband of hers had hurt her again...

"What's wrong, Moira?"

"Viv, I wasna expecting you so early," Moira greeted her woodenly, causing Vivienne to frown with consternation. "Ken you come back in a little while?"

That was a bold-faced lie, as this was the usual time Vivienne came. As soon as she was sure "Lord of the Douchebags" went to the mine or carousing with his loser ass friends. She was about to ask her friend what in the hell was wrong with her when a man shifted away from the wall he was leaning on behind Moira.

Violence.

It was Vivienne's first thought as she looked at the white man with the brown curly mullet, full lips, and light green eyes. He vibrated with it. If it wasn't for the left side of his face that was severely scarred with burn marks, he would have been teased for being a "Pretty Ricky". As it was, the vivid green of his eyes was a severe contrast to the pink, puckered flesh.

"Who's yer friend, Mrs. Sullivan?" The polite tone belied the vile, lecherous look in his eyes, as he strolled past Moira to stand in front of Vivienne a little too close for her comfort. His thorough once-over left her with an unclean and violated feeling. "Hello there, pretty lady."

"My eyes are up here," Vivienne replied icily, and he raised them slowly from where they'd lingered on her chest. "Do you mind stepping back? You're all up in my personal space."

"Yer lucky we ain't alone; otherwise, I'd be all up in somethin' else," he remarked lewdly.

"If ye dinna mind, Mr. Rumsford, I'd like to finish conducting our business," Moira spoke loudly in the hopes of distracting him from her pissed-off friend. An angry Vivienne was an insult hurler and would only infuriate this cur. "How much is needed to complete the transaction?"

Rumsford licked his lips a he leaned in and sniffed Vivienne's hair creepily. "Why don't you and I head back to your place, gal? Or you just scared yer gonna like it too much? I promise to go easy on ya...well, at least the first time anyway."

Vivienne set her recyclable coffee tray on a nearby washer and loosened the lid on one of the steaming hot lattes. "I promise that if you don't get away from me, you're going to get fucked up today."

He looked at the coffee in her hand and stepped back several paces and sneered, "Uppity bitch! Mrs. Sullivan, thanks to your unfriendly associate here, the price just went from two thousand dollars to five thousand dollars."

"Five thousand dollars! I dinna have five thousand dollars, Mr. Rumsford," Moira wailed, her hazel eyes filling with distress. "Please give me two more weeks ta see what I can do! I beg of ye!"

"What is this money for, Moira?" Vivienne demanded, not liking the fact that her friend was mixed up with this pig. What could they possibly have in common?

Moira refused to look at her as she mumbled, "I'm trying to settle Patrick's gambling debts so that nothing is hanging over my head. As you know, his grandfather lent me the money for this place, but he put his grandson on the loan as well. Patrick has borrowed money against it for his gambling debts. I'm just trying to pay it off, but the price has just gone up."

Vivienne was puzzled by the explanation, but she hated the fact that Patrick "the asshole" had put Moira in this vulnerable position. "I'll loan you the money. Tell your "friend" here to give me an hour, and I'll go get it."

"No can do, black beauty. It's gotta be now or I'm walkin', and the price will just keep goin' up." He raked her with another depraved look. "Unless you wanna take me up on my earlier suggestion?"

"You have a serious death wish, don't you?" Vivienne set the coffee down and unsnapped the heavy gold and diamond bracelet Alexei had given her for Christmas their first year together. She ran her fingers over the beloved piece, hating to part with it, but Moira looked so sad and desperate that Vivienne knew she had to help her.

She thrust her hand out at Rumsford, who eagerly came forward and she dropped it into his meaty palm. "Here, take it. It's worth four times her payment. Don't bring your ass around here again, motherfucker. Consider her debt paid."

"No, Vivienne! I canna let you do that!" a distraught Moira protested vehemently.

Rumsford laughed at her and gave Moira a wink as he addressed her. "Well, ain't you real clever? And here you had me feelin' sorry for ya and shit. I guess it pays to have rich friends, don't it?"

He headed toward the door. "We're square for now, but for your sake, it better be real because I wouldn't mind coming back here to do deal with you, black beauty."

"If you read the inscription, you'll know it's real, and you'll also know who'll be fucking you up if you're dumb enough to bring your ass around here again."

Rumsford held the bracelet up to the light and read the inscription and laughed long and hard. "Well, ain't that somethin'? Nice doin' business with y'all. I'll be sure to let my boss know that we're squared away, Mrs. Sullivan."

Vivienne made sure he got into his gold Isuzu Rodeo and drove away before releasing her breath. Her relief was short-lived as Moira grabbed her by the arms and confronted her angrily.

"Why did you do that, Vivienne? That was a foolish thing for you to do!"

She was sobbing as she sank into one of the waiting chairs lining the wall. The deep heartfelt sounds wracked her slender body, causing it to shake uncontrollably. Her Irish accent was even more pronounced as her agitation grew. "Y-Y-Ye shouldna done that! Alexei will be mad as hell if he finds out about yer involvement. Anyone can see he doesna approve of our friendship."

"Hmmmph! While I wasn't expecting you to react this way, a thank you would be nice for bailing your ass out! Let me worry about Lex." Vivienne plopped down next to her as a dizzy spell hit her.

"I don't feel so good, but I can't tell if it's because I haven't eaten, or the revolting bastard who was trying to get into my pants, or the fact that my best friend in the whole world lied to my face and expected me to believe her shit! Don't tell me what I shouldn't have done when you were obviously digging yourself into a deeper hole than you were already in with that animal! Now spill it, Moira, and don't you dare lie to me!"

Moira raised her splotchy face from her hands, and her miserable red-rimmed eyes were full of anxiety and stress.

"You just paid off the balance on Patrick's murder."

"WHEN I ASKED YOU ABOUT the bracelet, you said that you no longer cared for it," Alexei lashed out with thinly veiled contempt as he recoiled from her. "You lied directly to my face about it, Vivienne!"

"I promised Moira I wouldn't say anything about what she did!" Vivienne retorted defensively. "She was already terrified of you and how much you disapproved of our being friends! I couldn't take away her hope! It was all she had left!"

"No, it wasn't! She had three great children to focus on! I would have helped her!" Alexei raged. "I *despised* Patrick and would have helped her in any way that I could if she would have come to me! I was not going to interfere in her marriage if I'd never heard her speak ill of her husband let alone say five words to me!"

"Well, you certainly made it easy for her to fear you with your constant mean-mugging and telling me to stay away! All you wanted was for me to listen to and do what you wanted! You didn't care that I wanted my career back or that aside from you, Moira, and the boys, I was lonely here!"

Vivienne stood up with help from Kat and moved away from her husband, needing distance from his suffocating anger. "You hated that I was trying to start a business for myself and that it would take me away from you! All you wanted was for me to be waiting for you in bed with my legs open, ready to fuck or pop out a baby!"

"Jesus fucking Christ!" Darby howled, covering his ears. "Can we please concentrate on the matter at hand?!?!"

"And what was so wrong with wanting to spend time with my wife?! I didn't get married to distance myself from you, Vivienne! From the moment I saw you, I knew I wanted you forever! I never had a single doubt until the end when I worried about if I could make you happy because you were obviously so fucking miserable being married to me! Yet you always had doubts! You doubted yourself, you doubted me, and in the end, you doubted our marriage and ran away like a coward! You should have trusted me as your husband to take care of this situation and handle Patrick!"

Alexei could barely sit still he was shaking with rage. "Except by then, you were looking for an out to our marriage, were you not?"

"I never wanted to leave you!" she screamed. "I just wanted you to see me as more than a possession! I told you from the beginning that I refused to be contained, but all that mattered to you was that I understood your rules! We had a child and weren't in a good place, so I left to clear my head. I thought that—"

"You thought what? That I would come for you and beg you to come home???" Alexei thundered. "You left me! A man can only take so much! When times are hard you don't run! Had you trusted me, you have never been in this mess!"

"I was not willing to risk harming a hair on any of my childrens' heads! You couldn't guarantee protection one hundred percent! Look what happened with your loyal bodyguards!" She stalked over to him, jabbing Alexei in the chest, as he bent, bringing them nose -to-nose. "I think it's really funny that you should say that, Mr. Know-It-All! I don't think this has anything to do with me and everything to do with *you*!"

"What do you mean?" Jack asked sharply. "I need y'all both to focus on the topic! Viv, what did you mean by that?"

She was attempting to regain control of her emotions, but despair and anger were threatening to drown her. The way Alexei was looking at her let Vivienne know that he would not be forgiving her anytime soon and Laura's words came back to haunt her.

"His pain will manifest itself, and when it happens, it will not be pretty, my friend."

Vivienne was a fool to have left or to think they could ever move forward from it.

"Just things like Rumsford's delight when he read the inscription on the bracelet, to Patrick being alive when he should have already been dead, according to Moira," she explained. "And today Rumsford said that she was the job! Before she found out about Casey's injury, we'd been moving your toys, books, and clothes. Your mother would bring them to the laundromat, and I would take them from her and stow them away. When I ran into Patrick outside of the laundromat, he confronted me."

"What's the matter, spook? Ya look like ya seen a ghost?" He stepped closer to Vivienne, and she could smell the crazy coming off him. His hatred was threatening to suffocate her in its cloying waves. "I know what the both of ya's tried to do, and if it's the last thing I do, bitch, y'all are gonna pay."

"Your mother admitted that a man had reached out to her regarding Patrick's abuse and how he could make all her problems go away for a fee, and she agreed. But why would he raise the price on her at the last minute?"

"Because he knew her rich friend would bail her out," Kat spoke up, and they all turned to her.

"It makes perfect sense when you think about it. He conveniently shows up just a little bit before Mama gets there at the same time every day and freaks Aunt Moira out and upsets her in front of her loaded bestie? What else is Mama gonna do, especially when it has to do with the devil spawn husband that she wants Aunt Moira to be rid of? It's what any bestie would do if they had the means!"

"The man at the department store showed me my bracelet before he left and said he was keeping it as insurance," Vivienne murmured, staring at her husband as they were both coming to the same realizations.

"The deal was that I don't go back to Alexei, or he would go to authorities; he also threatened all of you...just to ensure that I would stay away."

"What man at the department store?!" the children chorused, and Vivienne waved their concern away as she paced the carpet.

"Don't worry; we're working on finding him," she told them as she paced.

"Rumsford was here the week Moira died," Alexei volunteered as he paced in the opposite direction. "He knew you and Moira were best friends-"

"And that *you* didn't approve! She even said that to me! "Anyone can see he doesn't approve of our friendship." Those were her exact words! So, he set this in motion, I'm sure to drive us apart, babe!"

"And it worked, but *who* exactly is he working for?"

"Bruno said you wouldn't win against him. The mystery man. That while you were good at war, this man was a master strategist and—"

"What did you say?!" Alexei grabbed her by her shoulders, and all three Sullivan brothers automatically rose. "He used those exact words, Vivienne?"

"Yes, but what does that have to—"

But Alexei wasn't listening as he threw the door open.

"Magnus, get your ass in here!"

CHAPTER *Fifteen*

SHE WASN'T SURE WHAT WOKE her, but Noelle knew before she opened her eyes that Jack wasn't in bed with her. Just to make sure, though, she reached out and sure enough, his side of the bed was empty, and the sheets were cool. An indication that he'd never come upstairs after she took the kids up. After leaving the Romankov estate, Jack had filled her in on *everything*, and to say her damn mind was blown was putting it mildly. She, Sidra, and Avery had exchanged meaningful glances on the way out, confirming that they would be meeting up tomorrow, or rather later today, to discuss things in great detail.

Noelle left the comfort of their bed to slip on her robe and look for her husband. Before heading downstairs, she checked on baby Jack whose crib was still in their room. The little boy's curls were standing up all over her head as he slept sprawled on his back with his hand down the front of his diaper.

Ugh! Why were boys like this?

Next, she went to check on Ruby and her special guest for the night. Poor Ruby had been so distraught by Daddy's anger, Nana's face, and the argument between Nana and Papa that everyone in the house had heard, she'd remained unnaturally quiet with a pensive expression for the rest of the day. Not even when baby Jack went into "Zilla mode" did she react in her usual defensive manner. Instead, she'd asked for D.J., who was now sleeping in the twin bed in her room while Ruby slept in her converted crib toddler bed curled into a ball with her fist pressed to her mouth.

Noelle pushed the door through and headed down the stairs wrapped in garland and eucalyptus with boughs of holly and red and white brocade ribbon for the holiday. The overhead light above the foyer was on and so was the one above the kitchen stove. Down the hall, she could hear the faint crackling and knew where she'd find her husband at this time of year as the wind howled outside. Noelle knew that tomorrow, snow would cover the entire town and Smoky Mountain range and enthusiastically looked forward to it. Although she was born a city girl, Noelle was really a country girl at heart. There was nothing she loved more than her family and friends who now all resided here as well.

Her fair aisle slipper-boots made no sound as she walked down the long hallway to the family room, where she found her husband sitting in front of the enormous Christmas tree he'd brought home yesterday morning. He was deep in thought as the flames flared brightly and he stared morosely at the bare tree, sipping amber liquid from a crystal tumbler.

They were so attuned to each other that Noelle wasn't surprised when without looking at her, he spoke.

"I'm sorry, I woke you, darlin'. I didn't wake the kids too, did I?"

"No; they're as snug as bugs in their beds, but you know I need you next to me, baby."

Noelle entered the room and took the glass from his hands with no resistance. She wrinkled her nose at the strong smell of its contents. The decanter on the end table next to him was empty, so she knew he'd been at it for awhile. Jack didn't appear to be under the influence as he took the glass from her and set it on the table before pulling her into his arms and down on his lap.

Her heart went out to him and her brothers-in-law. She knew that the news that Moira shouldn't have died and was trying to make a way out for them was a shockingly devastating blow to navigate. Noelle smoothed his disheveled black curls from his forehead while he silently watched her with tortured eyes. His combined scents of cognac, sage, lemongrass, and the clean fragrance of his soap tantalized her nostrils.

Jack closed his eyes as his wife's nails raked through his hair. Already, he felt more at peace just having Noelle near. She was his safe haven, whether she knew it or not. The demons from his past had chased him doggedly and slowly torn away at his soul until he married her, and they were eventually silenced.

That peace had remained unwavering until today.

There had been so much going on, and he'd tried processing it to the best of his abilities while remaining calm for his brothers and Kat's sake, but Jack knew he hadn't succeeded. Just seeing Mama Bear's face, all bruised and battered, had brought back so many nightmares! It had been enough to make him want to lose his shit. He knew his lil' brother felt the same way. Then after dropping bomb after bomb, Alexei, Holt, Papa C, and their town butcher for chrissake, had left together to God knows where.

"No one is going to think less of you if you let go, baby. I won't let you fall, Jack." Noelle urged, pressing her forehead to his.

Jack swallowed hard, trying to force back the lump in his throat. "How's Ruby? I know I scared her today, and I hate myself for it! Just seeing Vivienne's face like that took me back to my childhood. I'm sorry I let y'all—"

Noelle's finger to his lips stilled him. "Don't you dare apologize for being human, Jackson Connall Sullivan! How can you say such a thing after what you went through today? After everything all of you have been through?"

Jack opened his eyes to meet her smoky gray orbs. As always, they seduced him without even trying to be sexy. It was her love for him that Jack saw shining brightly that captivated him each and every time, and the reason he was always seeking her gaze.

"She was tryin' to do right by us. All this time, I've secretly harbored a little bit of resentment about why she stayed with him and we suffered, when she really was puttin' us first!"

Noelle cradled him close to her, and Jack wrapped his arms around her, burying his face in her bosom as his body became racked with emotions, but he was visibly shaking from the effort. *"I miss her every day, Noelle.* I have a million things to tell her, about all of us. I was lookin' forward to visitin' her grave in the New Year and sharin' everythin', but fuck! It feels like she just died all over again! And just when I felt able to celebrate the holidays again."

Morosely his eyes strayed over to the flames. "You've gone to so much effort to make sure we had new, great memories, which I'm eternally grateful for, but I'm afraid that the holidays will never be the same for me, sugar."

His wife kissed the top of his head. "Let it all out, babe. It's okay to cry."

Jack's hand slid up to her nape as he raised his head to brush his lips against hers. "I don't wanna talk anymore, darlin'. Gimme some sugar."

Noelle kissed him, slowly at first, but it intensified as his hands slid down to palm her ass and shift her, so her sex hovered over his firm erection. Her tongue slid between his lips to savor his taste, and his gave chase as Jack growled and squeezed her bottom and smacked it firmly.

"Damn, baby, you always know how to get me goin'."

Noelle hurriedly shucked off her red, chenille robe and tossed it on the floor as Jack pulled the straps of her white cami down to reveal her firm, lush breasts. He cupped the heavy globes, loving the weight of them in his hands as Noelle thrust them close to Jack's mouth. Dying for his touch, she gripped his hair in anticipation a whimper of need on her parted lips.

Jack smiled slowly as he stared up into his wife's heavy-lidded eyes. "Damn! You take my breath away, Noelle."

"Please! I need you, Jack."

"You have me, love. Forever and ever." He pushed her breasts together and slowly licked her straining nipples before suctioning them into his mouth. *"I ain't goin' nowhere."*

Noelle writhed in his lap, trying to catch her breath as Jack lavished her aching breasts. But that wasn't the only thing aching for his attention. Her pussy was slick and ready for him, as if it could be anything else with his skillset. He released her breasts to capture her mouth again as his hand slid under the edge of her nightgown and crept up her inner thigh.

Jack swallowed her harsh exhale as he stroked her through the damp fabric of her panties from her clit to where she ached most. He repeated the motion torturously as Noelle pushed up and down against his fingers frantically. The fabric was soon soaked as her arousal increased tenfold.

"So fucking wet. I want to taste you, Noelle."

He rose with her in his arms, and their mouths fused together. Jack set her on her knees with her back toward him as he pulled her back to him and filled his hands with her breasts, squeezed them firmly, and plucked roughly at her nipples, his tongue thrusting into her mouth when she turned her head toward him. Noelle reached behind her to clench his head to her as she drew on his tongue and his denim-clad thigh nudged her bare ones apart.

She was crazy for more of him and *needed* him inside of her right now. However, Jack was feeling a certain way tonight, and couldn't be rushed. Not that Noelle minded in the least, loving the pleasure-pain from his firm touch. Before she'd slept with Jack, she'd had no idea what she liked in bed and was frustrated with feeling disconnected from her body. Jack had shown her it was also the right partner that heightened the experience. Noelle had found she didn't care how he fucked her as long as he never stopped. He encouraged her to freely express herself because they both knew he'd be handlin' her ass, exactly the way she needed when he was ready. Jack released her breasts and gently pushed her forward until she was lying face down on the plush charcoal rug with her ass in the air, offering it to him.

Jack was shaking at the enticing sight his wife presented him—the full globes of her ass as her night slip fell to her shoulders and exposed her satiny smooth, brown sugar-hued body. The firelight made her skin gleam, and Jack could no longer control himself. He gripped her saturated panties on each side and ripped them from her ass, tossing them into the fireplace as he bent his head, hands spreading her ass cheeks and burying his face in her pussy to feast on her sweetness.

"Oooohhhh, Jack! Right there! Don't stop!"

Noelle brazenly threw her ass back at him, and he alternated between sucking on her engorged clit, plunging his tongue into her center, and then sliding up to tease her French star. Rubbing her face against the softness of the rug, Noelle's eyes rolled into the back of her head as Jack tongue fucked her mercilessly. *Goodness.* Now he was taking nips at her clit and then flicking the oversensitive nub with his tongue. She was dizzy with pleasure and welcomed the pricks of euphoria spreading throughout her body that signaled an imminent orgasm.

Noelle embraced it as she spread her thighs wider and rode his face. Her fists clutched at the soft rug strands as she combusted and damn near went blind with her release, moaning and wailing into the carpet before Jack flipped her over and undid his jeans, yanking them and the boxer's underneath down his thighs to sink his pulsating dick into her, loving the way her pussy spasmed around him. Noelle wrapped her legs around his thighs and kicked his jeans down further as he ground into her. She pulled him down by his shirt for a kiss, relishing in her flavor all over his mouth. Still convulsing, she undulated her hips, sprung for more of him.

"Mmm, you almost made me forget there was more coming, babe."

Jack gave a hoarse laugh and shuddered as his Noelle found his rhythm. He rammed deeper into her, loving how aroused she was for him. "You know me, darlin'; I'm the gift that keeps on givin'."

He threaded his hands into her hair and commenced to make love to his wife as if his life depended on it. Jack was thankful for the blissful reprieve Noelle provided him with for the next couple of hours.

It was only after the flames of the fire died out that they checked on the children once more and were finally snuggled together under the covers in their own bed, watching the snow fall outside did Jack address the issues again.

"Let's see how this shit plays out. I can't trust any of it, Noelle, and what I mean by that is that I don't trust any of *them*."

Noelle could hear the underlying pain in his words and pulled his arms securely around her. "We're a family, Jack! We will survive this together and then move forward together! That is what families do. At the end of the day, you need to realize that everyone had the best intentions at heart."

Jack buried his face in her tangle of curls and tried not to suffocate her as he held onto his anchor tightly. "I love you, Noelle."

"I love you too, husband," she whispered drowsily as they finally drifted off to sleep.

Chatham, New Mexico

THE BLUE SKIES WERE FILLED with fluffy white clouds, and desert landscaping as far as the eye could see. It was deceptively serene to the average viewer. Great postcard picture material. To Alexei, it was a bleak sight. The rapidly moving clouds gave the façade of trying to get the hell out of this desolate, tiny-ass, rundown town, and the tumbleweeds chased each other across the long stretch of highway in front of their vehicle. The dried-up branches appeared to be warning the group not to go any further, but they paid them no heed.

The fatigue green colored Land Rover drove past a bar, grocery store, a diner, movie theater, a Chinese and Mexican restaurant, laundromat, and convenient store with a three-pump gas station. All of the buildings were faded in color, rundown, and depilated. The few towns patrons who were out and about looked just as bad, including the women who also had a jaded quality about them. A half mile down the road was a gaudy, neon blue building with flowers and green vines painted all over it. The garishly flashing yellow sign above it read Petal Soft Comfort.

"Something tells me they're not selling mattresses," Cruz muttered.

He turned off the road and pulled up alongside a long row of motorcycles and turned off the vehicle.

Holt viewed it with distaste from the backseat. "Let's just do what we came to do and get the hell up outta here."

"You are such a spoilsport!" Cruz complained. "Everything with you is "get in and get out"! I sure hope that for your woman's sake you aren't like—Arrrgh!"

"Please believe that if he hadn't done it, I would have," Alexei reassured Cruz darkly when the Spaniard lifted his face from the steering wheel and touched his nose carefully.

"Count me in on that deal," Cedric chimed in grimly as he unbuckled his seatbelt and they exited the vehicle.

The quartet entered the packed brothel and all activity came to a standstill at the sight of them. The scantily clad women stopped entertaining their prospective clients. The lure of good looks, power, and money was too much for them to resist. They came clamoring across the floor of the large room to secure their next score.

"Welcome to Petal Soft," a brunette with Double F's greeted Alexei as a redhead linked her arms wit Cruz, and a blonde draped herself over Cedric. Holt ignored a naked woman dancing upside down on a pole as she crooked her finger at him in invitation.

"Bitch, get back here!"

A tatted up, bare-chested Latino man shouted belligerently at the transgendered woman from the chair at the table where he'd been playing cards. He rose, unbuckling his belt. and pulled it from his pants.

He staggered their way, waving it threateningly at her and slurring.

"I'm gonna beat your ass until you're callin' me Daddy!"

"Shake him for me, Daddy," Blondie whispered seductively in Cedric's ear, and he shot her a look of annoyance. "Shake him and I promise I'll do whatever you want me to do."

"Bitch, you ain't my damn type, but I hate to see a woman bein' disrespected." Cedric addressed Alexei. "This you right here?"

"Never seen him before in my life," Alexei said.

He moved the pouting woman out of his way and stepped away from his father-in-law, a sign that Cedric took as the green light to proceed.

Holt and Cruz did the same way as the man lurched forward with the belt raised high. But the blow never came. The pressing of the pistol to the center of his forehead froze him in place.

"I should shoot your dumbass just for bringing a belt to a gunfight, ya dumb motherfucker." Cedric wrinkled his nose. "Or maybe just for not bathing or brushing your teeth in this century!" He lowered the gun until it rested between the wary biker's eyes. "You makin' a move today or what?"

"W-What do you want me to do, man?" he pleaded, dropping the belt to clasp his hands, and plead for his life. "I didn't mean to disrespect you like that. I'm sorry!"

"Get down on your knees and say that."

The man did as he was told. "I meant no disrespect. I'm sorry!"

"I'm sorry—*Daddy*."

There were sniggers, chuckles, and outright laughter as the red-faced man gritted, "I'm sorry...Daddy."

Cedric kept the gun on him. "Good boy. Now run along, and don't bother her again."

Humiliated, the man scrambled to his feet and ran out the door without a backward glance, leaving his belt behind.

"Not bad," Holt praised Cedric and clapped him on the back.

"Hell, I don't have the skills that you boys do, but I ain't completely useless," Cedric mumbled as he peeled the blonde woman off him. "Run along now. He won't be bothering you anymore."

Alexei stepped into the center of the parlor and surveyed it. "I'm looking for the owner of this place, Danny Flannigan."

There was a commotion from a dark corner as a man shoved three naked women off his lap. "Who the fuck are you and what do you want with my da?"

"My name is Alexei Romankov, and I am searching for Danny Flannigan."

Again, all commotion stopped as the man stood up. He was a great hulk of a man, even his muscles had muscles. His head was shaved bald and covered in Celtic tattoos, and his blue eyes were splinters of ice as his expression turned downright menacing, triggering everyone to retreat as he crossed the large room until he and Alexei were twenty-five feet apart.

"So, you're the one who chopped off his hand! You don't look like a big bad wolf to me. Maybe more like a bitch, I'm thinkin'," he sneered, flexing his muscles.

"My apologies, I didn't catch your name," Alexei remarked as he casually glanced around the seedy establishment. Eighteen men in the room, but none looked ready to come forward and help this emotional hothead in his quest to die. "Not that it matters to me anyway. Now, if you would be so kind as to run and fetch your boss; I don't like having my valued time wasted," Alexei looked him up and down with a smirk, "on trivial matters."

"It's Kieran, little bitch." The man flushed with the dismissive tone he was being subjected to in his own family's establishment.

All his life, he'd heard of the legendary bastard who was Alexei Romankov. Especially when his father had company and he regaled them with tales of how he'd lost his hand. The old man hated what had been done to him, but his fear had paralyzed him from doing anything about it. Shame had played a big role in it as well. Their nationality wasn't called the "Fightin' Irish" for nothing. Instead, Danny had gone into hiding in this shitty little town and opened this brothel with Kieran's mother, whom he beat and berated regularly to compensate for his failures. That was another reason Kieran hated Romankov and had always known what he would do if he ever crossed paths with him.

That time had apparently come, and Kieran's hatred intensified with every breath he drew. Envy engulfed him as he sized up the expensive wool coat, watch, and shoes Romankov wore. He radiated wealth, power, and entitlement and deserved to be brought down to the nothingness he'd made Danny Flannigan feel and, in turn, expose his family to. Today was the day that Kieran would right the wrong against his family.

"Ain't gonna be no mo' little bitches up in here," Cedric said, tightening his grip on his gun.

Kieran stared down at him unblinkingly. "When I'm done with him, I'm going to stomp you to death, little man."

He turned back to Alexei. "If you want to talk to my father, you have to get through me first, little bitch."

"Why don't you just go and get him for me?" Alexei suggested, with an exaggerated yawn.

"Don't take that shit from him," Cedric said hotly before retorting, "Fuck you, bitch!"

"It'd be real fuckin' nice, if just *once*, someone rolled out the welcome mat, had a hot meal, and soft bed waitin' for us whenever they heard the Romankov name," Holt grumbled under his breath as he cracked his neck and accepted the rush of adrenaline surging through his body. "*Is he crazy?* We can't let his old ass fight that beast."

"Let's do 'heads or tails'," Cruz whispered. "My vision's still a little blurry due to some dumbass slamming my head on a steering wheel. But I am in agreement with you. Ms. Vivienne would kill us if anything happened to him. That bastard definitely has a score to settle, and it won't be pretty; he's even bigger than you! I'll take heads."

"I can hear the both of you," Alexei chimed in just as softly without taking his eyes off his adversary. "No worries. As much as I appreciate Cedric coming to my defense, I will not allow him to fight in my stead."

Silence met his comment, and despite the death threat in front of them, Cedric sniggered at his son-in-law's lack of comprehension.

"Uh, well that's good to know for future reference," Holt offered, and Cruz outright laughed.

Realization dawned on Alexei, and he was filled with outrage at their presumptions.

"You think I can't win?!" he hissed under his breath. "That I'm too *old* to beat him?!"

"Holt started it," Cruz deadpanned. "If I said anything offensive, I'm blaming it on my head injury. Clearly, I'm not thinking straight."

"Fuck the both of you! I'll deal with you when I'm done!" Alexei growled without turning around. He made a big production of glancing at his watch. "If you insist on doing this, I can spare you...about five minutes, so let's be quick about this, little boy."

The enraged younger man charged him like a bull, full speed with his head down. Alexei calmly leaned down and picked up the abandoned belt, neatly sidestepped Kieran and looped it around Kieran's neck. He used the leverage to swing gracefully onto the man's back and tightened the noose, by pulling the belt through the buckle. Tighter and tighter he yanked, causing Kieran to stumble backward. Alexei kept one eye on the bar as he pulled the bigger man in that direction.

A gasping Kieran spun Alexei around and around in an attempt to dislodge him but was unsuccessful. He reached back and pulled at Romankov's hair and punched his face, but the other man did not break. Kieran was losing air and realized the bar was his only chance at removing the bastard. He backed up to it full tilt, hoping to crack Alexei's back in the process.

Alexei smirked victoriously at his companions and held onto the belt with one hand while shifting his body to the sided. He jumped up and over the bar as Kieran slammed his back into it with all of his weight. Alexei jerked down on the belt as he landed in a crouched position behind the bar. The snap of the bones breaking in Kieran's neck were heard throughout the noiseless room. Only then did Alexei release the belt, allowing the lifeless body to crash to the floor. He leaned back against the bar, attempting to catch his second wind. His head was ringing, his jaw throbbing, and his right eye was starting to swell, yet Alexei would take the win.

He really was getting too old for this shit.

An image of Vivienne popped into his mind. The way she'd worried her bottom lip between her teeth as she packed his bag, her concern for his safety clouding her pretty eyes. Before leaving, Vivienne reached up on tiptoe and drew him down to her for a kiss. Despite his anger with her, Alexei had responded immediately in the way he always did to her touch. He pulled her flush against him, molding their bodies together as they prolonged the kiss. Crying silently, Vivienne pressed into him, her hand sliding down to cover his heart, as Alexei kissed the tears from her cheeks.

"Come back to me, Lex."

It was what she'd always said to him when he'd left in the past. For the first time in their relationship, he hadn't responded with his usual answer of, "Do not ever doubt it.".

Instead, Alexei kissed her forehead and walked away without looking back.

The sound of squeaking wheels caught his attention. A glance to his left revealed an older Danny Flannigan in a wheelchair. Resignation lived in his face as he met Alexei's lethal stare. He wore a prosthetic hand where Alexei had cut his off, and his eyes watered when he caught sight of his dead son.

"Not my boy! Oh, God! You heartless bastard!"

Alexei straightened up. "Since you don't look that surprised to see me, I guessing that I've been long overdue for a visit. It would appear that you and I have much to discuss."

CHAPTER *Sixteen*

"YOU CAN'T GET MAD AT me, Romankov," Danny argued desperately as he rubbed his prosthetic hand on his thigh, nervously. "When I left you that night, I did exactly as you said. I warned the gang and got the hell out of there!"

Alexei remained silent, his gaze predatory and it unnerved Flannigan just as it had that fateful night. What was equally discomforting were the twin towers standing behind him and the shorter black man who kept his gun visible as if he would shoot and ask questions later if he heard something he didn't like.

"I never went back; I swear to ye on a stack of bibles!" Danny insisted, trying to stall, but it was inevitable.

Danny knew his time had come, and his attitude changed from eager to malevolent.

"Ye have no one to blame but yourself, ye smug-ass prick! This whole thing is yer fault! Ye didn't clean up your loose ends! Had ye done so, none of this would have occurred! No one would have ever come seeking me for the truth! Mulroney's children have every right to want to see ye suffer!"

Alexei tried to hide his shocked reaction to his admission.

Mulroney.

His killing the Irish gangster had set off a chain of events that spanned almost three decades, most importantly, Moira Sullivan's murder, which had devastated his wife and was the catalyst that drove her away. Alexei loved Vivienne above all else, and her staying away from him had slowly deteriorated him over time, to not be with her, raising their child together. The few times she'd allowed him to get close to her, he'd felt hopeful, only for her to pull away again under the threat of blackmail. The boys losing their mother and everyone winding up in therapy was all his fault. Not Vivienne's.

He felt like a failure as his father's words came back to haunt him:

"Always kill them all: The targets, their children...Everyone, Alexei! If you don't; it will come back to haunt you."

His killing Mulroney and Taras had been impulsive, and he hadn't bothered checking into their backgrounds thoroughly. He'd been too enamored with Vivienne and focused on leaving the family business to look into the matter. Alexei should have known better, though, because it was the reason he'd selected specific targets in the past. The thought of killing innocents had never resonated with him.

"Their names."

"Bradan and—" Danny paused and realizing he had the upper hand because he now had nothing to lose, sneered, "Sorry, that's all you're getting out of me. What are you going to do? Kill a cripple?"

"I wouldn't dream of doing such a thing. Cedric, do you know why this man is missing a hand?"

"Is it because he masturbated too much?"

Alexei laughed mirthlessly. "Not quite. He lost it the day he decided to disrespect Vivienne in my aunt's bakery by implying that he was going to sleep with her without her consent. He also dared to grab her with that hand, so I cut it off that night as punishment for insulting the woman I love and using racial slurs against her."

Cedric's blood boiled with the knowledge that this man had blatantly disrespected his princess. "I could have gone the rest of my life without knowin' that, Mr. Flannigan. Would you fellas excuse us, please?"

Flannigan's first scream reached the trio as they exited the brothel. Through the glass reflection, Alexei could see his father-in-law pistol-whipping Flannigan. Kieran's body remained in the same place, while the good times resumed. He wasn't worried, though. Chatham, New Mexico appeared lawless and low on morality.

"That was nice of you," Holt commented.

Alexei shrugged nonchalantly. "I thought he'd appreciate putting some numbers on the scoreboard."

They leaned against the railing and waited patiently. While Holt and Alexei ignored the lusty looks from the women, Cruz perused them shamelessly.

"I love how free and European this little brothel is." He winked at a naked woman wearing a rainbow afro as she did splits in front of him, sucking her own nipple. "You know what my biggest problem with American women is?"

Alexei hazarded a guess. "They have standards?"

Before Cruz could answer, Cedric joined them. He'd removed his tie and used it to wipe his gun clean. "I got the names. Let's get the hell outta here."

Alexei called Magnus. "I want you to find everything you can on Jamie "The Gent" Mulroney's children."

It was time to finish this.

VIVIENNE FOUND IT HARD TO concentrate on doing anything except worrying about every man in her life. Even Ian wasn't returning her calls and that was so unlike him. It was unusually quiet, especially without Magnus underfoot. The Scot had gone back to his vacation in Bora Bora, and Alexei was generously footing the bill for the entire trip.

Vivienne decided to stay busy by decorating the estate with her security detail. If they were going to be attached to her ass, then they might as well work with her. Kat took a break from jewelry designing to come downstairs and help as well.

They'd decided on a Nutcracker-Sugar-Plum Fairy ballet theme done in shimmering pastel colors of blue, green, gold, silver, pink, white, and purple. Life-sized nutcracker soldiers, fairies, silver reindeer with gold antlers and pearls draped around their necks, and ballerina statues were placed by the front doors, and the staircases were surrounded by oversized white boxes wrapped with gold and silver velvet ribbons to form spectacular gigantic bows. Plush, chenille mouse-shaped pillows were perched on top of the boxes to complete the look.

Balsam Fir Christmas trees were placed in every room on the lower floor and the landing in the middle of the double-sided staircase and lavishly decorated in pastel ornaments, keeping with the theme. Deco mesh wreaths of varying sizes, laden with pastel ornaments, hung from the ceilings in the foyer and on the doors. The staircase landings and fireplaces were draped with garlands made of faux eucalyptus, silk white and pink roses, and gold tulle. As much as Vivienne wanted to do real roses, she knew they would be a pain to upkeep.

"I think it looks fabulous, Mama! That husband of yours is going to love it!" Kat gushed and instantly regretted it at Vivienne's wistful expression.

"I hope he does. I'd planned on this Christmas being very special because I knew how much he was looking forward to it." Vivienne kept her eyes focused on twining the life-like roses and ribbons around the branches.

"It will be, Mama! You just have to believe," Kat assured her as she gave her a long hug. "So, we hit a rough patch; it's nothing we haven't done before. We'll get through it! Are you trying to tell me you're giving up just like that?"

Vivienne threw the arrangement down in frustration. "Never! I was a fool to not confide in your father, and I will never make that mistake again. I just don't know if I've made it clear enough. Or if it's even enough anymore, now that he knows the truth. On a scale of one to ten, how mad do you think the boys are at me?"

"Pretty mad," Kat said cheerfully. "Don't stress, Mama. They just need a moment to process everything. I know Holt's identity threw Casey and Jack for a loop, but Darby didn't seem that surprised. Cruz, for sure, was a surprise to all; there's plenty to work out, but have faith and believe in a Christmas miracle."

The front doorbell chimes echoed through the house, and Kat stepped away from her mother and dragged her toward it.

"Let's go! I figured you needed a pick me up today and took the liberty of calling in reinforcements."

The doors opened just as they arrived, and D.J. and Ruby ran in, greeting her in unison.

"Hi, Nana!!!"

Sidra, Avery, and Noelle followed behind them.

"Well, isn't this a wonderful surprise!" Vivienne hugged the children as the women surrounded them and offered her hugs and kisses on the cheeks. "Where's my sweet baby Jack?"

"He's hanging out with the boys today since he woke up sniffling," Noelle explained.

"Please tell me you've got something cooking," Sidra begged as she held her rotund belly. "We're starving!"

"How can you be starving? I just made you a bacon and egg breakfast sandwich with a side of fried potatoes that you inhaled in the car on the way over here!" Noelle challenged her.

"Ginger told me that she ordered a plate of lemon-pepper wings and tempura fried green beans at midnight," Avery added, dancing away from Sidra's attempts to pinch her.

"She also swiped a bag of mini green-chile chicken empanadas off the bar that Dean Amador brought over for Ginger, too. Daddy has re-watched the video like a hundred times. He said he's tempted to put it on Hooligan's Facebook page." D.J. bestowed a reproachful look on her. "Aunt Sid, you better get right with Jesus before Santa puts you on the "Naughty List"."

Ruby's eyes went huge with horror, and she slapped her hands on her round cheeks with a scandalized, "No "Nawsee Liss"!"

"Lawd, you get around, Sid," Kat giggled as she rubbed Sidra's belly.

"For your information, D.J., I prefer to buy my own gifts instead of accepting them from a stranger," Sidra informed him.

Unrepentant, she turned her nose up in the air and headed to the kitchen. "It's called being *independent*, you little tattletale! Oh, and tell Dean Amador to tell me to my face why he wants to deny my unborn child some nourishment!"

She stopped in front Avery. "You ought to be ashamed of yourself for allowing him to attend a school run by a tyrant! I swear you people don't listen to me! I keep trying to tell you that it's not me who's doing all these things! It's you know who."

The group watched her waddle off. Only when the coast was clear did D.J. voice his concern to no one in particular.

"Think she's ever been on the "Nice List"?"

Vivienne wrapped her arm around him and led the way to the kitchen. "I'm sure it hasn't been since God was a little boy, baby."

"I think she's the reason the "Naughty List" was invented," Kat offered mischievously. "Can I get an amen?"

"Amen," they laughed and followed Sidra, who was already charming Marta.

SEVERAL HOURS LATER, VIVIENNE WAVED goodbye to her family from the front steps. As always, time spent with them did wonders for her soul. Kat had also taken leave to do some early Christmas shopping and meat up with her best friend, Autumn. She promised to be back in time for dinner. Vivienne had just entered the house when her phone rang. She frowned when she saw it was Stuart Royce.

"Hello, Stuart. What can I do for you?"

"Vivienne, I'm calling because I'm extremely concerned about some pictures and bank statements that I received anonymously," Stuart stated furiously. "When I first reached out to you, you assured me that your firm's reputation was above reproach, did you not?"

"Yes, I did, and that has never changed or come into question," Vivienne retorted immediately put on the defensive as her mind raced at the implication. *Had the blackmailer struck again?* "I don't particularly care for your tone, Stuart. I'd highly recommend you adjust it and your words before you go any further. When you are able to do that, then you may further elaborate."

"Then why am I being blackmailed on your behalf?!" Stuart seethed, stunning Vivienne into silence. "As you know, I'm going to be speaking at a charity dinner tomorrow, and the blackmailer is requesting that I resign from your firm or these documents will somehow be released to all the Washington insiders. I'll be the laughingstock of D.C.!!!"

"Stuart, I can assure you that is not going to happen at all," Vivienne spoke calmly, even though her heart felt like it would leap out of her throat. The word blackmail was enough to send her into a tailspin.

Magnus had insisted he'd taken care of everything...

"Really?! I don't even feel reassured of my level of importance as your client because Ian isn't returning my calls, and neither is Jack! I've just arrived at the Miramar Resort and checked in, hoping to speak to one of you since only God knows what Ian is up to! How dare you pass my business on to your apathetic partner! This needs to be fixed before my speaking engagement! My reputation is on the line, and so help me, Vivienne...if your husband is behind this-"

"You can shut the fuck up right there, Congressman Royce!" Vivienne was now on the warpath for his blood and shaking with fury, consumed with rage at his implications.

How dare this limp-handshaking, spoiled jackass imply anything about her husband! If he even knew what Alexei was capable of...she doubted his name would even leave his mouth.

"My husband is an honorable man. If he has a problem with someone, he will bring it to them personally. Not resort to such a low and despicable thing as blackmail! When this matter is all straightened out, you and my lawyer will be having a meeting about besmirching the reputations of good men and businesses. I'll see you in thirty minutes."

Vivienne went to get ready and called and left Alexei a voicemail before sending a group text to Ian and Jack.

New York City

Ian juggled the bags of groceries in his hand and smiled his thanks at the doorman holding the glass paneled entrance open for him. He rode the elevator the twelve floors back up to the apartment. Although Ian could have arranged for the groceries to be delivered, he liked being out in the streets on New York City, especially during the holidays when the city vibrated on a whole other level. The tree at Rockefeller Center was festively lit, and all the stores, from the neighborhood bodegas to Cartier participated in holiday decorating. It was a spectacle to behold as people carried their live Christmas trees home by foot, car, subway, bicycle, and even rollerblading. The how didn't matter as long as the tree got there.

This morning, Ian had taken a walk to clear his head and tried to figure out what he really wanted out of life. If Vivienne and Alexei could get their shit together, then so could he. Otherwise, all Ian's relationship and life advice was for naught. He would end this current "relationship" once and for all tonight. It was just too convenient and unhealthy for him. He couldn't continue to hook up and have mindless sex in an attempt to fill an unfillable void.

Tonight, Ian would leave for Whiskey Row and stay until the holidays were over. Spending time with the family would do him some good and hopefully still the restlessness growing within him. He would take the kids on a shopping spree at The Rabbit Hole and pick up some exceptional liqueurs from the Wishing

Well. After eating take out for the last week, he was looking forward to Noelle's home cooking. Eating one of her comforting meals always made him feel closer to his beloved Harvey.

It was getting harder and harder to conjure up his image lately. It used to pop into Ian's head immediately, but now, it was Dominick's face that popped up so readily instead. With his kind eyes and bright smile, the singer was like a breath of fresh air that Ian wanted to inhale, but he refused to go there with the younger man whose life was just beginning again. The last thing he wanted to be was the jaded sugar daddy to a talented rockstar fresh out of the closet.

Ian used the keys he'd been given to push the door open with his knee as one of the bags tore at the bottom. He'd have to remember to come back and shut it. He walked down the hallway into the kitchen to set the bags on the counter, and as he opened the fridge, he called out to his lover.

"It's me! I picked up some groceries for you because I noticed your cabinets were bare. After I put them away, we need to have a talk."

Now that he was back here, Ian felt stifled and unclean. Yes, they needed to talk, and he would not sugarcoat shit. He'd been raised as a gentleman and would continue to remain so by hopefully parting as friends.

"Oh dear, that sounds very ominous, but I'm in agreement because I'd like to talk to you as well. Why don't you have a seat right now?"

The gun shoved against his temple took him completely by surprise.

"What the hell do you think you're doing?" he snarled, turning slightly to face his attacker. "Put that damn thing away, you fool!"

"I'm doing what I'd always planned to do, of course." Bradan's smile was soft, which made it that much more disturbing as he held up Ian's cell phone with his other hand.

"You left your phone here and have received some interesting texts that could screw things up for me. My brother wouldn't like it if anything went wrong when he was so close to completing his masterpiece. After all that he's done for me, I couldn't bear for him to be mad at me. You were a good lay, Ian, but at the end of the day, that's all you were."

This last was said with a penitent smile, for Bradan truly cared for Ian. He was everything he wanted in a partner— educated, suave, well-dressed, polished, witty, and talented in bed. But like everyone in Bradan's shitty life, except for two people, Ian did not love him and never would. That was the reason he was perfectly okay with killing his lover.

Ian gave a genuine smile that puzzled Bradan.

Why did he look very relaxed, and damn near happy for someone who was about to die?

"He's actually much more than that." An ominous voice came from behind him, sending chills down Bradan's spine. "He's family, motherfucker."

VIVIENNE ENTERED THE LOUNGE OF the Miramar Resort and found Stuart Royce waiting at the bar for her with a black dossier. He nodded curtly and stood up. His attempt to greet her with a cheek kiss was an epic fail as she held her gloved hand up to his face to stop him.

"That's not necessary." Vivienne surveyed the crowded area. "You picked this place to have the conversation? Where anyone could hear?"

"Well, I didn't think it was appropriate for me to invite you to my room as you're a married woman and I have a reputation to consider."

"Why don't you just put the red A on my chest, you sanctimonious ass?" Vivienne kept her smile in place as she took another glanced around. "Let's step out on the patio, then."

Stuart allowed her to proceed and even enjoyed the view. She hardly looked old enough to have a grown daughter and be a grandmother. Vivienne radiated passion, and the congressman would dearly love to find out exactly how much. They passed through the balcony doors, and the warmth from the outdoor heaters protected them against the chilly night. Her two guards stood by the doors, ensuring their privacy and Vivienne's protection.

Stuart pulled his coat closer around him, to ward away the frigid air, but Vivienne seemed immune in her mink coat. He could not believe that she was content to stay in this mountain town, hidden away from civilization. Would she not miss the glitz and glamor of D.C.?

She was such a beautiful woman, and Romankov did not deserve her in the least, he thought viciously, which was why he withdrew a gun with a silencer from his trench and fatally shot her two security guards.

The déjà vu feeling came over Vivienne as she watched the guards fall. She opened her mouth to scream and Stuart pointed the gun directly at her.

"Not a word, Vivienne. Unless you'd care to join them."

"HE WAS JUST USING ME the entire time."

Accepting the truth of his own statement was a bitter pill for Ian to swallow.

"To keep an eye on Vivienne and Alexei. The entire time I thought it was a mutual beneficial thing."

After Holt and Cruz rescued him, they'd driven back to the airport with Bradan stuffed in the trunk. By the time, they reached the private hangar, the man was a pale, pasty meltdown, rocking and stuttering. Uncaring of his state, Cruz had taken the shackled man and shoved him into the luggage compartment. Holt had turned the stereo on overhead to drown out Bradan's banging on the lid until the noise stopped.

Tiredly, Ian rubbed his eyes, weary with the guilty realization that he'd unknowingly conspired to keep his dearest friends apart and enable Vivienne to be kidnapped.

Holt poured him a shot of tequila from Alexei's bar on the plane and handed it to the older man. "I know you're a cabernet and cocktail kind of guy, but right now, I think you really need a shot of this instead."

Dismally Ian took the glass without looking and downed its contents. "That's ghastly stuff! Hit me with another, please. While you're doing that, you can fill me in on how things are going with Katerina."

"Everythin' is goin' great with Kat. I've given her some things to think about and hopefully, she makes a decision soon." Holt refilled Ian's glass and gave it back to him. "And before you ask, I have Alexei's approval, but am holdin' out for Ms. Vivienne's as well before gettin' on one knee."

"Good point, Holton. Vivi will appreciate that."

"Ian, I'm not gonna say anythin' about you bein' at Murphy's. The way I see it, that's your business. You were just as much a victim as everyone else in this sick affair," Holt stated with finality. "I know Cruz wouldn't mention it either if I asked."

"That's very kind of you, Holton, but I need to own up to clear my conscience. I despise putting my business out there, however, I do not want my friends to ever have doubt about me."

His phone buzzed, and he pulled it out and read the forwarded message from his secretary with a frown. Then Ian remembered what Bradan had said and pulled up his texts apprehensively. His frown grew as he viewed Vivienne's snarky one to him and Jack.

GENTLEMEN, ARE WE OR ARE WE NOT RUNNING A BUSINESS???:-/ STUART ROYCE WAS UNABLE TO REACH EITHER OF YOU, SO I AM GOING TO MEET WITH HIM AT THE MIRAMAR RESORT TO SMOOTH HIS RUFFLED FEATHERS. I'M SURE HE'S GROSSLY EXAGGERATING HIS SITUATION AND EVERYTHING WILL BE FINE. I WILL KEEP BOTH OF YOU POSTED.

After scrolling through his calls, Ian's alarm grew. "I think we have a problem, Holton. Vivienne said Stuart Royce tried calling Jack and myself, but I have no missed calls, and she's now meeting with him!"

Holt smiled grimly and poured himself a shot and tossed it back. "*We* don't have a problem. *Royce* is the one with a problem. He just doesn't know it yet."

CHAPTER Seventeen

"WOULD IT BE SAFE TO assume that you are not being blackmailed?" Vivienne snarked when Stuart shoved her forward and they continued their trek through the snow-covered field.

"That's correct. Now shut up! I need to concentrate and listen for the plane. If that stupid Russian hadn't deviated from the plan the first time, I wouldn't be caught in this shitty weather now," he growled. "Your husband is nowhere near done suffering as far as I'm concerned. You should have stayed away from him, Vivienne. Since you didn't, I have to figure out which punishment is more effective—killing you in front of him or vice versa?"

"Why didn't you just kill one of us a long time ago?"

"Don't think it didn't cross my mind. Honestly, I was having so much fun watching the two of you suffer being apart," he gleefully answered and chuckled spitefully. "That fucking sad sap sitting outside of your house, pining like a lovestruck fool!"

"You've gone to a lot of trouble for revenge, and I still don't know why. I'd appreciate knowing your reasoning before I die."

Stuart considered her statement, and Vivienne knew by the way his stiff demeanor relented that he would tell her. He pulled his wallet out and threw it at her. "Open it."

Vivienne's stomach clenched when she saw the picture of him and the man who'd threatened her in the dressing room. "This man is your employee?"

Stuart laughed at her obvious revulsion.

"He's more than an employee, Vivienne. Bradan and I are fraternal twins who didn't meet until we were twenty-two years old. Our mother Shanna O'Leary, of Irish, Scottish, and American descent, was a Texas oil heiress. She took a trip to Europe as a college graduation present and met Jamie Mulroney. She spent the summer with him and came home pregnant. When her parents found out about her pregnancy they quickly married her off to a suitable prospect from a well-to-do political family, my "father" Senator Malcolm Royce, without telling him about her little problem.

Their marriage was doomed from the start, and he despised the idea of playing daddy to another man's child. He even went so far as to threaten to divorce her and expose the dirty scandal. Her family agreed that she would go back abroad and say that she lost the baby, but her grandmother would secretly raise the baby in Scotland. It seemed like the perfect plan except there were now two babies to get rid of. When we were born, she did not want to give us up and honor the agreement, so she stayed in Scotland with us for three months.

Finally, Malcolm went to retrieve her, and he found her at the park playing with me as Bradan was ill at home with her grandmother. They argued and it drew the attention of other people at the park. One couple in particular paid especially close attention and decided to investigate further. They turned out to be friends of Malcolm's family and were ecstatic to know they'd had a baby! Malcolm had no choice but to let Mother bring me back to the states, but under no circumstances could Bradan come."

Stuart's face was a mask of vicious hatred. "In public, our life was perfect, but privately, my life was a living hell with this man who despised Mother and me. He belittled every little thing we did, and no matter how hard I *tried*, nothing I did was ever good enough, and I never knew why! Mother tried comforting me by being both a mother and a father, but it wasn't enough. It never stopped me from trying to earn Malcolm's love. If she'd even had admitted he wasn't my father, I would have accepted it and stopped putting forth the effort, but on her deathbed, she confessed that all of our luxuries would've been taken from us and how would we have lived?"

Stuart laughed crazily, and Vivienne's alarm grew at the rate that he was briskly unraveling. She kept her eyes on the gun in his hand, ready to make a move if an opportunity presented itself. Vivienne knew she had to stall Stuart by keeping him talking.

"Would that have bothered you?"

"No, it wouldn't have bothered me! I just wanted him to love me and for us to be a normal family!"

"I can only imagine how hurt you must have felt. I didn't have a normal childhood, either. I never knew my mother either," she confided.

"Do you know how my mother died, Vivienne?" Stuart's voice was spookily calm. His disturbingly serene expression caused her to break out in goosebumps.

"Wasn't it a stroke and she fell down the stairs?"

"That was the story Malcolm gave the papers, but she was actually murdered. *I* pushed her down the stairs after finding out whom Bradan was and that she'd been traveling to visit him every year, leaving me behind."

"How did you find out about that?"

"One night, Malcolm and my mother went out. I brought my girlfriend at the time home. She said she was cold, and I went to my mother's closet and tried to retrieve a sweater from the top shelf. I couldn't reach it, so I grabbed a hat box and stood on top of it. I got the sweater but lost my balance and fell off the box. It rolled on its side and the lid fell off. There were tons of pictures with Mother and this boy, piquing my curiosity. I flipped them over and read the words "Bradan and Mommy" repeatedly.

When they came home, Malcolm retired to his study, and I confronted her. Mother confessed to everything." The façade of the handsome politician had slipped, revealing the maniac. Malcolm's eyes were feral, his voice shaking with rage, spittle flying from his lips.

"How I hated her! Instead of being helpful, she'd hurt me worse than Malcolm ever could by denying me my blood family! After she was done confessing, I pushed her as hard as I could. She broke her neck in the fall. Malcolm came out to see what had happened and I told him. I also told him to clean up my mess, or I'd go to the papers and expose his scandal. After the funeral, I moved out, and a week after her will was read, I went to Scotland. I met my brother and found out that Mother had passed herself off as his 'Aunt Shanna'. He was underweight and had been verbally and physically abused by the miserable old bitch who hadn't wanted to be saddled with a kid. After we killed our great-grandmother and disposed of her body, we traveled to Ireland and found Jamie "The Gent" Mulroney."

"Was he everything you ever dreamed off?" Vivienne asked sarcastically.

Stuart's eyes took on a faraway look. "He remembered Mother and was happy to meet and readily accept us. Bradan and I spent five months with him, and it was the best times of our lives. We knew he was part of a criminal organization but didn't care. We wanted to follow in his footsteps, but he said we had to do it the smart way. He was planning to take America by storm and that I should go into politics as I'd previously planned."

He laughed sadly. "I can still remember him saying that politicians were the real gangsters and that

I'd be able to help him better in that way. The last thing he said to both of us before we left is that he'd see us in America. I made plans for Bradan to get a visa as well and returned home. I visited Da twice in San Francisco where he was taking over a Russian territory. We would sit around with his men, and they'd regale me with tales of their wild times in Ireland and try to drink each other under the table."

Stuart's eyes misted over. "The last time my Da saw me, he held me and said, "Business is good, boyo! The Russians aren't putting up a fight, so I'll be expanding soon. Get yer brother here so we can conquer this fooking country! I'm proud of ye, Stuart." Then a week later I received a call from his second-in-command, Danny Flannigan telling me he was dead at the hands of your husband."

He started to move, pacing in circles around Vivienne. "You'll never know how deeply I mourned him. Or maybe you felt that way when your bestie, Moira was murdered?"

"Go to hell," Vivienne whispered, remaining still, yet tense with anticipation.

"Oh, I've been there, Mrs. Romankov!" Stuart jeered. "Your husband put me and Bradan there and it's exactly where I plan to send him! I know everything there is to know about you and your husband. I've spent years studying him and conjuring up ways to take him down without having scandal attached to my political name. Ruining his businesses and reputation? Not good enough. Robbing him? Not good enough. What would it take to make the "Alexei The Great" feel pain, hmm?"

Stuart came up behind her and she recoiled when his lips touched her ear.

"You are his one true weakness, Vivienne! There is nothing he would not do for you. It has always been about you for him. That's why we decided to work another angle and make it about you as well. Drive a wedge between the two of you. My brother was the one who hired that buffoon Ermines McNall to kidnap Magnus for us. Rumsford is a poor relation in the Royce family and always looking to make easy money. Greedy but not so bright, which is why he got exactly what he deserved. Danny Flannigan also shared the information of what happened to Taras that night, and I knew Bruno wouldn't mind a little revenge. Did you know Bradan has been fucking Ian Rusnik? That enabled us to keep closer tabs on things. Also, the reason I hired your firm. Everything has been leading up to this moment for what Romankov did."

"You bastard! You murdered Moira and then turned her family's company to represent you?"

Vivienne pivoted around and kicked him in the knee with her stiletto heel. With a howl, Stuart dropped the gun. She bent to pick it up and he rushed her, knocking her on her back and viciously slapping her across the face. The blow stung against her frozen flesh. From the corner of her eye Vivienne saw a jagged rock and seized the opportunity. She grabbed it, knocking his hand away to slam it upside his head. Stuart reared back in pain, and Vivienne hit him in the nose with it, gushing blood followed the sickening crack and it ran down his face.

She pushed him off of her and rolled to her knees, trying to scramble to her feet. Her fashionable boots slipped, and Vivienne lost her balance, falling forward. Stuart pounced on her, yanking her around to face him, and punched the side of her face.

"I'm going to kill you!" he screamed and raised his leg to kick her.

Suddenly, a massive blur exploded into their altercation. Flying over Vivienne, it knocked Stuart back. The enormous form of fur and teeth growled and shook him like a rag doll while he shrieked and cried out in pain. A sharp whistle, and the Caucasian Ovcharka dropped Stuart but stood sentry over him menacingly.

"Vivienne! Are you okay, my love?"

Alexei fell to his knees next to her, frantically scouring her from head to toe.

His voice was music to her hears and she sobbed with the relief of knowing that he was safe.

But what about Bradan?

Clinging to him, Vivienne cried harder. "I'm fine, Lex, but he has a brother! Ian —"

"Sshhh, Vivi. Everything is fine now. You will see, my love." Alexei kissed her forehead tenderly.

She heard more footsteps and then Jack's voice heavy with concern. "How is she?!"

"See for yourself, Yakov." Alexei carefully picked his wife up and passed her to their oldest son.

"Dammit, Mama Bear," Jack said hoarsely. He pressed his cheek to hers. "I got your text, but your phone kept going straight to voicemail. Luckily, Magnus was able to track you. The boys and I met up with Alexei at his house when he came to pick up Muffin to track your scent."

More footsteps crunched through the snow, and Vivienne bawled uncontrollably when Casey and Darby surrounded them. If she could have seen clearly, she would have seen tears in their eyes also as Casey took her from Jack and held her close to him.

"Muffin?! That beast's name is *Muffin*?" Vivienne gave an exhausted laugh when the dog gave a happy yelp, hearing her name.

Darby brought her gloved hand to his lips and kissed it. "Yeah, V. There's Muffin, Snickerdoodles, Brownie, and Shortbread."

Alexei snatched Stuart by his injured arm and squeezed, relishing in the howling politician's misery. The Russian showed no mercy as he dragged him along.

"It is now time for you to join your brother."

BRADAN WAS WORRIED SICK OVER Stuart's absence.

His older brother and their father Jamie were the only people who'd tried to make his life better. Their great-grandmother had abused him and only took care of him for money. 'Aunt Shanna' hadn't loved him enough to stand up to her husband. Only Stuart had cared enough about him to better Bradan's life. Except he'd failed him. Who knew where his older brother was now?!

The door opened, and a Russian guard motioned for Bradan to accompany him. In the hallway, he saw a resigned Bruno with a guard as well and tried to speak, but the glowering guard told him to shut up. Quietly, they walked from the estate and across the vast grounds to a large barn-like building. They were quickly shoved inside the building, and Bradan's worry turned to relief when he saw Stuart sitting there in the middle of the floor.

"Stuie! I was so worried about you! I'm sorry I failed you!" Bradan said shamefully.

He threw himself at his older brother and hugged him. Stuart yelped in agony, shoving him away with his good arm.

Stuart's eyes were full or sorrow and bitterness. "I'm the one who failed you, Bradan, but don't worry; I'm going to sue Romankov as soon as I get the chance! He can't keep us here like prisoners. I'm a congressman, for God's sake! He *will* pay one way or another!"

Bruno chuckled derisively and they both turned to look at him. "You still don't get it, do you? You Americans are so spoiled and entitled!"

"What does he mean, Stuie?" Bradan addressed his brother with confusion. He was starting to worry because his normally confident brother looked anything but.

From above them in the darkness, Alexei spoke. "He means that you've already been tried for your crimes and found guilty. *This* is where you will meet your punishment."

"You can't do this to me!" Stuart shouted, panicking. "My staff will be looking for me!"

"Oh, but I can," Alexei returned smoothly. "The three of you conspired to bring me down to avenge your loved ones that you held in the highest regard, despite their wrongdoings. I'm sorry that I drove you to take such drastic measures. Now I'm going to make it up to you by reuniting you with them."

The bright lights came on above them, and they saw Alexei, Cedric, Ian, Jack, Casey, Darby, Holt, Guy, Cruz, and all of Alexei's guards watching from the railings as four stall doors opened and Muffin, Snickerdoodles, Brownie, and Shortbread emerged.

The brothers were frozen with fear while Bruno met the disgusted gaze of each of the men he'd betrayed. He nodded his head in acceptance of his fate as Alexei spoke again.

"Playtime, children! Get your toys!"

The dogs attacked viciously then retreated as their "toys" screamed in miserable agony. They repeated this brutal pattern until the floor was stained crimson with blood from the chunks of flesh flying everywhere. When their toys screams were forever silenced, the dogs licked their muzzles clean and retreated to their stalls. Only then did the guards file out, leaving the family alone to view the massacre below them.

"You know, I was really angry when I found out what y'all were up to and all the secrets, but I'm suddenly feelin' much better," Casey acknowledged grimly. "I just don't want to be kept in the dark about shit ever again."

"I second that motion," Jack chimed in, looking away from the scene and treating Alexei, Cedric, and Holt to a hard stare. "We're a family! It's not just a damn title; it's the code we live by. If we don't have that, then we don't have a damn thing, agreed?"

"Agreed," they chorused remorsefully.

"You'll never know how much I deeply regret any of this happening," Alexei lamented thickly. "I'm sorrier than you will ever know-"

"Stop! How could you have ever known any of this would happen?" Darby said forcefully.

His father's face was carved in agony. "If only I had been more like my father. He would have known to tie up loose ends—"

This time it was Ian that cut him off. "That same father who turned his back on you for wanting to be with the woman you loved? The wonderful mother to these boys and your daughter? Forgive us for being grateful that you didn't emulate yourself after him."

"I know that I was shitty to you for a long time, Alexei, but I only wanted the best for my daughter," Cedric added humbly. "I was too fucking blind to see she already had it. You've shown me there are no lengths that you won't go to not only for her, but your children as well. I'm sorry, I doubted you, son. I'm going to be leaving here and meeting Clarissa for the second part of her cruise. If it's alright with you, I'd like to come back to spend time with you guys?"

"*Da,* we would like that very much, Cedric," Alexei spoke solemnly, and the two men exchanged a handshake.

"Awww, hell! C'mere, son!" Cedric threw his arms around his son-in-law.

"Y'all don't even know how many times I wanted to tell you about my secret but couldn't," Holt spoke up. "I took a vow as well, and that's all I'll say on the matter. Actually, I'll say a little more. All you'll ever need to know is that I'll always have your backs should you need me."

"That goes both ways, doesn't it, fellas?" Guy's gave Jack and Casey a challenging glare. "You were there for us when Ms. Moira died and Miguel as well, Holt. Enough said. We don't doubt you. Carryin' a secret like that couldn't have been easy. Hell, look what Ms. Viv's secret did to her marriage. We got your back, Thor."

"This is so touching. I hate to cry and go, but I have a store to run. *Adios, mi amigos.*"

"From associates to friends, da? I like it. I'm forever indebted to you. Should you need anything, do not hesitate to call on me, Merada." Alexei engulfed him in a bear hug, as did Holt, and then Cedric.

"I'll keep that in mind, Romankov." He nodded goodbyes to the other men and left whistling "Say You Say Me".

Behind him, Cruz heard Guy ask, "What's up with the song?"

Alexei and Holt exchanged a laugh.

"I guess he just likes it." Alexei offered, and Guy grunted.

Cruz smiled to himself as his phone buzzed. He pulled it out of his jacket and the smile died.

"I HAVEN'T RECEIVED ANY PICTURES! WE HAD A DEAL, MERADA OR HAVE YOU FORGOTTEN?"

As a matter of fact, he had.

For a brief moment, Cruz allowed himself to forget that he'd made a deal with the Devil.

CHAPTER *Eighteen*

TWO WEEKS LATER

"HOW ARE THINGS GOING WITH Alexei?"

Ian waited as Vivienne supervised the servers leaving the kitchen with trays of smoked salmon blini puffs, spoons laden with seared scallops and parsnip cream, prosciutto-wrapped pears with baked brie, spinach and artichoke stuffed mushrooms, mini beef wellingtons, and chicken pot pie turnovers.

"I wouldn't know; I've hardly seen him, Ian. He leaves early in the morning and only comes to bed when I'm asleep."

The only reason Vivienne knew that was because in the wee hours of the morning, Alexei drew her close to him. In the morning, the only proof that he he'd been there was the indentation in his pillow and his uniquely, addicting scent that seduced her senses. Vivienne tried to speak with him, but her husband was avoiding her at all costs.

Except for this evening, as they had a house full of guests.

Alexei had entered the bedroom to get ready just as she was exiting. His smoldering gaze undressing Vivienne of the floor-length, fitted black velvet sheath with the sweetheart neckline. She left her hair down in big waves and curls, and his eyes lingered on the diamond pendant that skimmed the top of her revealing cleavage. The temperature in the room skyrocketed as their gazes merged.

"I laid your tux on the bed. Our guests will be arriving shortly. Don't be late."

Vivienne walked past only to be yanked back against his chest as his beard brushed her bare shoulder. It was followed by his lips, evoking a tremble from her when he bit down lightly. "You look exquisite, Vivi."

"The guilt is eating away at him, no matter how many times we've all reassured him that none of this is his fault!"

Three of the servers came back frazzled with empty trays, and Vivienne scowled ferociously at them. "Did you *throw* the food at my guests? How did those trays empty so quickly?"

"You seriously have to ask, Vivienne?" Ian's look was full of pity as they stumbled over each other to answer her.

"There's a beautiful pregnant woman—"

"With an *extremely* aggressive attitude—"

"Her husband said we'd better not make her cry. The 'or else' was implied," the last server finished meekly.

"Just fill the trays and keep them that way! Give her whatever she wants!"

Vivienne waited until they left and held out her wineglass out to Ian who filled it to the rim and then carefully clinked it with his. She downed half of the wine in one gulp.

"Come on, Rusnik. Let's go mingle."

The Romankov holiday party was in full swing. Holiday music mixed with top forty from the speakers and everyone appeared to be having a good time mingling and dancing. From across the room, Vivienne's eyes sought and held Alexei's, and she forgot to exhale at the smoldering desire and love she saw in his. He was resplendent in his black tuxedo with his shoulder-length hair slicked back. Vivienne could see more silver in his beard, and it only made him more devastatingly handsome to her.

Alexei was equally affected by Vivienne's appearance. Despite her recent harrowing experiences, she was stunning tonight in that form-fitting dress. The richness of the black velvet set off her honeyed hue exquisitely. He wanted to peel it off of her but keep the diamond nestled above her breasts on. Alexei wasn't blind to the admiring but well-deserved glances she was receiving, and he'd made sure to hold the stare of each man with the exception of family.

He kept waiting for her to blame him for Moira's death and announce she was leaving him once and for all. That if it wasn't for him, she would still be alive, but Vivienne had said nothing. The weight was killing him.

"Never thought I'd see the day "The Wolf" feared a slip of a woman," Holt remarked off-handedly. "Go dance with your woman, Romankov."

"She's not just any woman" he murmured. "I hate to say this, but you're right, Brammer."

Alexei approached her and Ian. "Dance with me, Vivi."

It wasn't a request. Any other time, Vivienne would have bristled and delivered a sassy comeback. Not tonight when her husband was initiating contact and conversation.

With a radiant smile, she stepped into his arms. "It's about damn time, Romankov."

However, awkward silence ensued, and they absorbed the words to Lady Gaga's "Million Reasons".

You're giving me a million reasons to let you go
You're giving me a million reasons to quit the show
You're givin' me a million reasons

"This song is different," Alexei spoke cautiously. Insecurities creeping in, he held on tighter than his normal possessive hold. The thought of letting Vivienne go was unbearable. If she decided to leave, he'd probably have to lock her away—in a non-creepy, non-stalkerish way of course.

"I find it to be very fitting, Lex. There have been so many instances in our relationship where you could have walked away yet didn't. Thank you for that," she said quietly. Her fingernails brushed the black waves at his neck, and she loved watching his eyes flare in response. "And now here we are."

If I had a highway, I would run for the hills
If you could find a dry way, I'd forever be still
But you're giving me a million reasons
Give me a million reasons

"Where exactly is *here*, Vivi?" Alexei tried to keep the desperation out of his voice but knew he'd failed miserably when she averted her eyes to focus on a point off to his right. "Are you saying you want a divorce or you're here to stay? Because I refuse to let you go!"

"Then act like it!" she cried, the strain of the last couple of weeks causing her to snap. "Act like you want me around for more than just warming your bed, Romankov!" Vivienne stressed under her breath, smiling as they passed other dancing couples.

Suddenly Alexei released her. Vivienne would have stumbled if he hadn't grabbed her by the hand and led them from the dance floor. As they passed by their amused family members, Alexei growled, "Watch the damned party for us!"

The gang watched as they swiftly exited the banquet room.

"I got five hundred dollars that says they don't come back. Who's in?" Kat inquired cheerfully, but no one wanted to take the bet, so they all split up to do what they were told.

ALEXEI UNLOCKED HIS STUDY, RELOCKING it after they entered.

"We have guests, Alexei. You wanted to host a Christmas party, and now, thanks to you, we're being rude!" Vivienne scolded him but couldn't hold back a giggle as he kicked off his shoes, unzipped his pants, pulled them down, and then dispersed himself of his jacket. Her pussy throbbed as she saw how ready he was, his erection jutting proudly from the dark nestle of curls.

"Let them wait, Vivi. Take off your panties!" Alexei ordered as she backed away with a playful shake of her head.

The tiny, naughty smile dancing about her lips was driving him crazy, just like only she could. Alexei was burning up for her.

"I don't think so, Mister! If I don't go and host this party my husband wanted then he'll think that I'm unreliable and am not one hundred percent committed to him and our marriage. I can't have him thinking that about his wife who loves him insanely."

A slow smile spread across his face as he realized what she was saying. *Vivienne wasn't leaving him.* He crooked his finger at her.

"Come here, wife."

She ran to him, and he picked her up and leaned her against the door. Her dress fell around her waist, and he glanced down at her in surprise. "Why aren't you wearing any underwear, Mrs. Romankov?"

Vivienne snaked her arms around his neck as he lined himself up at her entrance and slid into her effortlessly. She was drenched in her arousal for him and sighed with bliss as she felt him tapping at her spine. Against his lips, she breathed, "Rule number five: *Romankovs stay ready for any situation, husband.*"

"Indeed, they do," Alexei lips quirked as he solemnly agreed, eyes shining with love for her. "I love you, Mrs. Romankov. Forever and ever."

"It's you and only ever you, Alexei. Until the end of time," Vivienne cosigned as he spoiled her with sweet slow strokes of his cock while they exchanged tender, lazy kisses.

She leaned into him as he reached behind her to unzip her dress. Vivienne untied his bow tie and unbuttoned his shirt to press fevered kisses down his neck. Alexei leaned her back against the door, and the velvet fabric fell away to reveal her pert breasts. Lovingly, he trailed kisses down her neck and shoulders before lavishing her nipples with his mouth. Vivienne groaned her pleasure as she leisurely rose and fell on him, savoring the fullness inside of her and basking in his love that surrounded and engulfed her. They went slower than slow to prolong this moment, but per usual, it was just too fucking good to last.

"Vivi, Vivi, Vivi," he serenaded her with her own name as she gripped fistfuls of his hair, and held on for dear life, both of them feeling the release threatening to erupt.

"I don't want this to end, Lex," Vivienne moaned as he bit her nipples. She bowed her back, hungry for more of his tongue. *"Make it last forever, baby."*

Alexei suckled the tender pulse at her neck as the slickness of her arousal hurled him closer and closer to the brink. *"We have a lifetime filled with these moments ahead of us, my love. Come with me."*

Despite the slowness of their lovemaking, their release was anything but. The orgasm catapulted them into nirvana and the door shook repeatedly under Alexei's straining into Vivienne's tight sheath. It overtook them and finally did what nothing else could and brought the great Alexei Romankov to his knees as he continued to fill his wife with his release and prolonged her orgasm as they whispered their love to each other, secure in the knowledge that there was no feeling or love greater than theirs.

EPILOGUE

GUY FELL DEEPER AND DEEPER into Fern's luminescent eyes as they danced. He glowered when Jack and Noelle danced by them and his friend made kissy faces at him while Noelle mouthed 'serves you right'!

"What's wrong, G? Is there something on your mind?"

His cock stirred automatically at the sound of her voice. Her voice, smile, scent, looks, laugh…fuck it, his cock got hard just because it was *Fern*.

"Everythin' is fine. Just thinkin' about some orders I need to get to when I return to work," he assured her.

Valiantly he tried to keep his hands on her slim waist, but it was hard because they were curious. Guy's palms itched to feel just how supple the tempting, plump globes of her ass really were. All night long, the tomato red silk fabric of her dress caressed her body as it shifted and moved in a seductive dance when she did, letting him know she was blessed in all the right places.

"I love how passionate you are about your job. The broom you designed for Max and Georgie's wedding was stunning. I'm sure they're in heavy demand, right?" Her small pink tongue darted out, and she licked her lips nervously under his fiery gaze.

It was too much for Guy. He knew that Fern was just as aware of the attraction between them, but she wouldn't act on it out of loyalty to his brother.

But Miguel, may he rest in peace, was dead, and *he* was alive and feeling her on levels Guy hadn't even known he was capable of reaching. He glanced up with a sinful smile and then fell back a couple of steps, prompting Fern to automatically follow.

"We're under the mistletoe, Fern. Make a move," he challenged.

She looked up and saw he was correct. Her heart was hammering so hard, she was finding it hard to function. She closed her eyes and fought to control it. To fight the temptation that was Guiles Keetowah-Marquez. Nothing compared to being in his arms and feeling his hard, lean body pressed against her much softer one, reminding her how long it'd been since she had intimate contact with the opposite sex.

But never like this. Guy's touch reminded Fern that she was a woman that used to have a healthy sexual appetite. His full lips indicated that it was made for doing unmentionable things that would bring Fern hours of wicked pleasure. The decadent look in his eyes confirmed it. At what cost to her psyche was the million-dollar question.

Guy's firm fingers gently gripped her chin and tilted it up. Fern opened her eyes to find his face hovering right above hers.

"You're overthinkin' it, darlin'. We can go as slow as you want as long as we're movin' forward in the same direction."

"What do you want from me, Guy?" Fern questioned him, panic rising at the intimacy swirling in his eyes. If she wasn't careful, he would have her handing him her heart on a silver platter.

"Everythin' I'm ready and willin' to work for, Fern," he vowed. "But I'll start with your trust first."

"Just don't hurt me, Guy," Fern pleaded right before she pressed her lips to his.

"Never that, darlin'," he swore fiercely, his tongue flicking the corner of her lips temptingly.

Neither Fern or Guy noticed Pearl Mignon, practically shielded by the Christmas tree in the corner of the room, stalking them with a possessive glare.

"I'M GLAD EVERYTHING'S BACK TO the 'new' normal around here," Kat commented as Holt gallantly whirled her around the dance floor. She tipped her head back and laughed with delight as they twirled in time to the music. "Maybe now, we can pick up where we left off..."

Kat waited for him to take the bait as she focused on the deco mesh wreaths and sugar plum fairies dancing above her. Holt slowed the spin as he brought her back up to face him.

He enjoyed the becoming blush in her cheeks and admired the way it traveled down her slender neck to the lush swells of her breasts on display. They were revealed by her plum corset underneath her sapphire blue satin pantsuit.

"Please refresh my memory on where that was, darlin'."

"Eyes above the neck, pervert," Casey hissed at him as he danced by with Sidra. It was more like danced behind her and sway to the beat of the music as he had not one but two dancing partners in his wife and baby Moira.

Kat rolled her eyes at him as she lowered her arms and encircled them around Holt's waist. Eyes wide with innocence she remarked, "Did you hear that, Mr. Brammer? How lucky am I to get an introverted pervert?! It's like the gods are smiling on me. And I was referring to you getting back to the business of sweet-talking me into your bed, of course."

"Baby, you know that's not our deal." He lowered his lips to her ear. "Do I need to discipline you for lyin'?"

Kat swallowed hard at the provocative, edgy image his words evoked. "Promises, promises, Holton."

He covered her lips with his, and Kat clung to the lapels of his tuxedo jacket and welcomed his sensual onslaught.

"Cryin' all night!" Darby muttered as he and Avery danced by and they broke apart.

"Pay them no mind," Kat whispered to him, staring up at him drowsily. He was looking particularly fine in his navy-blue suit, beard, and man bun. Sometimes, she wanted to slap herself to see if he was just a dream because frankly, Kat couldn't believe he was all hers.

"Do I ever?" he drawled. Someone coughed discreetly, and Holt sighed with resignation, certain it was Jack's turn to give them hell.

It was not Jack, but his father, Rudii. The older man smiled warmly at Kat. "*Hej,* Ms. Romankov. Please excuse us, I need to have a word with my son."

"Hej!" Kat enthusiastically returned the Swedish greeting for hello. "Of course, Mr. Brammer. I'm going to dance with D.J."

Holt watched her strut away and immediately wanted her back in his arms. "What's goin' on, Dad?"

"Short story? Due to your refusal to take your rightful place with them, the family is displeased with your recent involvement in affairs that they don't consider to be any of your business," Rudii said bluntly. "They're also not happy with the way your cousin Otto is mishandlin' things and are highly offended that you would take up for Romankov's cause but not your own blood's."

"What are you sayin', Dad?" Holt ground out. "You know good and well it was my business also."

Rudii was filled with sympathy for his only child. He'd watched the way Holton had stared at the vision that was Katerina Romankov when he thought no one was looking. They were years in the making. "She means that much to you, son?"

Holt's answer was revealed in the ignited blue flames of his eyes as he regarded his father silently.

"Then you have a choice, Holt," he informed his son sternly. "Give them what they want. They're willin' to offer a year max."

"A year of my life?! Like hell," Holt fumed. His large hands curled in frustration and anger at the thought of choices being made for him regarding his life. "What's the alternative?"

Rudii was silent for so long that Holt wondered if he'd even heard him. "Then they will come to you. *Here.* Do you remember that movie "30 Days of Night"?"

The cult horror film focused on a small town plagued by depraved creatures that terrorized its helpless residents for a thirty-day period. Yep, the comparison sounded about right.

Except the vampires were way nicer.

Holt looked around at his friends and family all celebrating and enjoying life. His beautiful Kat laughing as D.J. tried to spin her around. The small velvet box was burning a hole in his pants pocket because he was impatiently waiting for her horny-ass parents to leave Alexei's study and speak to Ms. Vivienne alone before proposing in front of everyone.

He caught Kat's eye, and she winked saucily at him. As usual, her impish smile made his heart expand with love. Holt tried to return the gesture but knew he failed miserably when her smile fell. With a concerned gaze, Kat began to make her way back to him.

"How much time do I have to decide?" he gritted out, already knowing the answer.

His father placed a hand on his shoulder and squeezed compassionately. Holt closed his eyes briefly, wanting to rage at the unfairness of it all.

"The family plane is waiting for you as we speak."

THE END

OTHER BOOKS

By D.A. Young

Whiskey Row Series

Sweet Obsession
New Beginnings
The Pursuit of Happiness
Perfectly Imperfect
No Greater Love

Baymoor Series

The Farmer & The Belle
Lost & Found
Take A Chance on Me

Circle of Friends Novella Series

Second Chances
Forever Yours

The Ties That Bind Series

Book One
Book Two

Baxter Park

Winner Takes All

ABOUT THE *Author*

D. A. YOUNG IS A DAUGHTER, mother, Gigi, wife, and work in progress who loves God and the life she's been blessed to create with her family and friends. Food, traveling, reading, and music are her passions. Raised on dramas such as "Dynasty" and "General Hospital", D. A. Young is an author of adventures featuring multiple characters and subplots.

Interested in what I'm doing next?

FOLLOW ME ON FACEBOOK!

https://www.facebook.com/D-A-Young-1695356880704195/

Made in the USA
Middletown, DE
23 May 2020